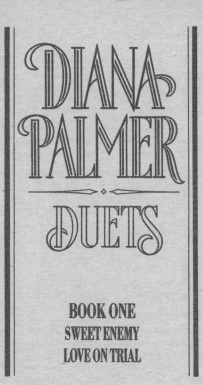

DIANA PALMER

DUETS

BOOK ONE
SWEET ENEMY
LOVE ON TRIAL

Silhouette Books®

Published by Silhouette Books New York
America's Publisher of Contemporary Romance

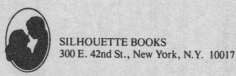

SILHOUETTE BOOKS
300 E. 42nd St., New York, N.Y. 10017

First published in North America as a MacFadden Romance by
Kim Publishing Corporation.

First Silhouette Books edition published March 1990.

DIANA PALMER DUETS
© 1990 HARLEQUIN ENTERPRISES LIMITED

SWEET ENEMY © 1979 Diana Palmer
LOVE ON TRIAL © 1979 Diana Palmer

ISBN: 0-373-48222-1

SWEET ENEMY

Maggie Kirk had always been wary of Clint Raygen, her best friend's older brother. So why had she chosen his ranch to recover from a broken heart? Could it be that when Clint wasn't on the warpath, he was as gentle as a spring morning...or that when her sweet enemy smiled, he took her breath away?

LOVE ON TRIAL

Attorney Hawke Grayson was known as a ladies man around town. But reporter Cyrene Jameson felt she was immune to his magnetism. And yet, after being assigned to do a story on Hawke, she found herself wondering if *her* defenses would hold up. The man had a way of getting under her skin...and he was quickly making his way to her heart!

Dear Reader:

Back by popular demand! Diana Palmer has long been a favorite of Silhouette readers and it is with great pleasure that we bring these impossible-to-find classics back into print.

Sweet Enemy, Love on Trial, Storm Over the Lake, To Love and Cherish, If Winter Comes and *Now and Forever* are some of the first books Diana Palmer ever wrote, and they've been unavailable to readers for ten years. We've received many letters requesting these stories and all of us at Silhouette were thrilled to put together these three volumes of Diana Palmer Duets.

The six novels contained in the three "Duets" show all the humor, intensity, emotion and special innocence that have made Diana Palmer such a beloved name at Silhouette. I'd like to say to Diana's present, past and future fans—sit back, relax and enjoy!

Best wishes,

Isabel Swift
Editorial Manager

Contents

Books by Diana Palmer

A Note From Diana Palmer

Dear Readers:

It is a great pleasure to see these books in print once again. These stories were written ten years ago and they came under the category of light romance—in other words, they are not as racy as the books we see in some of the lines today. In 1979, when I wrote for the original publisher of these books, I knew nothing whatsoever about how to write a romance. But I worked for two marvelous editors who did: Anne Gisonny and John Collins. Together, they pushed me in the right direction and kept telling me that I had enough talent to make it in the world of romance writing. Without their faith and support, I don't know that I would ever have made it at all.

There are two other people who deserve a mention here. One is Ann Vandiver, my friend for almost twenty years and my co-worker for ten at a small-town newspaper called the *Tri-County Advertiser* in Clarkesville, Georgia. Ann made me take my old moldy manuscripts out of my closet and send them off to a publisher. She kept telling me I could do it, even when I was sure I couldn't. She was, and is, one of the best friends I have in the world.

The other person I owe my career to is my husband, James. He has been my support and mainstay for eighteen years of marriage. He believed in my talent and did everything he could to make it possible for me to write, including giving me the freedom of time to create after our son was born. James was never too proud to change diapers or give bottles; he was never too selfish to take care of our baby while I wrote at night, after working all day at my newspaper reporting job. He has stood by me through family crises, the loss of both my parents, financial troubles and persistent illnesses that have plagued me. He has always been there for me when I needed him, a rock to keep me anchored in the roughest seas. I love him with all my heart, and I owe him whatever success I have achieved. He is a good man, my husband and my friend. Our marriage has been, and is, one of the best. He and our son are the light of my life.

There are plenty of other people who inspired me to write: my parents, my newspaper editor Amilee Graves—a woman of rare and unique intelligence—and any number of fellow reporters who shared the sorrow and delight of news-gathering with me. It was newspaper work that taught me about life and people. The lessons were hard sometimes, and I saw things I don't like remembering, but I like to think that I did a little good along the way. What I learned, I put to good use when I became a writer of novels.

The books in this particular Duet were written at a very special time in my life.

Sweet Enemy was written while I was carrying our only child, Blayne Edward Kyle. I had been married for eight years when I became pregnant, and James and I had really resigned ourselves to being just the two of us. Since I didn't expect to get pregnant, I didn't realize what was wrong with me until I was three and a half months along and finally went to see a doctor. I was convinced I had cancer and was dying. Well, the rabbit died. I didn't.

I was over the moon when I knew about the baby. He went with me to meetings of the chamber of commerce and the county commission, to interviews with the fire and police chiefs and civil defense director, and even to cover news stories. He was very portable at that time, and I enjoyed my pregnancy as I have enjoyed nothing else, except for writing. The plot for *Sweet Enemy* developed as I walked down the streets of Clarkesville, a very small town with wonderfully friendly people, en route to interviews. It was early spring when I finished the book and sent it to Anne Gisonny.

I'd been so afraid of going into labor, of not realizing it, or of being at the wrong place and not getting to the hospital on time. As it happened, I did make one false trip to the hospital that resulted in my being sent home. But the next morning, the pains started again with a vengeance. I went to work, as I had for almost the total nine months of pregnancy, and was sent out to cover a filling station fire. I waddled around with Fire Chief Claude Marcus and my camera, took photos, did an interview. Then I went back to the office, handed in the photos, wrote the story, and drove myself to the hospital. Because by that time, the pains were about five minutes apart.

James came with some friends to take my car home, and the long wait began. Thirty-six hours after I'd originally started into labor, they gave up on our natural childbirth training and wheeled me into the operating room to do a cesarean section. At 4:30 p.m. on July 3, 1980, Blayne Edward Kyle was born.

I can remember being delighted at the thought of having a son, and fascinated with the look of his tiny face. The nurses brought him to me for feeding, and it was incredible to hold him and know that he was part of us. The next day was the Fourth of July, and I had plenty of visitors. Then, on the fifth, James brought me a package from my publisher. It contained a T-shirt, a congratulations card and copies of *Sweet Enemy*!

I was still hurting, but when I saw the cover of *Sweet*

Enemy, the pain dwindled pretty quickly. It was a tremendous treat to have the book come out at such a nice time. I showed it to everyone, along with the baby, who still ranks as my greatest creative achievement.

Newspaper reporters and people who work in manufacturing companies don't get rich in small towns. Some weeks we had very little left over after we paid the bills and bought baby food. It took us a year to pay off the hospital. Those were rough years. Getting my novels published was our very first financial break. I discovered that if I wrote fast, the company published fast, and I did ten books in one year. All of a sudden, we could afford a walker for Blayne, a car that only had sixty thousand miles on it and a real stereo of our very own. Luxuries!

I was already working at three jobs—at the *Tri-County Advertiser* full-time, as a stringer or district correspondent for *The Times* in Gainesville, an afternoon daily, and doing free-lance feature work. I even did a stint for about a year as a stringer for the *Atlanta Constitution*, mostly police news in my area. In my spare time at night, I wrote romances and thanked God for the work. Supporting a baby and ourselves was almost more than James and I could manage.

Sweet Enemy was my fourth MacFadden. By then, I had sort of learned the basics of writing romances, and I was really enjoying my work. Clint and Maggie were special to me, because they were my first really warring couple. Having Maggie tie a bow on the cow's tail was rather borrowed from life—a few years earlier, I had tied a big pink bow on the bumper of a coworker's car.

The heroine's first name in *Sweet Enemy* was the same as my mother's. Everyone knew my mother as

Eloise, but her given first name was Maggie. I called her "George" and worshiped her. She and I were like overgrown juvenile delinquents together. She was pretty and smart and full of fun, and we were best friends as long as she lived. We wrote for rival newspapers, and had a ball competing for "scoops." She was a fragile little thing, never in really good health, but her good days were *good days*. She enjoyed life more than anyone I ever knew. Even the bad times never got her down or broke her spirit. The heroine in *Sweet Enemy* was another riposte in our unending quest for one-upmanship. (She had recently poured ice cubes on my father's chest while he was sleeping in the middle of the night and we were watching a late movie together. Dad came running, screaming, out of the bedroom and George calmly put the ice tray in my lap.) I handed George the copy of *Sweet Enemy* and showed her the heroine's name. She gave me a knowing smile and I knew revenge would be forthcoming. Sure enough, her next column for the newspaper was all about my attempts to learn to play the trombone—under her bedroom window at dawn.

Love On Trial came next, and the first scene in that book reflects one of my—and my mother's—favorite hangouts in Atlanta. It was a little coffee shop at Park Place Plaza, a place with white linen tablecloths where they served exquisite *kaffee mit schlag* and delicate pastries with real butter. George and I would go there and drink coffee, our mutual favorite beverage, and talk about what we were going to do when we became famous authors one day. George had already had an article published in *Atlanta Magazine* and scooped me on a major news story just before she and Dad moved back to Atlanta. Then I sold my first book to Mac-Fadden and got pregnant later the same year. Ho, ho,

Ho, ho, ho, I was ahead by four books, even if George was ahead by one child. (My sister, Dannis, was twelve years my junior and is still my baby sister, even though she's married and has a daughter of her own.)

Anyway, the little coffee shop had a pride of place in *Love On Trial* because of its pleasant associations. The hero was an attorney because I had spent some time as a legal secretary and had a special fondness for lawyers. Siri, the heroine, was a reporter, too; a profession I knew quite a lot about by then.

The only real regret I have about these books is that when I read them now, with ten years of experience as a novelist to fall back on, I see so many things that I would love to change. I can't, of course. These are first books by, at that time, an unknown author. I know so much more now than I did then about characterization, about plotting, about continuity, about motivation. But it gives me great pleasure to be able to look back on these early efforts and see how much I've learned since they were written. I still enjoy the characters, because they are like old friends to me, and it's nice to be able to visit them and remember what my life was like at the time they lived in my mind.

I was thirty-three years old when I wrote *Sweet Enemy*. Now I am forty-three. I wouldn't have believed that my ideas, my interests, my outlook on life, could have changed so much in that short period of time, or that my life could have changed so much.

Since 1980, James has had open-heart surgery—a dangerous operation to replace two worn-out valves in his heart with artificial ones. My mother died of pneumonia in 1982—before my first Silhouette was published. My father remarried and died of cancer in 1988. I had my first mainstream romance accepted by Warner Popular Library, under the title *Diamond*

Spur. I write for two lines at Silhouette—Romance and Desire—and I have no plans to give up short contemporary fiction.

I hope you'll enjoy reading these books as much as I've enjoyed telling you about them. Life is sweet, and each age has its own particular beauty. The two years these books represent in my life were two of the best I've ever had. They burn like candles in my memory, lighting me through the dark times back to the warmth of living parents, special friends, happy times and challenging hardships. As the song goes, even the bad times were good. I hope your lives are as blessed as mine has been, with laughter and love, and always hope. Thank you for your loyalty and your friendship. God bless you, my friends.

Much love,

Diana Palmer

SWEET ENEMY

1
*

I won't go!" Maggie Kirk said stubbornly, and turned away from her friend's cajoling pleas. "It's like asking me to walk into a Bengal tiger's cage with a sirloin roast tied around my neck!"

"But, Maggie," Janna protested, her dark eyes pleading softly, "it's just what you need. Remember how we used to escape to the ranch when we were in school, how we looked forward to riding and picnicking by the river?"

"My memories are a little different," the slender brunette said with a grimace. She perched on the edge of the bed, studying the legs of her brown denim jeans. "I remember being put over Clint Raygen's knee for riding that surly stallion of his, and being locked in my room for going on a picnic by the river with Gerry Broome."

"Clint did warn you about High Tide," her small friend reminded her, defending the brother she worshipped. "And you know what Gerry tried to do. Clint knew he was too old to trust you with."

Maggie blushed with the memory of Clint finding her fighting her way out of Gerry's furious embrace, and the sight of blood when his big fist connected with the younger man's nose. The lecture that followed hadn't been pleasant, either. She sighed. It had always been like that. She and Clint had been enemies from their first encounter, when she was eight and he was nineteen and she threw a baseball bat at him.

"It was a long time ago," Janna reminded her. "You're twenty now, and it was all right when we went down to spend a week with Clint and Mama last summer, wasn't it?"

"Of course it was all right, he was in Europe!" Maggie erupted. "This time, your mother's in Europe, and Clint's home, and Lida's just dumped him and he's going to be an absolute pain in the neck!"

"That's why I think you should go," Janna said.

Maggie gaped at her. "Janna, old friend, have you been tippling the brandy bottle again?"

"Well, here you are just getting over that rat, Philip," Janna explained, "and there he is just getting over that ratess, Lida..."

"Haven't you ever noticed that although your brother and I are probably very nice people when we're separated, we seem to turn rabid when we come face to face?" Maggie asked patiently. "The last time," she reminded the wide-eyed girl, "he threw me, fully clothed, into the river, I hit my...my embarrassment on a rock," she faltered.

"You kicked him," Janna replied. "Hard. On the shin."

"He called me an idiot!"

"Well, what would you call somebody who tried to stone a rattlesnake to death from four feet?" Janna threw up her hands. "Honestly, Maggie, when you get around my brother, you lose every ounce of sense you have."

"There you go again... Oh, never mind." She propped her chin on her elbows. "It's no use talking about it, anyway. Clint won't have me down to the ranch without you, and we both know it."

"Yes, he will. I asked him."

"What did you tell him?" Maggie asked suspiciously, her emerald eyes sparkling.

Janna shrugged. "That you and Phil had split, that's all."

"Just that...not how we broke up?" she asked quietly.

"I swear, Maggie. I'd never do that to you."

She forced a wan smile. "I didn't mean that. It...I guess it hit me a little harder than I expected."

"Clint said you could fill in for his secretary while she's on vacation," Janna continued brightly, "and have a working holiday that you'll get paid for. He said it would be the best medicine you'd ever swallowed."

"And, knowing Clint, he'll add a teaspoon of arsenic just to flavor it," Maggie grumbled. "Arrogant, hard headed, bossy..."

"You are between jobs," Janna reminded her.

Maggie sighed. "If I were drowning, you'd toss me an anchor, wouldn't you, my bosom buddy?"

"Oh, Maggie, it's a golden opportunity I'm giving you. Three weeks with the most eligible bachelor in the Sunshine State, good-looking, rich, desirable..."

"I think I'm going to be sick," Maggie said, turning her gaze to the budding trees outside the window.

"Haven't you ever had a romantic thought about Clint, in all these years?" Janna persisted.

"Sorry to disappoint you, but, no."

"The best cure for a broken heart is to get it broken again."

"Golly, gee, Janna, look at the pretty bird on the limb here," Maggie said enthusiastically. "Isn't he just too gorgeous?"

"Okay, okay. Will you at least go to the ranch?"

"Next to hell, it's my very favorite place when Clint's there."

"It's pretty on the ranch right now—all the wildflowers are in bloom." Janna sighed. "Clint's always out on the range somewhere, with the cattle or the field hands, and you know he almost never gets to the house before dark."

"And there's always hope that he'll get captured by rustlers and held for ransom until my vacation's over, right?" Maggie grinned.

"Right!" Janna laughed.

Maggie was never really certain why she decided to take the bus. Perhaps it was because so many pleasant memories of her childhood were connected with it, when she had ridden from her parents' home in Atlanta to her grandparents' home in South Georgia on the big, comfortable bus. And from there, it was just a pleasant drive to Janna and Clint's family's ranch in Florida.

Maggie's eyes were drawn to that long, level landscape, where pine trees, pecan orchards, and spacious farm houses stood sheltering under the towering oaks and chinaberry trees. Her childhood had been spent here, riding over these fields on horseback with Janna. Usually Clint was in hot pursuit while she bent low over the horse's neck. The wind would cut into her face as she urged her mount on, after flinging back a challenge to Clint. The tall man's eyes always had a pale green glint to them when she challenged him, and he always gave her just enough rope to hang herself.

She smiled involuntarily at the memory. She and Clint had never actually decided on the boundaries of their relationship. The banter between them was usually friendly, although it could get hot. But it had never been really malicious or cruel. They were the eternal odd couple, always rubbing each other wrong, always wary around each other as if they held an uneasy truce and were afraid it might fall and break.

Clint was too rugged to ever be called handsome, but he drew women. He always had them hanging on his arm, and Maggie was determined from the beginning never to be one of those poor moths drawn to his flame. She resisted his charm effortlessly, because he never wasted it on her, and she was glad. She'd never been completely sure how she'd react to Clint in that kind of relationship. Because she was afraid of it, she worked minor miracles to prevent it from ever happening.

A buzz of conversation caught her attention, and she drew herself back to the present just in time to see the people across the aisle staring fixedly out the window. The bus slowly ground to a halt as a rider came straight toward it on a black stallion that gleamed like silk in the sun.

Maggie didn't have to be told who was riding the horse. The man's tall, easy arrogance was a dead giveaway, even without the cocky angle of his range hat and the khaki work clothes that seemed to be a part of him.

He reined up at the door as the bus driver opened it with a grin.

"Man, can you ride," he laughed, shaking his curly dark head appreciatively.

"I've had my share of practice," Clint Raygen said with a lopsided smile. His dancing green eyes found Maggie moving up to the front of the bus in her powder blue pantsuit and he raised a lazy eyebrow at her.

"Thank God you're still tomboy enough to wear pants, Irish," he said, throwing down the gauntlet effortlessly with that hated nickname from her childhood. "I don't have time to meet the bus. We're tagging some new cattle. Hop on."

"Hop...on?" she echoed weakly. "But...my luggage?"

"The driver can drop it off in town, can't you?" he asked the man. "We'll get it later."

"I'll do it," the driver said, "on condition if I ever get two days in a row, you'll teach me to ride a horse like that."

"I own the C bar R," Clint told him. "You're welcome anytime. Maggie, hop aboard."

There was a muffled giggle from behind her, and she didn't have to turn to know it was a couple of teenagers who were in the seat behind hers. She straightened her shoulders. There was no way out of this, for sure, not without becoming the object of everybody's conversation for the rest of the way into town.

"I haven't been on a horse in a year," she told him, as she took the lean, brown hand he held out.

"Step up on my boot and swing your leg over," he said in his best you-Jane-me-Tarzan voice, and she could almost see the teenagers swooning.

She managed to get herself up behind him without too much effort, but it was a disturbing new contact, and she had to hold on tight to his hard waist to keep from sliding off the big horse. It was like digging her fingers into solid steel, those whipcord muscles were so powerful.

"All set, Maggie?" he asked over his shoulder.

Sweet Enemy

"All set," she murmured in a low voice that wouldn't carry farther than his ear. "Ready to gallop away in a cloud of dust and leave your adoring public gasping in the wake of your dramatic exit!"

She felt his chest shake under her hand as he urged the stallion into a slow canter and headed out across the field.

"If this isn't dramatic enough for you, Irish," he said arrogantly, "I'll put Whirlwind into a gallop."

Both slender arms went around him and she held on for all she was worth. "Oh, please don't, Clint, I'll be good," she said quickly.

He chuckled deeply. "I thought you would. I'll drop you by the house on my way to the feedlot."

"You sure picked an unusual way to meet me," she remarked, watching the high grass wave along the path the horse was making.

"I didn't plan it," he said casually. "I just happened to see the bus, and I figured you'd be on it."

She wondered at that. Clint always seemed to know when she was coming. He always had. It was as if he had a built-in radar where she was concerned.

She stared at that broad, unyielding back. "Thank you for letting me come," she said quietly.

"Janna said you needed a job," he replied matter-of-factly. "And I happen to be between secretaries," he added in a taut voice. It went without saying that Lida had been the last one.

She turned her attention to the long horizon, dotted with pine trees and scrub palmettos and red-coated Herefords with their faces tiny dots of white in the distance. Involuntarily, a smile came to her face.

"Janna and I used to play cowboys and Indians in those fields," she murmured. "I always had to be the Indian."

He glanced down at her leg in the loose slacks. "You still dress like one," he said. "I've hardly ever seen you in a dress, Irish."

She shifted restlessly. "They're a little out of place on a farm, don't you think?" she grumbled. It was the old argument again, he never tired of chiding her about her preference for slacks.

"I hadn't planned on using you to tag cattle and bale hay," he growled.

She drew a sharp, angry breath. "How I dress is my business," she replied. "All you have to worry about is if I can type and take dictation."

He reined in abruptly and half-turned in the saddle, twisting his tall body so that he could look back at her. His narrowed eyes were a menacing pale green.

"I'll remind you once that there's a line you don't cross with me, little girl," he said in a soft tone that cut more surely than shouting would have. "Your whipped pup of a boyfriend may have taken backtalk with a grin, but don't expect the same consideration from me. I still say a woman's got only one use to a man, and I think you know what I'm talking about."

She did, and nothing could have prevented the blush that colored her high cheekbones. She looked away quickly.

He studied her quietly, his eyes tracing the delicate profile turned toward him. "Why do you screw your hair up like that?" he asked suddenly.

She gritted her teeth. "It keeps it out of my eyes," she replied tightly.

"And keeps a man's eyes turned the other way," he added. "How did that city dude ever get through the layer of ice around you, Irish? With a blowtorch?"

That brought her emerald eyes flashing around to burn into his. "Would you rather I'd have come in a slinky, skin-tight dress with my face plastered in makeup, batting my eyelashes at you?" she asked hotly.

His bold, slow eyes ran over her face, down to her soft mouth, further down to the full, young curves of her body. "You did that once," he recalled gently, meeting her shocked, uncertain gaze. "When you were seventeen, and I suddenly became the star in your young sky after Gerry Broome threw you over."

The memory was like an open wound. He'd never let her forget it. She couldn't forget, either, how she'd run after him shamelessly, finding excuse after excuse to follow him around the ranch that unforgettable summer. Until finally he'd gotten tired of it and shattered her pride into a thousand aching pieces by confronting her with the crush, a confrontation that had shamed her into hiding. She'd never quite recovered from the rejection, keeping it buried in her subconscious. It was one reason she fought him so hard, keeping anger like a safe, high fence between them.

She dropped her eyes to the broad chest in front of her. "That was three years ago," she said quietly.

"And now there's Philip," he added. There was a note in his deep, slow voice that defied analysis. "Isn't there?"

She clenched her jaw. "No," she whispered achingly, "there isn't. Didn't Janna tell you that we'd split?"

His eyes narrowed. "My sister doesn't tell me a damned thing. So you threw him over, Irish?"

She met that taunting gaze levelly. "I caught him with one of my bridesmaids after the rehearsal," she told him, "going into a motel room together."

He studied her thoughtfully. "Were you that cold, that he had to find another woman to warm him?"

She flinched. "Damn you!" she breathed. "I might have expected that you'd see anybody's side of it except mine. It's always been that way with us."

"It's always going to be that way," he said quietly, something deep and strange in the eyes that searched hers, "because you don't want me on your side. You want a damned wall between us for some reason. What the hell are you afraid of?"

"You can ask me that, with your reputation?" she scoffed.

A slow, mocking smile touched his cruel mouth. "Little girl, you flatter yourself. Even forgetting the fact that I could give you eleven years, you don't stir me in a physical sense, Maggie. You never have." His eyes swept along her boyish figure. "It would be like making love to a snow sculpture."

She kept her face cool. It would never do to let him know how much he could hurt her. "I thought I came here to be your secretary, not your whipping boy," she said coolly. "Or do you expect me to pay for Lida's sins, along with my own?"

She saw his eyes narrow, the muscles in his jaw moving ominously. "My God, you're asking for it," he warned softly.

She straightened, moving as far away from him as it was possible to move on horseback. "You started it!"

"I can finish it, too," he said curtly.

She looked away. "I told Janna it wouldn't work," she bit off. "If you'll kindly take me to the house, I'll get a cab back to the bus station."

"Running away, Irish?" he growled. "You're good at that."

Her lower lip trembled. "I won't be crucified by you!" she burst out on a sob. "Oh, God, I hate men, I hate men," she whispered. "Cheats and liars, all of you!"

His lean hand caught the nape of her neck and drew her forehead against his broad shoulder, as he twisted further in the saddle. "How many women were there before you found out?" he asked at her ear.

A sob shook her. "Four, five; I lost count," she whispered. "We were going to be married just two days after...he said I wouldn't melt in a...in a blast furnace," her voice broke again. Her small hand curled against the warm muscles of his arm. "And he...he was right. I didn't feel that way with him, I couldn't...!" She drew a long, sobbing breath.

His fingers tightened on her slender neck. "How old was he?" he asked gently.

She swallowed down another sob. "Twenty-seven."

"Experienced?"

"Very."

"Was he patient, Maggie?" he asked.

She drew a soft breath, her eyes closing tightly. "He...
took it for granted that I knew... well, that I..."

His chest rose deeply against her, and fell with a sound
like impatience. "It's just as well, Irish," he said at her ear.
"Better to find him out now than after the wedding."

"Clint, I'm sorry I jumped..." she began.

His cheek moved against hers, rough and warm. "Dry up,
little watering pot. I've got cattle to tend, and Emma's going
to be standing on her head wondering what happened to us.
Okay now?"

"Yes." She managed a wan smile for him. "Clint, I'm
sorry about Lida..."

His face was shuttered, but not angry. He flicked a care-
less forefinger against her nose. "Let's go home."

He turned back to the saddle horn and coaxed the stallion into a canter. He didn't say another word until they got
to the sprawling white frame ranch house in its nest of oaks
and pecan trees. He let her down at the white fence beside
the front porch.

Sitting astride the black stallion, he was an impressive
figure, tall in the saddle and ramrod straight. He lit a cigarette, his eyes studying her quietly for a long moment.

"Must you stare at me like that?" she asked uneasily,
shifting under the bold thoroughness of his scrutiny. "I feel
like a heifer on market day."

Something cruel flashed in his pale eyes. "I'm not putting in any bids," he replied innocently. "I'll have one of the
boys fetch your luggage. Emma'll get you something to eat.
I'll explain what I need done when I get in tonight."

The coldness in him, so sudden and unexpected, made
chills run down her spine. For years they'd been make-
believe enemies. But this felt like the real thing. He looked
at her as if... as if he hated her!

"I still think it might be better if I went home," she said.

"You'll stick it out," he countered sharply. "I can't get a
replacement at this short notice, and I've got correspondence backed up to the eaves, with a sale day coming up."

"Orders, Mr. Raygen?" she fumed.

A wisp of a smile touched that hard, stern face that was so much a stranger's, emphasizing the nose that had been broken at least twice and showed it. "Orders, Irish."

"Will you stop calling me that? You know I hate it!"

"By all means, hate it. Hate me, too, if it helps. I don't give a damn, and you know that, too, don't you, little girl?" he asked with a hellish grin.

She whirled on her heels and stalked through the gate onto the long white porch, with its rocking chairs and wide porch swing and pots filled with blooming flowers.

2

*

Emma was rolling out dough in the spacious, homey kitchen when Maggie walked in and, unmindful of the flour up to her elbows, she grabbed the younger woman in a bearish hug.

Maggie laughed, smothered in the ample girth of Emma's huge embrace, feeling really at home for the first time.

"It's so good to have another woman here, I could jump for joy," Emma grinned, running one floury hand through her short, silver hair. "Clint Raygen's been like a wild man for the past month. I'll swear, I never thought a hussy like that Lida Palmes could affect him in such a way. If you ask me, it's just hurt pride that's eating him, but it doesn't make any difference to his temper."

"So I've noticed," Maggie sighed, and sat down at the long kitchen table where Emma was making bread. "What did she do to him?"

"Walked out on him without a word. Not even a day's notice." She shrugged. "Found herself a rich Florida millionaire, they said."

"He couldn't have been that much richer than Clint," Maggie remarked.

"He wasn't," Emma smiled. "And he had twenty years on him, to boot. Nobody understood what got into her. One day she was queening it over me and the ranch hands, the next she was gone."

"Was it very long ago?" she asked idly.

"Let's see—hard to remember things at my age, you know. But . . . oh, yes, it was the day Janna called to tell us we were invited to your wedding." She laughed. "We didn't even know you were engaged, you secretive little thing."

Maggie's eyes fell. "I guess you knew we called off the wedding."

Emma's floured hand touched hers gently. "It's for the best. We both know that, don't we?"

She nodded with a misty smile. "I wasn't desperately in love with him, but I did like him a lot. I guess my pride's hurt, too."

"You'll get over it. When one door closes, another opens, Maggie, my dear."

"You're right, of course," she managed cheerfully. "Janna sends her love. She said she'll try to get her vacation early and come on down in a few weeks."

"That would be nice, to have both of you home for a while. Well," she said, kneading dough rhythmically, "tell me all the latest news."

It was well after dark, and Emma and Maggie were just getting everything on the dining room table when Clint came striding in the front door. His jeans were red with mud, his shirt wet with sweat, his jaw showing a shadow of a beard. He barely spared them a glance before he went down the long hall that led to his room.

"Whiskey," Emma remarked with a nod, and poured a glass two inches deep of the amber liquid before adding a touch of water and two ice cubes to it. "I can tell by his walk."

"Tell what?" Maggie asked.

"What kind of day it's been. The cattle must have given him fits."

"Not the cattle," Maggie replied wearily. "Me. We got into it on the way home. I should never have come, Emma. It's just like old times."

"Is it, now?" the older woman asked curiously. "Maybe. And maybe not. We'll see."

Clint came back looking cooler, his dark hair damp from a shower, his face shaven, the work khakis exchanged for a pair of sand-colored slacks and a beige patterned shirt that clung to his muscular arms and chest like a second skin.

His green eyes slid down Maggie's slender figure in pale yellow slacks and a tank top, moving back up to rest narrowly on the familiar bun.

"Welcome back, tomboy," he said with thinly veiled sarcasm.

"Thanks," she replied sweetly. "Emma poured you a drink."

He turned away, found it on the table and threw down a large swallow of it. "Well, sit down," he growled at her, "or do you plan to eat standing up?"

She dragged out a chair and plopped down in it, pointedly avoiding his gaze as Emma brought the rest of the food and finally sat down herself across from Maggie.

"Do I get combat pay?" Emma asked Clint when she caught the icy glares that were being exchanged.

"Put on your armour and shut up," Clint replied, but there was a glint of humor in his tone, and in his pale eyes.

Emma glanced at Maggie with a grin. "Welcome home, honey."

Dinner was pleasant enough after that, but when the last of the coffee was gone, Clint motioned Maggie to follow him, and led her into the darkly masculine den with its gun cabinet and oak desk and deer head mounted over the mantel.

"Get a pencil," he told Maggie. "You'll find one on the desk."

She picked one up out of a pen holder, and borrowed one of the empty legal pads as well before she sat down in the chair beside his big desk.

He turned, his eyes studying her quietly, angrily, for a long moment before he spoke. "How old are you now?" he asked unexpectedly.

"Twenty," she replied quietly.

"Twenty." He lit a cigarette, but his eyes never left her. "Twenty, and still unawakened."

She felt the color rush into her face, and hated it, hated him.

"You're sure about that?" she asked hotly.

He held her eyes for a long time. "I'm very sure, honey," he said softly.

Unable to hold the penetrating gaze for another instant, she dragged her eyes down to the blank sheet of yellow paper and concentrated on the bluish lines that ruled it.

"I thought you wanted to dictate some letters," she said in a tight voice.

"You don't know what I want, little girl," he replied. "And if you did, it would probably scare the hell out of you. Got your pencil ready? Here goes . . ."

He was dictating before she had time to puzzle out that cryptic remark.

The first few days went by in a rush, and Maggie fell into an easy routine. Clint left the correspondence on her desk every morning, all outlined, so that she could work at her own pace. At night, he signed the letters and checked the records she typed for him, and they both worked at holding their tempers.

She finished early the fifth day and couldn't resist the temptation to go for a ride. Clint had given her a gentle little bay mare for her seventeenth birthday and it was still her favorite mount. Melody was the name she gave it, because of the horse's easy rocking motion as she walked; like a blues melody.

It stirred her emotions to revisit the haunts of her childhood on the large, sprawling farm. Near the tall line of pine trees was the aging, majestic pecan tree that she and Janna climbed long ago—their dreaming tree. Then a little farther along was the thicket where dogwoods grew virgin white in the spring and little girls could gather armloads of them to dream over.

Then, too, there was the river. Maggie reined in the mare and leaned over the saddle horn to watch it flowing lazily like a silver and white ribbon through the trees. The river, where they waded and swam, and where Clint had hurled her—fully clothed—the day she kicked him.

She couldn't resist that cool, inviting water in the heat that was thick and smothering even in the shade of the hardwoods on the bank. She tied Melody to a sapling and tugged off her boots and thick socks.

The water was icy to her bare feet, the river rocks smooth and slippery. She wobbled cautiously near the bank, grabbing onto a low-hanging limb of the bulky oak tree to keep her balance.

With a sigh, she closed her eyes and listened to the watery whisper of the river, the sound of birds calling and moving the leaves over her head as they jumped from bough to bough. The peace she felt was indescribable. It was as if she'd come home. Home.

She remembered Clint's mother baking biscuits in the oven, laughing as she teased Maggie about her pigtails. And Clint, maddening even that long ago, swinging her off the floor in his hard arms to welcome her when she got off the bus at the station. Twelve years ago. A lifetime ago.

She opened her eyes and followed the path of the river downstream with an unseeing blankness in her stare. It was hard to say just when she and Clint had lost that rapport. When she was fourteen—fifteen? There had always been pretend arguments, but as she reached the middle of her teens they had suddenly become real. Clint seemed to provoke them deliberately, as if sparking her hot temper were important, to keep her at a distance. It had been even worse in her seventeenth summer...

She blotted out the thought. As long as she lived, she'd never get over that humiliation. To an already withdrawn teenager, the effect had been devastating. Not until Philip came along had she even tried to open her heart again. Only to have him shatter her pride to tiny bits.

A strand of her hair tumbled into her eyes and rather than try to put it up again, she removed all the pins from her hair and stuck them in her pocket, letting the rich black waves fall gently around her shoulders. It had been a long time since she'd worn her hair down like this outside the privacy of her bedroom. That, too, dated back to Clint's cruelty.

He made no secret of his fondness for long hair, and Maggie had let hers grow to her waist in the months before that summer vacation. She'd even shed her favorite slacks outfits for some frilly sundresses and dainty sandals, all in the hopes of catching Clint's eye. But all she'd caught was Gerry Broome's, and Clint had come to the rescue just in time. Gerry couldn't get away from her fast enough, and Clint always thought that was the reason for her one-woman campaign to reel in his heart. But none of it had worked.

"Save your schemes for a boy your own age, little girl," he'd warned her venomously after a lecture that her cheeks still reddened from three years later. "I want more than long hair and doe eyes when I take a woman in my arms. The only thing about me that you arouse is my temper. I don't want you, Maggie."

The words echoed in her mind for days afterwards, even when she got back home and was caught up in her father's lingering illness and her mother's grief. She'd cut her hair then, and even when it grew again, she kept it tightly capped in the bun. It hadn't come down even for Philip, who loved long hair himself, but wasn't persuasive enough.

With a sigh she sank down on a big boulder at the river's edge, trailing her bare toes through the cold, rippling water, her hair hiding her face from view as she relived the memories.

"Sunning yourself, mermaid?" a taunting voice asked from close behind her.

She whirled with a gasp, almost unseating herself into the stream as she faced Clint. He was leaning carelessly against the trunk of the tree, one dusty boot propped on a chunky root, his forearms crossed over his knee—just watching her. His stallion nibbled at leaves on the oak tree nearby.

"You move...like wind," she accused breathlessly, smoothing the hair away from her face.

"An old hunter's trick. Your mind was far away, little one," he said gently, his eyes sketching her face in its frame of waving black hair.

"I guess it was." She turned back, automatically winding her hair into a braid so that she could pin it up.

"Leave it!" he said, in a tone like a whiplash.

She stiffened with her hands up against her nape. "It . . . gets in my way," she said tightly.

"We both know that isn't why."

"You flatter yourself if you think you're the cause of it," she said with practiced calm, reaching into her pocket for some bobby pins. "I'm not seventeen any more, Clint. I'm not vulnerable anymore."

He was behind her before she realized it, arrogantly sweeping the pins from her hand. He jerked her up by the elbows and held her on her tiptoes in the cool, rushing water.

His green eyes narrowed, darkened, as he looked down into her frightened face. It wasn't Clint's familiar, taunting eyes that looked down into hers. He was a stranger—unsmiling, somber, studying her with an intensity that rippled along her nerves.

"Was that a dig, Maggie?" he asked gruffly. "Or did you think I'd forgotten what happened?"

She averted her face and tried not to feel the steely excitement his fingers were causing. "It was a long time ago," she said as calmly as she could with her heart beating wildly.

"And you're all grown up now, is that it?" He pulled her close against his tall, lean body. "How grown up are you, little girl?" he whispered, and she felt his breath, smoky and warm, whipping across her face.

She pulled furiously against his merciless grip, fighting him for all she was worth. "Let go of me!" she flashed, her loosened hair flying as she twisted against his hands.

"Irish," he taunted softly, holding her easily in spite of her flailing efforts to resist him. "As Irish as a shamrock. Calm down, little tigress, I'm not going to force anything on you."

She did calm down, but more because of her own fatigue than the soothing words. "You beast," she muttered, glaring up at him out of eyes like an angry cat's.

His hands slid up her arms to her throat, holding her flushed young face up to his, and all expression seemed to go out of his own face, leaving his eyes narrow and dark as they looked deep into hers.

"Fire in you," he said gently. "Soft flames, Irish, that could burn a man alive. Did Philip ever see that white-hot temper?"

The intensity of his gaze confused her, shook her. "He didn't know I had a temper," she said unsteadily. Her eyes narrowed, temper coming to her rescue. "You wouldn't know I had one, either, if you'd stop picking on me!"

"I like it when you fight me," he said softly.

She looked up in time to see the light in his leaf-green eyes flare up with the words, and a ghost of a smile touched his hard, chiseled mouth. It was like no look he'd ever given her before—appraising, calculating—almost sensuous. It made her heart tremble, because the way he said it conjured up a picture of a woman fighting the crush of a man's hard arms, the sting of his mouth...

She dropped her eyes to his chest, and suddenly he released her, moving away to light a cigarette with long, steady fingers.

She rubbed her chafed arms. "If... if you want those records typed today, I'd better get back to the house," she said, turning toward the bank. "And," she threw over her shoulder as she bent to wipe her wet feet with a handkerchief, "you owe me a package of bobby pins."

She felt his eyes running over her as she pulled on her boots.

"Leave it down, Irish," he said carelessly, his eyes never leaving her as she got up and untied Melody's reins. "I won't make any more remarks about it, but leave it loose."

She gaped at him, puzzled at the anger in his deep voice— anger that was meant more for himself than for her. With a shrug, she mounted and rode away without a backward glance.

He stood and watched her until she was out of sight, his eyes narrowed against the sun, his face thoughtful and solemn.

3

Emma only set two places at the supper table, noting Maggie's puzzled glance with a smile.

"Clint's got a date," she explained, leaving Maggie to put the silverware at the places while she went out to the kitchen to bring the food in.

A pain like being shot went through Maggie's slender body, and she wondered at it. For all that her pride had been crushed by Philip, her heart had never been touched by any man—except one. She hated the rush of feeling, the green surge of jealousy that thinking about Clint and a woman, any woman, could cause. It had always been that way, always. And she managed to keep it hidden because of what he'd already done to her stubborn spirit. But it was still there, inside, glowing and sweetly burning like a candle no amount of wind could blow out. And she hated Clint for causing it.

He came in from the feedlot just as Emma and Maggie were finishing up the dishes, and to avoid him, Maggie retreated to the front porch and glued her lean body onto the porch swing. It was warm and sweet-fragranced, that long porch in the darkness. In her childhood, she had sat in it while the thunder shuddered around her, feeling the misty whip of rain in her face while she closed her eyes and heard the soothing squeak of the swing in motion.

The sudden blinding glare of the porch light brought a surprised gasp from her lips; she sat stark upright as Clint came into view.

It was always a shock to see him in a beige linen suit and coral silk tie, the white of his shirt bringing out his swarthy complexion, his dark hair. He could have passed for a very masculine model, sophistication clinging to his tall, muscular body like the spicy cologne he favored.

His eyes were a dark green as they swept over her blue-jeaned figure, rigid in the porch swing. He eyed her through a small gray cloud of cigarette smoke, moving closer like some big, graceful cat.

"Hiding, Irish?" he asked quietly.

She dragged her eyes down to his broad chest. "I felt like some air."

One dark eyebrow went up. "You fell out of that swing on your head once," he recalled. "You and Janna were using it for a rocking horse, and you went head over heels."

Her fingers touched the dark green wooden frame and the cold metal chain gently. "You like to remind me of the unpleasant things, don't you?" she asked carelessly.

"Would you rather be reminded of that day by the corral when you did everything but go down on your knees and beg me to make love to you?" he asked mockingly, a harsh note in his voice that cut as much as the humiliating words.

Her eyes closed at that memory, at the pain of it. There was a streak of cruelty in him, she thought miserably; there had to be or he wouldn't enjoy taunting her like this. She got out of the swing, still avoiding his eyes, and started past him.

One lean, steely hand shot out like a bullet and caught her arm roughly, hauling her up against him as easily as if she'd been a child.

"No comeback, Irish?" he growled. "Where's that hot temper now?"

She couldn't find it. Her body trembled in his grasp, and she couldn't even fight him.

With a gesture that was barely short of violence, he threw his unfinished cigarette off the porch and caught her by both shoulders, his fingers hurting, his green eyes blazing down into hers.

"Let me go!" she burst out, panic sweeping through her because of the new sensations he was causing her to feel as he bruised her body against him.

"Why?" he asked shortly.

Her full mouth trembled as she searched for the words that would free her. "You're...hurting me," she managed.

"Where?" he murmured, and his eyes began to sketch her small, flushed face like an artist's brush.

"My...my shoulders," she stammered.

His crushing hold loosened, became warm and sensuously caressing, his fingers burning her through the thin cotton blouse. "Does this hurt?" he asked gently.

She couldn't get the words out. He was burning her alive with that slow, tenderly soothing touch, making her heart dance, making her lungs feel collapsed. Her small hands went to the silky shirt, pushing halfheartedly against the warm, unyielding muscles of his broad chest.

Soft, deep laughter brushed her ears. "Can't you talk to me, little Maggie?" he whispered deeply. His hands left her shoulders to cup her face and hold it up to his eyes. The warm strength in them drained her of protest, the tang of his cologne was permeating her senses. Her fingers, where they pressed against him, were so cold they felt numb. And still she couldn't move, couldn't look away from the mocking gaze that had her hypnotized, trapped.

His eyes dropped to her soft young mouth, and one thumb came up to brush across it like a whisper. "I could break your mouth open under mine like a ripe melon right now," he murmured sensuously, "and you wouldn't lift a finger to stop me, would you, Irish? You're still mine to take, any damned time I want you!"

With a sob of exquisite shame, she broke free of him, catching him off guard, and she ran every step of the way back into the house, ignoring Emma's stunned queries as she took the steps two at a time.

All the long night she lay awake, staring at the dark ceiling, planning a way, any way, out of this nightmare. Even going back to her old job, seeing Philip again, didn't hold the terror that staying here did. She had to get away. She had to!

She climbed out of bed and into her clothes numbly as the sun began to climb out of the early morning clouds. She packed before she went downstairs, her mind made up, her eyes red and dark-shadowed from lack of sleep. She'd have breakfast and explain to Emma, then she'd get a cab to the bus station, and Clint would never...

He was still at the breakfast table, where he normally wouldn't have been at this hour of the morning. His own eyes looked as if he hadn't slept, and she wondered bitterly what time he'd come home, reasoning she must have dozed off eventually because she never heard him come in.

"I'll get you some coffee, honey," Emma said quietly, patting her on the shoulder as she passed toward the kitchen.

She made a big production of unfolding her linen napkin and smoothing it on her lap, of studying the tablecloth, of doing everything but meeting the watchful gaze across from her.

"Did you sleep at all?" he asked finally, his voice deep and slow and bitter.

"Oh, I...I slept fine, thanks," she managed.

"Like hell," he scoffed.

"Shouldn't you be out with the cattle?" she asked.

"Not until you convince me that you're not going to be on the first northbound bus," he said flatly.

That brought her eyes jerking up to meet the question in his, and he had all the answer he needed.

"I thought so," he said, leaning back in his chair to study her through narrowed eyes. "Running never solved anything, Maggie."

She glared at him, feeling something break inside her. "I need your advice like a hole in the head," she snapped, her face wounded. "What are you trying to do to me, Clint? Wasn't what Philip did to me enough without you trying to shatter the few pieces of me he left intact? Why do you enjoy hurting me?"

"Don't you know, honey?" he asked in a dangerously quiet tone.

It was the stranger's face again, not Clint's, and she stared at him curiously. "I...I don't think I know you at all sometimes," she said involuntarily.

"You don't." He gulped down the remainder of his coffee and lit a cigarette. "You're wallowing in self-pity, Irish, or didn't you realize it? Poor little girl, betrayed by her fiancé, left alone at the altar...well, I'm fresh out of sympathy. He was a damned two-timing cheat, and you're well rid of him. All he hurt was your pride, little icicle," he said ruthlessly. "You wouldn't recognize love if it came up and sat on your foot."

"I suppose you would, being such an expert!" she flashed.

His eyes glinted at her over a mocking smile. "That's more like it," he chuckled.

She frowned. "What?"

He rose, pausing by her chair on his way out, one long arm sliding in front of her as he leaned down. "I told you before, baby," he murmured at her ear, "I like it when you fight me. That's the easiest way to tell that you aren't trying to bury your head in the past."

She flushed, suddenly understanding—or, almost understanding—his behavior last night.

"I don't want to spend the whole two weeks fighting you," she grumbled.

His fingers caught her chin and raised her eyes to his. All the levity was gone from his hard, dark face now. "Why don't you get Emma to pack us a picnic lunch?" he asked softly, "and bring it down to the feedlot around noon. We'll go down by the river and eat."

"B...but, the sale; all those invitations, and the...the publicity...?" she stammered.

One long finger traced the soft curve of her mouth in a silence that made her unsteady breathing audible. "I'll lay you down under that gnarled old oak," he whispered deeply, holding her eyes, "and teach you all the things Philip should have had the patience to teach you."

She blushed furiously and tore her eyes away. "I...I really don't need any lessons, thank you," she said shortly. She jerked away from his lean hand. "Once burned, twice shy, Clint. You won't bring me to my knees again, not ever!"

He didn't seem to be fazed by her passionate outburst. He only smiled. "Won't I? Don't underestimate me, honey."

"I learned early not to underestimate the enemy," she replied.

He went out laughing just as Emma returned with the coffee and a plate of eggs, bacon, and fresh biscuits. "Now, what's got into him?" she asked curiously.

"The devil," Maggie said tightly.

Maggie was just finishing an advertisement on the sale for the local weekly paper when she heard a sudden loud pounding at the front door, and Emma's quick footsteps going to answer it. There was the snap as the door opened, and a sudden jubilant cry from Emma, and then two voices mingling, Emma's excited one and a laughing, pleasant male one.

"Maggie! Come here!" Emma called.

Puzzled at the commotion, Maggie stuck her head around the door and found her eyes held by a pair of dark blue ones in a deeply tanned face outlined by thick blond hair.

"Well, hush my mouth, if it isn't the girl I swore undying love to on the stage in our sixth-grade play!" Brent Halmon grinned, his eyes sparkling at her from the hall.

"Hi, Sir Got-A-Lott, where's your hawse?!" she laughed back.

He threw open the door and swung her up in his lean arms, planting a smacking kiss on her cheek. "By gosh, you've grown, Maggie!" he teased, giving her a lengthy appraisal as he set her back on her feet. "Did you really get this pretty in just four years?"

"This isn't my real face, you know," she whispered *sotto voce*. "It's the mask I wear so my green warts won't show!"

"Still got 'em, huh?" he said in mock resignation, shaking his head. "I warned you about kissing those frogs, didn't I?"

"You two!" Emma laughed, eyeing them. "Always into mischief of some sort or other. You gave Clint gray hairs when you were kids."

"Speaking of old Heavy Hand, where is he?" Brent grinned.

"Out putting diapers on his baby cows," Maggie told him. "And ribbons on their mamas, and evening jackets on their daddies. There's a sale day coming up next week."

"I know," Brent told her, "that's why I came. I've got my eye on that prize Hereford bull of Cousin Clint's."

"Speaking of mammoth ranches," Maggie said, "how is Mississippi?"

"Green and beautiful. Why don't you ever come to visit me?"

She shrugged. "Work. As a matter of fact, I'm Clint's temporary secretary for the next couple of weeks. That's why I'm here."

He nodded. "I heard about Lida taking a powder on him," Brent said with a harsh sigh. "It was no less than I expected. I thought Clint of all people would have more sense..."

"And I think everyone's got the wrong idea," Emma said quietly. "Clint wasn't in love with Lida. He wasn't thinking of marriage, either. He's a normal, healthy man, and she was a sophisticated woman who knew the score. And that's enough about it. Come on, Brent, I'll show you up. Clint will be so surprised...!"

"See you in a few minutes, Mag," Brent called over Emma's bright conversation.

Brent was changing for supper when Clint came in, dusty and tired and in a gruff temper. His eyes narrowed as they settled on Maggie, finishing one last letter at her desk.

"Weren't you hungry?" he asked without preamble.

She stared at him blankly. "Hungry?"

"At dinner," he said flatly.

She remembered what he'd told her at breakfast and began to bloom with color. "You were joking..." she said weakly.

"The hell I was," he shot back, his eyes narrow, threatening.

She opened her mouth to speak just as Brent came in the door and clapped Clint on the back.

"Hi, Cousin!" he said cheerfully as Clint wheeled, stunned, to face him. "Surprise, surprise!"

"My God, what are you doing here?" Clint asked irritably.

"I came for the sale," was the imperturbable reply. "You did invite me," he reminded the older man.

"For the sale, not the summer!"

Brent's eyebrows went up, but he cheerfully ignored Clint's ill humor. "Bull gore you or something?" he asked pleasantly, studying the taller man's dusty clothes for sign of blood.

Maggie stifled a giggle, but not before Clint shot a narrow glance her way and saw her face.

"Oh, you're home!" Emma smiled at Clint from the doorway. "Just look who's here. Isn't it nice to have Brent back again?"

"Enchanting," Clint agreed. "Pardon me while I go upstairs and put a gun to my temple in honor of the occasion."

Three pairs of puzzled eyes followed his tall figure as he thudded up the stairs.

"He doesn't *look* drunk," Brent remarked casually.

Clint's temper seemed to have improved when he came back downstairs, his dark hair still damp from a shower, in a pair of dark slacks and a green patterned silk shirt open at the neck, in a shade that matched his eyes. He seemed to go out of his way to be pleasant to Brent, dwelling on the subject of cattle and land management to such an extent that Emma and Maggie ignored them and talked clothes all through the meal.

"I haven't been around back yet," Brent said as they relaxed over coffee in the living room. "Is the pool still there, and filled?"

"It is," Clint said pleasantly. "Feel like a swim? Maggie?" he added, glancing at her.

"If you'll let me wear a bathing suit, instead of pushing me in fully clothed," she said sweetly.

"Honey, it'll be a pleasure," he said in a voice that made chills run down her spine.

"Did I miss something?" Brent blinked.

"Last summer," Maggie explained, "he threw me in the river with my clothes on."

"You kicked the hell out of me first," Clint replied imperturbably.

"What was I supposed to do, stand there and let the stupid snake have first bite?!"

"Did you think you could stone the damned thing to death with a handful of pebbles?"

"They were stones, and I . . . !"

Brent stood up. "If you two want to do this thing properly, why don't you appoint seconds and meet in the lower pasture at sunup?"

Clint gave him a look that sent him toward the stairs. "I'm going after my trunks. Coming, Maggie?"

She glared at Clint. "Why not?"

4

___ * ___

The pool was Olympic-sized, and the water was pleasantly
cool. Maggie floated quietly, her slender body scantily covered in an aqua two-piece bathing suit, her long hair float-
ing behind her. She and Brent had done two laps paralleling
each other when Clint joined them. Swimming was something he rarely did in company, and never among strangers.
A long, jagged white scar ran from the center of his broad,
hair-laden chest along the bronzed skin of his flat stomach.
Another was visible on his muscular thigh. Souvenirs, he
called them, of a long-ago conflict when he hadn't quite
dived away in time to miss a shower of shrapnel. To Maggie, they weren't in the least unsightly—the only thing about
him that shook her was the sight of that powerful, dark
body without the veneer of clothing to make it less sensuous. But Clint was touchy about his scars nevertheless, so
she never mentioned them, nor did Brent.

They relaxed in the soothing water without talking for
lazy minutes, until Emma shattered the peace by calling
Brent to the phone.

"They find you wherever you go," Brent groaned as he
pulled his slender body out of the water. "Carry on without me, Maggie. Clint'll save you if you go down for the
third time."

"Want to bet?" she murmured, but he hadn't heard her.

Clint surfaced beside her, shaking his dark head to throw
his hair out of his eyes, and his lean hands caught her bare
midriff, sending a wild shudder of pleasure through her slim
body as he righted her in the water and pulled her body
against him roughly.

"What was that crack supposed to mean?" he asked, his eyes burning into hers, his muscular legs entwining with hers under the water.

"That you'd probably enjoy drowning me," she said unsteadily. Chills began to run over her. "Please let me go. I'm cold."

"Cold or excited?" he asked, his face solemn, his gaze level and questioning. "You always had a soft spot for Brent, didn't you, Irish?"

"We get along very well."

"And you and I don't," he said flatly.

"That goes without saying. Clint..." Her hands pushed against him, touching the thick scar at his breastbone. Her eyes drifted down to it lying under the thick tangle of wet hair that felt strange and new to her touch. Her fingers traced it gently, then they moved over the broad, hard chest that was cool from the water. A shock went through her as she realized what she was doing and she jerked her hand away as though his flesh had scorched her.

He caught her hand and lifted it to his shoulder, holding it there as he studied her downcast face. "Maggie, don't," he said gently.

"I'm sorry," she murmured in a whipped tone. "I didn't mean to..."

He caught a handful of her wet hair and pushed her face against him until it was smothered against the cool, bronzed flesh, the curling hairs tickling her nose.

"My God, I like it when you touch me," he whispered at her ear, a husky, strange note in his voice. "There's nothing to be ashamed of. It's natural for a woman to be curious, especially when she's innocent." His fingers tightened at her nape. Against her, under the water, she could feel the heavy, hard beat of his heart. "Come here, honey," he whispered, and both arms went around her, swallowing her, in an embrace that brought the stars down into the pool with them. His hold tightened slowly, holding her, crushing her, hurting her...

"Give me your mouth," he growled huskily.

Burning, hungry, she lifted her face to his blazing eyes
and saw them shift to her lips with something like awe. This
was Clint—Clint, who teased her and tormented her, who
was as much a part of her childhood as the ranch, the
horses, Janna. But it had never been like this, not in all her
wild young imaginings. He was a man, older than she, experienced, confident. And her inexperience was no match
for the hunger she read in his face.

"And now," he whispered roughly, bending his dark
head, "now I'm going to teach you sensations you never
knew you could feel, little innocent. I'm going to show you
how to be a woman . . ."

She was trembling, helpless as she waited breathlessly to
feel his hard, chiseled mouth on hers. She started to speak,
to say something, anything, just as the patio door opened
and broke the spell.

She felt the shudder run through Clint's hard body as he
released her and dove under the water. Brent came running, his bare feet thudding on the wet concrete, and dove
into the water with a resounding splash.

Maggie went riding with Brent the next day when she finished Clint's terse correspondence, which he left for her on
the Dictaphone.

"I love this place," Brent said with a smile, drinking in
the lush green forest around them. "I spent a lot of my
childhood here."

She smiled, too. "So did I. Janna and I used to play
cowboys and Indians here, remember? Once we ambushed
you from the top of one of those pines."

"And got ticks, both of you," he remembered gleefully.

She shuddered. "It was awful!"

"No doubt." He stopped and looked down at her,
frowning. "What got into Clint last night?" he asked suddenly.

She felt the blush rising, and averted her face. "Bad temper," she said flatly, remembering how he'd left the pool
without a backward glance just after Brent's return. He had

left the house not long afterward, and it had been early morning before Maggie heard the car return. By the time she and Brent got to the breakfast table, he was already at work. She closed her eyes on the memory of what he'd been about to do—what she'd almost let him do. She could still see his hard mouth poised just above hers, feel his warm, smoky breath mingling with her own. She'd wanted that kiss so much that it was like being torn apart when Brent had interrupted them. But it was better this way, she reminded herself. Clint had all the women he needed, that was obvious. He liked to humiliate her, anyway, so she should have been better armored. Perhaps now that Brent was here...

"Where are you?" Brent asked, waving a hand in front of her eyes.

She glanced at him with wide eyes. "Mars," she whispered theatrically, "out there! Exploring strange and exotic places with my mind!"

He grinned. "Why not try exploring me with your lips?" he leered, raising and lowering his eyebrows for effect.

She burst out laughing and let Melody flow into step beside his horse. "You're just what I needed. Oh, I'm so glad you came!"

"I'm glad *you* are," he replied.

"What do you mean?"

He glanced at her speculatively. "I mean, Cousin Clint isn't. Look out, my long-ago leading lady. Clint in action is a force to behold."

"I don't understand."

"He wants you," he told her nonchalantly.

Her heart stopped, then started again. "He's only playing games, Brent. Lida ripped at his pride and..."

"He wants you," he repeated quietly. "I've never seen him look at a woman exactly that way before, but the intent is all too familiar. I wouldn't like to see you hurt."

His concern was comforting. She reached out and touched his thin arm. "I don't want to see me hurt, either," she said with a smile. "I've got both eyes wide open. I'm not burying my head in the sand."

He shook his head, smiling back. "My sweet, you've been in love with him most of your life, pseudo-fiancés notwithstanding. He may not see it, but I do."

She chewed on her bottom lip, staring down at the pommel of her saddle. "I thought Philip would..."

"...Compensate?" he finished for her. "You knew better, didn't you? Maggie, you shouldn't have come here."

She laughed softly. "It's a little late now."

"Come home with me when I leave," he said quietly.

She stared at him, trying to read his thin face.

"No, it isn't like that," he laughed. "Maggie," he added, solemn now, "I know how you feel. There's a woman back home...I'd give everything I own, and more; she doesn't feel that way about me. And, like you, I know that nobody else could take her place. Don't let yourself be drawn and quartered like this. We'll console each other."

"A shoulder to cry on, Brent?" she asked softly.

"That's all I can offer you," he replied, more serious than she'd ever seen him. He grinned suddenly. "Did you think I was offering you a grand passion?"

She laughed feverishly. "Let me think about it. Right now, I'm doing a job, and I gave my word."

"It's up to you what you do," he replied. "I never try to actively interfere in anyone else's life. But I'm offering you a refuge if ever you need it. And he'll never find you."

She nodded. "Thanks for the option."

He winked at her. "You're more my cousin than he is. We always were a pair of rascals."

"We still are." She leaned toward him conspiratorially. "Let's swipe the rotor out of his jeep."

"You're on!"

Clint eyed both of his innocent-looking guests over the supper table.

"A strange thing happened to me today," he remarked casually. "I tried to start my jeep and the rotor was missing."

"The rotor?" Emma exclaimed, pausing in the act of lifting a forkful of mashed potatoes to her mouth. "The rotor was gone?"

Maggie raised both eyebrows and met Clint's searching gaze levelly. "How strange," she said impassively.

Brent strangled on his coffee and had to excuse himself from the table.

"Never fear!" Maggie called after him, rising. "First aid is on the way!"

For the next few days, she and Brent fortunately were able to keep out of Clint's way—just. But his temper was shorter than ever, and getting things ready for the mammoth sale wasn't helping it.

"Hey, Maggie," Billy Jones, the foreman called, "Clint wants to see you!"

She looked up from the porch where she was getting a checklist ready for the midday barbecue at the sale. "Well, here I am!" she called cheerfully. "Tell him to look to his heart's content!"

Billy went away shaking his head, and Maggie was instantly sorry. Brent had just been called away on business that morning and she was afraid to push Clint too far without Brent's protection. But the tension was beginning to get to her...

"So there you are, you damned little witch," Clint muttered, coming up the steps, his hat cocked over his brow, fury in every line of his hard face.

She felt herself cringing, but she kept her eyes raised. "Yes?"

He stopped just in front of her and swept off his hat, slinging it onto the nearby table. He leaned down, one hard-muscled arm on either side of her where she sat in the big, high-backed rocking chair, trapping her.

"If I were you," he said in a dangerously soft voice, "I wouldn't push too hard. I've had about all I can take from you and Cousin Brent!"

She felt the raw power in that lean body at the proximity, and it was disturbing. "Just because we hid your rotor..."

"...*And* tied pink ribbons on the tails of two of my milk cows, *and* put bubble bath in the swimming pool, and..." he growled hotly.

She flushed. It had really been funny at the time. "Your trouble is that you don't have a sense of humor," she grumbled.

"You've got enough for both of us!" he shot back. His eyes were like a panther's—green-gold in that swarthy face, narrow and threatening.

"Even when Brent and I were kids, you managed to make us feel like criminals every time we played a prank," she told the open front of his blue-checked shirt, where dark, curling hair peeked out, damp with sweat.

"You damned near turned my hair white a few times," he recalled, and some of the anger drained out of him. He smiled.

"So I see," she murmured, and involuntarily her fingers reached up to touch the silver at his temples. "You're absolutely *sure* it isn't a sign of old age?" she added mischievously.

He chuckled softly. "You brat."

All the years seemed to fall away when he laughed like that, and he was the Clint of her childhood, the bigger-than-life creature her dreams were made of, invulnerable and indestructible.

"Clint, I am sorry about the bubble bath," she said, "but it did look so pretty..."

He tweaked a long strand of her hair. "Brent's a bad influence on you. And from now on keep your little hands off my jeep."

"Yes, Clint."

"So meek!" he drawled. His eyes dropped to her mouth and lingered there for a long time. Abruptly he caught her tiny waist with both hands and jerked her up against him, holding her so tightly that she cried out involuntarily.

"You beast, will you let me go?" she gasped angrily.

His breath was warm at her temple. "It's dangerous to stop fighting me, Irish," he murmured in a stranger's husky voice. "I'm a man, not a boy like Brent, and I'm not used to limits of any kind. Are you too innocent to understand that, or do you want me to spell it out?"

She felt the lean, hard body against hers go taut as his hands put her away, and she moved to pick up the sheets of paper and pen that had fallen to the floor.

"I seem to remember your telling me that I didn't... appeal to you *that* way," she said through tight lips, avoiding his watchful gaze.

There was a long, static silence between them. "Do you have a list for Shorty?" he asked after a while, and she heard the click of his lighter just before a cloud of smoke drifted around her. "He'll need to get those supplies today so that he can start cooking early in the morning."

"I've just about finished it," she replied, sitting back down. "I thought I'd have him get some paper tablecloths and plates and napkins, too, and plastic utensils."

"Thrifty little soul, aren't you?" he asked gruffly. "Am I supposed to be impressed?"

"The only thing that might impress you," she returned hotly, "is a steam roller!"

"More depressing than impressing, surely," he said with a flash of a grin.

She drew a hard sigh. "You are without doubt, the most maddening human being...!"

"With your hair loose like that," he murmured, "and your eyes like green buds in early spring, you're pretty maddening yourself, honey. Just make sure you don't fling any of that sweet magic in Brent's direction. I'd hate like hell to have to throw him off the property."

"What I do with Brent...!" she began.

"...Is *my* business as long as you're on *my* ranch," he said flatly, his eyes daring her to argue about it. "Don't make the mistake of underestimating him, either. He's a man, and the kind of teasing you do with him can be just as inviting as a come-on."

Her mouth flew open. "Clint, for heaven's sake, I've played at words with him all my life!"

"And while you were still eight, and he was ten, it was safe." His dark green eyes swept over her lithe figure in the soft tan blouse and slacks. "Baby, you're a hell of a long way past your eighth birthday. Don't tempt fate."

"How strange that you should be warning me about Brent," she flung at him, "when just the other day he was warning me about you!"

One eyebrow went up and she could see the mischief sparkling in his eyes. "What did he say?" he asked.

Her mouth opened to say the words just as she realized what they were and shut it again. Her face burned like fire.

He laughed softly. "Well?" he prodded. "You know I'm not going to let that drop until you tell me. What did he say, Maggie?"

She shifted uneasily. "He said you were a force to behold," she said finally.

"And what else?"

"That was . . . all," she faltered.

He studied her for a long time, idly drawing on the cigarette. "I think I can guess," he mused. "And he's right, up to a point. I can have damned near any woman I want. But, Maggie," he added, his voice soft now, "I don't rob cradles."

She kept her eyes down, inclined to argue, but too smart to open that can of worms. "How soon do you need this list?"

"In an hour. I've got to send Shorty into town anyway for some wire I ordered. Since mother's not going to be back for two or three more months," he added, "you'll have to act as hostess."

"Can't Emma . . . ?"

"Honey, there's nothing like a pretty, sexy woman to keep buyers happy," he taunted.

The open glare she shot up at him was as potent as words. "I will not be used as a . . . !"

He leaned down, his warm breath mingling with hers, stopping the tirade effectively just by moving close. His eyes burned deep into hers. "Twelve years," he murmured, "and you still can't tell when I'm teasing and when I'm not. I don't intend using you as bait. And if any man lays a finger on you, I'll break both his arms. Satisfied?''

Her eyes widened, her whole expression puzzled. "Clint, why do you . . . ?''

His finger tapped her nose lightly. "Finish your list. I'm up to my neck in work.''

He turned abruptly and left her staring after him.

Sale day came all too soon the next morning as the buyers started arriving by car and plane. In no time at all, the lush grounds were covered with them. Shorty was trying to be ten places at once, busy with roasting huge carcasses for barbecue, stirring baked beans, making rolls—Maggie volunteered to help, but he wouldn't hear of it, gesturing angrily at her flowing white dress and demanding to know how she'd ever get grease spots out. She left him to do it with a smile and a wink. Seconds later, Emma barged in with her apron already spotted and stained, and started watching the beans. Shorty almost fell on her shoulder and kissed her.

Maggie supervised the temporary help, getting tables set up, coffee urns arranged, tea made and tubs brought in for soft drinks and beer. She remembered sale days in her childhood, when Mrs. Raygen had made this seem so easy. It was anything but.

Unconsciously, she searched the nearby stalls for Clint and found him with her eyes. A tall, slender, beautiful blond woman held onto him while he talked cattle with an elderly man beside her. There was something so familiar about the woman; she searched her memory and came up with a name. Sarah Mede. Little Sarah, who'd grown into a siren, and was chasing Clint as wholeheartedly as Maggie ever had at the precocious age of nine. Maggie sighed wearily. Janna had said something about Sarah and her father being on vacation in Europe. Apparently they were back, and she didn't need to ask who Clint had been dating recently. That possessive little jeweled hand said it all.

She turned back to her chores, wishing with all her heart that Brent could have made it back in time to give her some moral support. She felt as if she'd never needed it more. If only she'd never come!

"Well, hello," came a smooth masculine voice from behind and she turned to find a fortyish, rather attractive man in a rust-colored leisure suit standing behind her.

She smiled automatically. "Hello. Here for the sale?" she asked.

He smiled down at her. "That's why I came," he drawled with a laugh in his voice. "But I hear Clint's cousin already put in a bid for Bighorn. I sure had my heart set on that old Hereford bull."

"Sorry," she said with a smile. "But Brent did, too."

"You one of the family?"

She shook her head. "I'm Clint's temporary secretary. But I grew up just a few minutes north of here. I've known Clint and Janna and Brent most of my life."

"I hate to be pushy, but do you think I could get a cup of coffee while we wait on that barbecue?" he asked. "I flew out of Austin without breakfast, or coffee, or a kind word from my housekeeper, and I'm just about dry."

"There's beer if you'd rather," she said, thinking he looked more like a beer man than a coffee one.

He grinned, making extra lines in his swarthy face. "Can't stomach the stuff," he said with quiet honesty. "Although I will admit to a taste for aged Scotch. But right now all I want is coffee."

"Then, that's what you'll get, Mister...?"

"Masterson," he replied. "Duke Masterson. You?"

"Maggie Kirk."

"Just Maggie?" he probed.

She shrugged. "Well, actually, it's Margaretta Leigh," she told him, "but nobody ever calls me that."

"Why not?" he asked gently. "I think it's lovely."

She felt very young under those quiet, dark eyes, and out of her depth. "Let's see about that coffee."

He was a cattleman, as she guessed, with a large ranch near Austin as well as real estate and oil holdings. He was also an attractive man, with a charm that put her immediately at ease.

"I've been overseas for a month or so," he told her over a cup of steaming black coffee. "In Greece."

The question was out before she realized it. "Did you go to see Pompeii?"

It seemed to startle him. "Why, yes, I did. And Troy, and the Acropolis." He leaned forward. "Don't tell me you're an archaeology nut."

"I spent my childhood climbing over Indian mounds, and I read everything I can lay my hands on about new digs," she admitted.

"By God," he whispered. "Sounds like me. I used to follow my father down the rows as he plowed and pick up arrowheads, and pieces of pottery. I spend as much time as I can..."

"Tired, Masterson?" came a quiet, deep voice from just behind Maggie.

Masterson chuckled. "Beat, Clint," he admitted. "I got two hours of sleep last night and flew out without breakfast or even a cup of instant coffee. Margaretta took pity on me."

Clint moved into view with Sarah Mede still attached to his arm. He looked down at Maggie with strange, probing eyes. "Margaretta?" he murmured curiously.

Maggie bristled. "It is my name."

"And a very pretty one," Masterson added, sipping his coffee. "Clint, how about letting me borrow her for the evening? Just long enough for company at the supper table, at least."

The question seemed to surprise Clint as much as it did Maggie.

"I'd love to!" Maggie said without thinking. "We can talk some more about archaeology!"

"Archaeology?" Clint burst out, his eyes narrow and darkening. "What the hell do you know about that?"

She glared at him. "Quite a lot, in fact. I had two courses in it at University, and I spent two months on a dig just last year!"

"I don't see what you're so upset about, Clint, honey," Sarah murmured softly, and smiled at Maggie. "It isn't often that two people find something like that in common. And so quickly, too. Well, as you and I both like country-western music, Clint," she explained.

"I'll take care of her," Masterson told Clint, and something in his eyes seemed to convince the younger man. "I think you know me well enough, don't you?"

"I do," Clint said finally, his voice deep and quiet. "And you can take that as a compliment. There aren't many men I could say that about."

"What is this?" Maggie grumbled, glaring at Clint. "I'm a grown woman. I don't need a watchdog!"

"Grown," Clint scoffed. "Twenty, and you've got all the answers, is that it?"

"But, Clint," Sarah cooed, "I'm just twenty-one, and you never fuss about me..."

"Shut up, Sarah," he said flatly.

"You'd never say that to me," Maggie told him. "I'd flatten you like a...!"

"Go to hell, Maggie," Clint said with a hellish smile, and turning, drew Sarah along with him. "Get her home by midnight, Masterson," he called over his shoulder. "She turns into a pumpkin if you don't."

Masterson smiled at her. "Do you?" he asked, watching the emotions working on her wan face.

"I wish he would," she whispered hotly. "I don't need a big brother any more."

"I think you do." He folded his arms on the table and studied her. "I'm forty-two years old, little girl. And I'll guarantee that if Clint didn't know me personally, you'd never set foot outside this yard with me. But I don't have designs on you, and he knows that, too. I just need company, and it's very pleasant to have a conversation with someone who understands carbon dating and the lure of ancient tombs.''

She smiled. ''Thank you.''

Both his heavy eyebrows went up. ''Thank *you*. Now, how would you like to hear about Pompeii?''

''Oh, I'd love it!'' she replied, and settled down to listen, trying not to hear Clint's last angry words, trying to forget the hatred in his eyes . . .

The sale was over, the guests leaving, bare bones where the barbecued steer carcasses had been, when Maggie left with Masterson for the restaurant.

Clint had gone off with Sarah, and it was a blessed relief. She'd had about all the battle she could stomach for one day.

Over a nicely grilled steak, Masterson shared some of his journeys with her, smiling at the rapt expression on her young face as he described places she'd have given worlds to see.

''I've always wanted to see Stonehenge,'' she told him.

''Then why not go?'' he asked. ''Air fares aren't all that high, you know.''

She smiled. ''And I could always volunteer for a dig. It's just time. There never seems to be enough.''

Something darkened his eyes for an instant. ''I know. Don't let yours run out before you do a few of the things you want to do, little girl.''

She shrugged. ''I've got plenty.''

''No,'' he said softly, his eyes distant. ''No, none of us has plenty.''

It was midnight on the nose when Masterson pulled his rented car up in front of the ranch house.

''I enjoyed that so much,'' Maggie told him with a smile. ''If you ever get to Columbus . . .''

''That's not on the books, little one,'' he said gently. His dark eyes smiled at her. ''Thank you for keeping an old man company. Someday you'll understand how much it meant.''

''Old man? You?'' she asked incredulously.

He chuckled. "Now, that was a compliment. Goodnight, Margaretta Leigh."

"No goodnight kiss?" she asked saucily. "I think I'm insulted."

"You little minx..." He pulled her against his big, husky body and kissed her, hard and slow and with an expertise that was shattering. "Thank you, Maggie," he whispered, as he let her go.

"Goodnight," she told him, sliding reluctantly out of the car.

"Goodbye, honey," he replied softly. And in seconds, he was gone.

She stood watching the car's taillights as it wound around the driveway toward the highway, and for just an instant she wasn't in Florida at all. She was standing on the ruins of an ancient civilization with the breeze stirring her hair and drums pounding in her blood. And he was there, too, but his name wasn't Masterson. She shivered. Another time, another place, those dark eyes had looked into hers and today in a few hours out of time his soul had reached out to touch hers. She felt ripples of emotion tingling through her taut body. How strange to meet and instinctively know all about him—as if in another life...

"Come inside, little one."

She turned to meet Clint. He was still wearing his suit pants and his white shirt, but his tie and his jacket were gone. He looked dangerously attractive.

"I...I was just watching the car," she murmured as they went up the steps. The shiver went through her again and without thinking she slid her cold hand into Clint's, like a child seeking comfort. For just an instant his hand tensed. Then it curled, lean and hard, around hers and squeezed it.

"What's wrong, honey?" he asked.

She shook her head. "I felt...as if I'd known him somewhere before. And something was wrong, I felt it!"

"Déjà vu?" he asked with a smile, leading her into the house, and then into his den.

She shrugged, dropping wearily down onto the sofa. "I guess. I don't know. It frightened me." She watched him pour a neat whiskey, drop ice into it, and toss it back. "Tell me about him."

Clint moved across the room and went down on one knee beside her, his darkening eyes almost on a level with her in the position. His hands caught hers where they lay in her lap.

"He's got cancer, honey," he said very gently. "There's nothing they can do for him, and from what he told me himself, he's got less than two more months."

A sob broke from her and tears rolled down her cheeks. "I like him," she murmured through a pale smile.

"So do I. A hell of a man, Masterson. I've known him most of my life." He took his handkerchief and mopped her eyes. "You know, he accomplished more in his forty-two years than most men do in a lifetime. He didn't waste a second of it. It's hard to grieve too much for a man like that."

She looked into his quiet eyes for a long time. "I...I can't picture you grieving for anyone," she said softly.

"Can't you, honey?" He smiled at her, gently, his hand smoothing the hair away from her damp cheeks. "Do you still think I'm invulnerable?"

"I don't know." She studied his dark, quiet face for a long time. "I don't know very much about you at all. I...I didn't even know you liked country-western music."

"I like any kind of music. And storms, the wilder the better. And sensitive young women with liquid jade for eyes," he whispered deeply. "And if you weren't still cherishing that kiss Masterson gave you out in the car, I'd take your mouth and make you beg for mine, little girl."

She blushed to the roots of her hair, and tried to steady her breathing so that he wouldn't notice the effect those soft words had on her fragile emotions.

"I...I might not even...even like it," she replied, struggling for even a small surge of indignation to use against him.

"You've spent the past four years wondering how my mouth would feel on yours," he said quietly, his eyes biting into hers. "We both know that."

Shakily, she got to her feet and moved around him toward the door.

"When are you going to stop running from me?" he asked, as her hand went to the doorknob.

"Goodnight, Clint," she replied, ignoring the question.

"Don't trip on your way to the nursery," he growled.

She could taste the bitterness in those harsh words, and it served him right to be thwarted. For pure conceit, he was unbeatable.

"Margaretta."

The breathless sound of her name on his lips, so strange, so unfamiliar, made her freeze. She turned to catch an expression on his face that she couldn't understand.

"Go riding with me tomorrow," he said gently. "I'll take you down to that little branch of the creek where you and Janna used to go wading."

She hesitated. "Why?" she asked.

"Maybe I want to get to know you again," he said carelessly.

"Did you ever know me?" she asked him.

He shook his head. "I'm beginning to think I didn't. Will you come?"

She chewed on her lower lip. "If . . . if Brent isn't home, I will."

His eyes narrowed, a muscle in his jaw working. "Brent isn't coming back," he said tautly. "He called while you were out and asked me to ship his bull to Mississippi. He's on his way to Hong Kong."

"Oh." She turned away.

"Don't look so damned lost! My God, Irish, how many men does it take for you lately?" he growled hotly.

"What does it matter to you?" she shot back.

He still hadn't answered her when she went upstairs.

5

 ***

He was waiting for her at the breakfast table, a red knit shirt stretched across the broad expanse of his chest with bronzed flesh and curling dark hair just visible in the V-neck. His pale eyes searched hers for an instant before they dropped to the eggshell blue blouse over her blue jeans. They narrowed on the thin ribbon that bound her hair at the nape of her neck.

"Why did you drag your hair back like that?" he asked quietly.

"It gets in my eyes when I ride," she replied, taking her seat at the table.

"How do you want your eggs, sweet?" Emma called from the kitchen.

"None for me, Emma! Just coffee this morning," she called back.

"No appetite?" Clint chided.

She looked up into his eyes. "No," she said in a voice that sounded breathless even to her own ears.

Smiling, he studied her over the rim of his coffee cup. "No makeup?" he asked gently.

She watched the light catch the silver threads in his hair and make them burn. "I . . . I haven't put it on yet."

He held her eyes across the table, his face solemn. "Don't. I don't like the taste of it."

Her lips parted on a protest, but Emma came in with a steaming cup of coffee and Maggie gave it her whole-hearted attention.

It was a perfect morning for a lazy horseback ride. Even the sweltering heat was unnoticeable under the shade of the mammoth pecan trees in the sprawling orchard. Maggie never failed to be impressed with the orderly lines they'd been planted in so many years before.

"I wonder how old they are," she murmured absently.

"The trees?" Clint smiled. "Older than either one of us, that's a fact."

"Speak for yourself, Grandpa," she returned impishly.

He slanted a vengeful glance her way and pulled his hat low over his brow. "Dangerous ground, Maggie."

"I'm not afraid of you," she teased. "Your poor old bones are so brittle they'd probably break if you chased me."

He reined in his stallion and glared at her. "I think Brent had a point," he told her. "How about guns at fifty paces tomorrow morning?"

"Are you sure your hand's steady enough to hold a gun...?"

"Damn you!" he laughed.

She laughed back, and the years nearly fell away. "Race you to the meadow!" she called, and put her heels to Melody's flanks.

She thought she had him beat as they rode across the green pasture with its scattering of wildflowers and headed toward the woods. But before she could reach them, Clint passed her as if the small mare she rode was backing up. No one, she thought miserably, could beat him at this. He was a superb horseman, almost part of the horse he rode, and a study in masculine grace and power.

"Where've you been?" he asked as she reined up beside him. He paused in the act of lighting a cigarette to grin at her flushed, angry face. "Sore loser!"

She made a face at him. "Why do you always have to win?"

"It's my land," he replied nonchalantly.

Her eyes swung over the lush, grassy pasture to the fences far away in the distance, to the herds of cattle that looked like red and white dots. "It's beautiful," she murmured softly.

"You didn't always think so," he reminded her. "And you were right. Ranch life has its drawbacks, Maggie. There isn't much night life around here, much excitement. It can get pretty lonely."

"Is that how I strike you?" she asked with a wistful smile. "A city girl with a passion for nightclubs?"

He studied her narrowly over his cigarette. "Definitely a city girl. You always were."

She let her eyes follow the flight of a vivid yellow and black butterfly nearby. "I'm glad you know me so well."

There was an explosive silence. "If you hate the city so damned much, why do you live there?"

She flinched at the quiet fury in his voice. "What else could I do? All I know how to be is a secretary." She glared at him. "There aren't many jobs available for women cowhands, in case you've forgotten. Or is it," she added coldly, "that you just never noticed I wasn't a boy?"

His eyes twinkled with humor. "To tell the truth, honey, I never gave it much thought."

She touched the mare's flanks gently and urged her into a walk. "Thanks."

The path through the woods was wide enough for both horses to walk abreast—more a fire road than a trail. The peace was hypnotic, only broken by the soft swish of the pines in the breeze, the near-far sound of bubbling, soft-running water.

"This way," Clint said, turning his mount down a smaller, less clear path.

She followed him to what seemed to be a wall of underbrush. He stepped down out of the saddle and tied the stallion, motioning Maggie to tie the mare several yards beyond.

He held the branches back for her, and as she strode forward into the small clearing, it was suddenly like stepping back through time. The tiny stream where she and Janna once spent lazy summer afternoons wading and sharing dreams over a picnic lunch was there. As clear and sweet and sandy as ever.

"Watch where you walk," he cautioned her as he settled his tall form under a low-hanging oak. "I've had cattle mire down in that soft sand."

She glared at him as she sat down to pull off her socks and boots. "If I moo politely, will you haul me out?"

He grinned under the concealing brim of his hat, as he lay back with his hands under his head. "I might."

She waded into the clear stream, delighting at the feel of the cold water on her bare feet, the damp smell of sand and silt and sweet wildflowers along the banks.

"I used to come here when I was a boy," he remarked lazily. "I learned to swim just a few yards downstream where it widens out."

"And catch tadpoles and spring lizards, too, I'll bet."

"Nope. Just water moccasins," he replied.

She froze in her tracks. "In . . . here?" she asked.

"Sure. It used to be full of them."

Chills washed up her arms. She froze in the middle of the stream, warily looking around her. Suddenly every thin stick she saw was a hissing enemy.

"C . . . Clint? What do I do if I see one?" she asked.

"What did you used to do when you and Janna came here?"

"We never saw any."

"Pure luck," he remarked. He lifted the edge of his hat and peeked at her before he let it down again. "Well, Maggie, if you do see one, you'd better run like hell. It won't do a lot of good, of course, they're fast snakes and they've been known to chase people . . ."

She was sitting beside him with her boots and socks in hand before he finished the sentence.

He burst out laughing. "My God, I was teasing," he chuckled.

"You know how afraid I am of snakes," she muttered.

"After last summer, I've got a pretty good idea," he agreed.

She dried her feet with her socks, ignoring him.

"What did you do for amusement in Columbus?" he asked.

She wound one of the socks around her hand and stared at the diamond-sparkle on the water. She shrugged. "I spent most of my time digging up the backyard and planting things in the spring. In the summer, I liked to fish on the Chattahoochee. In the fall I'd go to the mountains with some of the other girls and watch the leaves turn. In the winter, I'd drive up to Atlanta to hear the symphony or watch the ballet." She studied the crumpled sock. "Dull things like that. I'll bet you can't stand classical music."

"In fact, I do," he said quietly. "Although my tastes run to the old masters—Dvorak, Debussy, Beethoven. I don't care for many contemporary compositions."

She stared at the hat over his face. "Sarah said you liked country-western."

"I do. And easy listening." His hand fished blindly in his shirt pocket for a cigarette. "I like art, too, little girl. I used to drive all the way in to Tallahassee for exhibits."

"When the King Tut exhibit was in . . ." she exclaimed.

"I saw it," he broke in. He removed the hat and tossed it to one side, while he lit a cigarette and looked up at her with eyes a darker green than the leaves on the tree overhead. "Let your hair down. I don't like it tied back like that."

"You just want it to flop in my eyes so I can't see," she pouted, but she loosened the ribbon all the same, and let the black waves fall gently to frame her face.

He reached out a long arm and his fingers caught a thick strand of it, testing the softness. "Long and thick and silky," he murmured quietly. "Black satin."

She couldn't seem to get her breath. Her eyes drifted to the tree trunk behind him. "Do. . .do you still like to hunt?" she asked breathlessly.

"Only venison," he murmured. "Your eyelashes are almost too long to be real, did you know that?"

She caught a shaky breath. "Clint, hadn't we ought to. . ."

"Ought to what, sweetheart?" he asked softly.

She met his quiet, searching gaze and lost the rest of her breath as her eyes widened with something like shock.

Without taking his eyes from her, he flipped his cigarette into the stream and began to draw her closer to him.

"Clint...!" she whispered fearfully, pressing her small hands against his broad chest as he leaned over her, easing her back into the dry leaves and pine straw that blanketed the hard ground.

His lean fingers touched her face, gently exploring it in a silence that throbbed with controlled emotion. "What are you afraid of?" he asked softly.

"You," she whispered shakily, trembling as his fingers lightly traced her nose, her high cheekbones, her mouth.

"Why, Maggie?" he asked, his gaze dropping intently to her mouth as his thumb rubbed across it, parting it, testing its silky softness.

Her heart raced under the soft, sweet pressure, and her eyes closed helplessly. The silence was as pure as dawn, broken only by the gentle swish of the tree limbs with their long gray beards of Spanish moss—and the erratic sound of her own breathing.

His lean fingers speared into the soft hair at her temples, holding her flushed face firmly as he bent; and she felt his firm, chiseled mouth touch her closed eyelids. His broad chest eased gently down against her in a contact that sent a shudder of pure pleasure rippling through her slenderness.

"Don't be afraid of me, little girl," he murmured against her ear. "I'm not trying to seduce you."

She blushed, swallowing nervously, and she felt his deep, soft laughter vibrate against her. Over the thin cotton shirt, her small hands pressed against the warm muscles of his chest.

His mouth, slightly parted, caressed her high cheekbone, the soft line of her jaw, her chin. "Unbutton it," he murmured absently.

"W...what?" she managed, drowning in new sensations.

"My shirt," he breathed at the corner of her mouth.

Her slender hands curled against him. "I...I can't!" she whispered shakily.

"Don't you want to touch me, little innocent?" he asked quietly. "You did that night in the pool—until you realized what you were doing."

"Clint, must you...!" she moaned.

"Hush," he whispered, his mouth moving until it was poised just above hers, so close that his warm, smoky breath mingled with hers. His hands moved on her face to tilt her chin up. "I need your mouth now, little girl, under mine, soft and warm and sweet."

Her eyelids opened briefly so that she could see him, and the look on his face made her tremble. "Clint..." she whispered tremulously.

"Tell me you want it," he whispered huskily.

A sob caught in her throat. "Oh, Clint...!"

His lips brushed against hers in a slow, unbearably tender tasting kiss that was everything she dreamed it could be. Vaguely she felt his fingers slide under her head to cup it, felt him stiffen as he began, ever so gently to deepen the kiss until it grew suddenly from a tiny spark to a bellowing flame between them.

A gasp broke from her lips at the fury of it, and her hands trembled as they went up to clutch at the broad shoulders above her. Clint. This was Clint, who taught her to ride, who bullied her, who broke her young heart that unforgettable summer—who was teaching her a lesson in ardor that nothing would ever erase from her mind or her heart. Clint, who was...loving her...!

All at once, he tore his mouth from hers and looked down at her with eyes that seemed to go up in green smoke.

One lean finger traced the soft, slightly swollen curve of her mouth in a lazy, tangible silence. "Margaretta Leigh," he whispered, his eyes sketching every line of her face. "What you know about lovemaking could be written on the head of a pin."

She jerked her eyes down to his chest. "I never pretended to be sophisticated," she said tightly. "I'm sorry if I disappointed you. May I get up now?"

"You didn't disappoint me," he said quietly, tilting her reluctant face up to his.

An irritating mist blurred him in her sight, and she hated the burr in her throat. "I don't know anything...!" she mumbled miserably.

"It makes for a hell of a change," he told her, and smiled patiently down at her. "I'm used to good-time girls who know everything, not sweet little innocents who need teaching."

Involuntarily, her fingers went up to touch the hard, firm mouth, feeling its sensuous contours. He kissed her fingers absently, his own going to the top buttons of his shirt to snap them open. He caught her searching hand and moved it down inside the opening, against the warm, slightly damp firmness of bronzed muscles and curling black hair.

With a gasp, she jerked her hand away as if it had been burned by the brief contact with his body.

His dark brows drew together, his eyes narrowed. "My God, is even that too intimate for you?" he growled. "You damned little icicle, do you think the touch of those slender young hands, untutored as they are, could send a man into a web of uncontrollable passion?"

She flinched at the anger in his deep voice. He rolled away from her to sit up, curbed violence in the way he put a cigarette between his lips and lit it.

"Put your boots on, little miss purity," he said roughly, "and I'll see you safely home with your honor intact."

"Clint, I'm sorry, please don't...!" she began tearfully.

"You heard me." He got to his feet, making a swipe for his hat on the ground and slamming it on his head. He moved through the underbrush to the horses, leaving her to follow.

She tugged her boots on over the damp socks, fighting tears, and blindly made her way to the little mare. She swung into the saddle, refusing to even look his way. She turned her mount and kicked her velvety flanks, startling her into a gallop.

"Maggie...!" Clint called after her.

She leaned over Melody's neck, her fingers clinging to the soft mane, and urged her on recklessly. She wanted nothing more than to get away from him, and in a haze of pure panic, she forced the mare into a run.

It happened with incredible speed. One minute she was firmly in control. The next, she caught a glimpse of blue sky, a glimpse of green grass, and her body came into shuddering contact with the hard ground.

She was vaguely aware of a voice calling her, of a touch that was none too gentle. She was too winded to answer, and her head hurt. She moaned as she opened her eyes and the sky, along with Clint's dark, tight face, came into blurry focus above her.

"You damned little fool!" he thundered at her, and the look in his eyes was frightening.

"I...fell," she managed in a winded whisper.

"And it's too damned bad you didn't break your stupid neck," he growled mercilessly. "I just may do it for you. Where do you hurt?"

Her lips trembled shakily. "My...head," she murmured.

His hands ran over her helpless body, feeling surely for breaks. His face was lined as she'd never seen it, emphasizing his age, and there was a pallor around his mouth that hinted of strain.

"M...Melody?" she got out.

"She's all right," was the terse reply. "No thanks to you," he added.

That was the proverbial straw. Tears began to flow down her cheeks in agony, her chest rising and falling jerkily with suppressed sobs.

"If you cry, so help me, I'll hit you, Maggie," he threatened darkly.

"You...big bully!" she wept. "I hate you!"

"That's no news." His arms went under her knees and her back, lifting her gently against him. "If I put you on Melody, can you hang on until we get home?"

"Yes," she replied doggedly. She'd hang on until hell froze over, just to spite him.

"We'll go slow," he said quietly, easily lifting her onto the small mare and making sure she had the reins firmly in hand. "Can you make it?"

She glared down at him with fierce green eyes. "You can bet on it," she said icily.

He ignored the anger, and the ice, and swung into the saddle himself. "Let's go."

It was the longest ride she could ever remember, and she was bathed in sweat when they reached the ranch house. Clint reached up for her just as she swayed dizzily in the saddle and carried her upstairs yelling for Emma as he went.

"What in the world...?" Emma asked in concern.

"Annie Oakley fell off," Clint said roughly. "Stay with this stupid child while I call Dr. Brown."

"I hope you trip and fall down the stairs!" Maggie called after him tearfully, wetness burning her eyes as she lay panting and disheveled, sore and miserable on the coverlet of her bed.

Emma sat down beside her and smoothed the wisps of hair out of her eyes. "Oh, my poor baby," she cooed, frowning in quiet empathy. "Does it hurt much?"

She began to cry, burying her face in Emma's apron. "I hate him," she sobbed. "Oh, I hate him, I..."

"I know," Emma said gently. "I've always known. Men can be so very blind, Maggie, and so hurtful. That one more than most. I've never known him to care about a woman. It's as if he's afraid of any deep emotional involvement. Even Lida—that was a physical thing, you know."

"Everything...with him is...physical," she wept.

"His father loved his mother deeply," Emma recalled, gently smoothing the dark waving hair on her knee. "But Mrs. Raygen was never able to return that love, even though she was fond of him. Perhaps the age difference was really too much. But Clint sensed that lack of balance in his parents' marriage, and it affected him. Love is a word he doesn't understand, my darling,'' she sighed. ''I'm sorry it's taken you so many years, and so much heartache, to learn it.''

"Oh, Emma, so am I," she whispered.

6

DR. Brown wanted to see her immediately, and she went reluctantly with Clint to his office to spend over an hour being X-rayed and probed and checked from head to toe. It was a mild concussion, and she was sent home with orders to stay in bed for at least twenty-four hours and for Clint to contact him if there were any nausea or unusual sleepiness.

"I'm sorry for the inconvenience," Maggie said tersely on the way home, drowsy already from the office visit and emotional stress. "I'll make up my work."

He took a long draw from his cigarette. "No sweat, Maggie," he said.

She leaned her head against the window, closing her eyes. She was already asleep when they got back home, not even aware of being carried upstairs and tucked in her bed. Not aware of the tall, solemn figure that sat quietly watching her for the better part of an hour with an intensity that would have shaken her if she'd seen it.

The next day, she was sore and stiff, but the headache had eased, and some of the heartache with it. Another week and she could go back to the apartment, and Janna, and a new job, and leave all this behind. All this. Clint. Clint! Her eyes closed miserably. This time, she'd have to leave him behind for good. No more trips to the ranch, ever, not even for a few days in the summer, and Emma wouldn't understand and neither would Janna. There'd have to be a very good excuse by then. Maybe if she had an overseas job...

"You'll have premature wrinkles if you keep scowling like that," Clint remarked from the doorway.

She spared him a quick glance, noting that he was dressed in a neat gray business suit instead of his jeans, and his dark

head was bare. He looked more like a businessman than a
rancher—and devilishly attractive.

"Going away, I hope?" she asked sweetly, concentrating
on her cold hands.

"For a few days," he replied, a mocking smile touching
his hard mouth. "I thought that might cheer you up."

"It's doing wonders for my disposition," she agreed.

There was a long pause before he shouldered away from
the door and came to stand beside the bed, his eyes dark
green and strangely solemn as he looked down at her.

"Head better?" he asked.

She nodded. "Lots, thanks."

"Look at me."

The quiet note in his deep voice brought her eyes up to
meet his in a silence laced with tension.

"I want to know," he said, "why you were afraid to touch
me that day by the stream."

She felt and hated the color that warmed her cheeks. "It's
over, can't we just . . . ?"

"Hell, no, we can't!" he shot back, his whole look
threatening. He sat down beside her on the bed. "Tell me."

She pressed back against the pillows in an effort to escape any physical contact with him. "It's just a game with
you," she said quietly. "You know a lot about women and
you can tie me in knots without really trying, and you enjoy taunting me with it. But I'm not a toy, Clint, I'm a human being, and I don't like being . . . used!"

He stared at her without any expression at all in his dark
face. "You thought I was . . . playing, Maggie?" he asked.

Her eyes riveted themselves on the silken knot of his tie.
"I should never have come," she said softly, regret in her
tone. "That summer I made a fool of myself is still there,
like a curtain you like to pull down often enough that I'll
never forget what I did. Don't you think," she asked bitterly, "that I've been punished enough, Clint?"

"I'll agree with you on one point," he said curtly. "You
shouldn't have come. Why I let myself be talked into it . . ."

"I'll be gone in another week," she reminded him.

"Back to what?" he asked then, his eyes narrow and assessing. "Back to the two-timing boyfriend? Back to your old job in his office?"

Her lower lip trembled. "Where I go and what I do is none of your business, Clint Raygen!"

His smile was mocking. "Thank God," he replied.

She sighed heavily. "You are, without a doubt, the most maddening man I've ever known!"

"So you're going to run out on me," he taunted. "Leave me here with no secretary and no prospects of finding one before you leave."

"You said two weeks," she reminded him narrowly.

"Make it four."

"Clint . . ."

"Just until Janna comes, little girl," he said quietly.

She avoided his eyes. "You don't want me here."

"No, I don't," he said, suddenly serious, "and remind me one day to tell you why—in about five years."

"Is it going to take that long to make up an answer?" she asked pertly.

He studied her face for a long time. "No," he said finally, "but it looks like it's going to take that long for you to grow up enough to understand the answer."

"Will you still be around then, you poor old doddering thing?" she asked in mock innocence.

His hands caught her face and held it in a vise-like grip on the pillow. "You damned little irritating cat, will you stop throwing my age at me?"

"Turn about's fair play," she said sweetly. "You take every opportunity to remind me of mine."

"And you've never stopped to wonder why, have you?" he growled.

She pushed against his hard chest. "Don't you have a plane or bus or train or something to catch?" she muttered.

His lips made a thin line as he glared down at her. "Can I trust you not to pull any more harebrained stunts until I get back?"

"Harebrained?" she replied hotly. "And just who upset me in the first place...!"

"If you hadn't panicked while I was making love to you..."

"You were *not*...!" she gasped.

His thumb pressed against her lips, stopping the indignant protest. "I would have been," he said quietly, "if you hadn't chickened out."

Her eyes flashed up at him. She jerked her face aside. "You flatter yourself that I'd have let you!" she returned.

"Or Philip?" he asked quietly. His eyes narrowed at the color in her cheeks. "I don't think I've ever known a woman as chaste as you are. You're so damned afraid of anything physical, Maggie, that I thought it was coldness for a long time, but it isn't. You're afraid to let go with a man."

"Am I?" she returned calmly, careful not to let him see how close to the truth he was. "Or is it soothing to your pride to think I am?"

"You little brat!" he growled, and, leaning forward, he caught her face in long, merciless fingers, spearing them into the hair at her temples to hold her. "Was it too close to the truth, Maggie?"

Her hands went up against his chest, pushing at it helplessly. "Let go of me! You think you know so much...!"

The fingers holding her head suddenly released it to catch her wrists like traps and slam them up over her head, pinning them to the bed.

There was something strangely ruthless in the way he looked down at her struggling, twisting body, in the burning half-smile that flamed on his chiseled mouth. "Fight me, wildcat," he murmured in a dangerous, low tone. "I love it when you fight...!"

She twisted instinctively, but his body went down to half cover hers, pressing her slenderness into the mattress, leaving only her eyes free to struggle.

The look on his dark face frightened her almost as much as the green fires that burned deep in his eyes, as he looked down at her with something like triumph. His glittery gaze shifted to her parted, trembling mouth.

"Don't!" she protested shakily as his dark head moved down.

He only laughed, softly, confidently. "Try being a woman instead of a cowering child," he said against her soft mouth as he took it.

An outraged cry broke from her under the punishing force of the kiss. She was aware of struggling briefly, fighting him until she felt the sting of his teeth against her soft lips, until the warm, steely nearness burned through the bedclothes against her, until he forced her trembling mouth to part for him and taught her sensations she'd never been capable of feeling.

She began to relax involuntarily when his mouth eased its pressure and became caressing, seductive, arousing. He released her wrists and his warm, long-fingered hands came down to cup her face, tilting it gently as he deepened the kiss in an intimacy she'd never shared with a man. A soft, barely audible protest broke from her.

"Not yet," he murmured deeply, his breath mingling with hers as he nipped sensuously at the soft contours of her mouth. "Kiss me back."

Her wet lashes opened lazily over misty, confused eyes, to find him staring back at her. He was so close that she could see the tiny lines around his eyelids, the dark eyebrows above them. Wonderingly, her fingers went up to trace them down to the hint of a frown that wrinkled his brow.

He drew back slowly, studying her. Her mouth was parted, her hair wild and disheveled, her eyes shimmering with mingled pleasure and awe.

"Beautiful little cat," he murmured, and his breath came heavily with the words. His hands slid into the thick tangle of hair at her ears, gently caressing. "Your eyes are like emeralds. I like the way you feel under me, Maggie."

Her lips parted as she tried to catch her breath, her heart racing under the warm crush of his chest. "You...hurt me," she whispered.

"That's what it's all about, little girl," he said quietly. His mouth brushed hers tenderly. "You bit me," he whispered against the moist, bruised softness.

She sighed against the drugging brush of his warm mouth, drowning in pleasure. "You . . . you bit me back," she murmured.

He laughed softly. "With a vengeance. I was afraid I'd drawn blood," he mused, studying the bruised little mouth so close under his. "I've never fought so damned hard for a kiss."

Her lips pouted up at him, her eyes clouding. "Well, don't think I enjoyed it!" she muttered.

"Didn't you, honey?" he asked deeply, and leaned down to tease her mouth with his in a heady, coaxing pressure that tore a moan from her throat as she raised up against him in a silent plea.

But he drew away and stood up in a smooth, graceful motion to bend a calculating gaze down at her. His dark hair was ruffled, his mouth sensuous from the contact with hers. The silk tie was disarranged, and he looked altogether masculine and disturbing.

He turned away to straighten his tie and his hair in her mirror. "What are you going to do while I'm gone?" he asked carelessly.

She fought to regain her composure, clutching the bedclothes around her as if they were a lifeline. "Work, I suppose. Did . . . did you leave any letters you want done?"

"Not a word," he replied coolly. He pulled a cigarette out of his pocket and lit it. "Take another day or so before you start back into the routine, little one. I don't want you to have a relapse."

She rubbed her bruised arms and wrists gingerly, darting an accusing glance his way. "That concern is a little late, isn't it?"

He smiled rakishly. "Did I bruise you?" he asked without a trace of sympathy in his deep voice.

"Yes!"

"And you loved every second of it, you little hypocrite," he taunted. "I'm almost sorry I stopped. Another few minutes and you'd have been clawing my back to ribbons."

She gasped at the insinuation. "How dare you!"

"You sound like something out of a very old Victorian novel," he observed, mischief in every line of his face. "Did it shock you that you could feel that kind of violent emotion with a man, Maggie—violent enough to make you bite and claw?"

She dropped her eyes like hot irons, concentrating on the clasped hands on the bedcovers. "It wasn't like that," she whispered. "I was fighting you, not..."

"I hope you'll remember this the next time you decide to use those formidable young hands on me," he remarked.

"What do you mean?" she grumbled.

He caught her eyes with a narrow, level gaze, and there was no humor in it. "I want you," he said bluntly, with no warning. "I don't take much encouragement, either, and that's something you'd better remember. You're not the little girl I used to carry around on my shoulders anymore. You're a woman, and you feel like a woman, and, God, I like touching you!"

She blushed to her toes. "If you think I'd let you...!"

"You just did," he countered.

"You didn't...touch me!" she flashed.

"We both know I could have," he said patiently. "You fought me like a tigress at first, I'll give you that. But you didn't stop me, did you?"

She glared at him, but she didn't deny it. She couldn't.

He took a long draw from his cigarette and studied her through narrowed eyes. "I never thought there was any danger of this happening, but I've just found out how wrong I was. Watch yourself, little girl. I know a hell of a lot more about it than you do, and I'm not above using every dirty trick in the book when I'm aroused. No man is."

She avoided his glance. "You always used to say I didn't affect you like that," she told the bedcovers.

"Honey, you're not any more shocked about it than I am," he replied tightly. "I was just teasing you that day by the stream, the same way I'd been teasing you ever since you came here. But when I laid you down under that tree, and felt that soft mouth under mine for the first time... My God, Maggie," he breathed, "if you hadn't drawn your hand back when you did, if it hadn't just happened to hit me the wrong way..." His eyes narrowed as he moved to stand beside the bed, looking down at her broodingly. "You little fool, couldn't you feel my hands trembling, or did you just not know what it meant?"

She ducked her head so that the cloud of dark hair hid her face from him. "I didn't know what it meant," she admitted miserably.

"I'm not trying to embarrass you, little innocent," he said gently. "I'm not trying to seduce you, either, but I'm not immune to you. Maggie, you're not the kind of woman a man uses. You were meant for a white wedding and children—and those things have no place in my life. You know that, don't you?"

She nodded. "I've always known it, Clint," she said quietly. "You've never made any secret of the way you felt about marriage."

"I don't like being tied down," he said harshly through a veil of smoke. "I can't bear possession, Maggie. In plain language, I've never found a woman I wanted that much, and I've never loved one. It isn't in me."

Her eyes shot to his face. "I don't remember proposing to you," she said.

He chuckled, the seriousness gone from his dark face. "It's just as well, Irish. We'd kill each other the first week."

"Amen." She traced the pattern on the bedspread. "For what it's worth, I don't like possession, either. Or being bullied," she added impishly.

He was quiet for a long moment. "Then why were you marrying Philip?"

"He didn't dominate me."

"Didn't, or couldn't?" he challenged. "Could you lead him around by the nose? Was that the attraction?"

"You go to hell!" she told him.

He only smiled, his lips mocking her. "You're going to take a lot of taming," he said speculatively. "I almost envy the man who'll get to do it."

Only a man like Clint, though, would enjoy it, she thought, would look on it as a challenge and make of it a pleasure that even imagination couldn't do justice to.

"The right man wouldn't have to fight me," she murmured defensively.

His face was quiet, solemn, as he searched hers. "What a waste," he said gently. "I don't like you submissive, Margaretta Leigh."

"How would you know?" she challenged. "You've never seen me that way!"

His eyes narrowed. "I don't think I'd want to," he replied quietly. "You're fierce when you fight, Irish. I think you'd love a man just as fiercely. Submission from you would be like possessing a wax doll." His eyes dropped to her full lips. "I'd like to feel that soft mouth on fire with passion just one time."

Her eyes fought him. "You won't," she threw at him. "Not ever!"

"Don't bet on it," he murmured softly, and she felt her heart stop at the look in his eyes when he said it. He turned and opened the door, glancing back at the picture she made. "Miss me."

"Please, hold your breath waiting for me to." She smiled sarcastically.

"Stay away from the horses while I'm gone," he returned, and, with a wink, he went out, closing the door firmly behind him.

With a cry of rage, she buried her face in the pillow.

7

*

Several days later—his few, plus some—she was back on her feet and too restless to sit still. Walking idly in the pecan grove under a spreading canopy of natural arches, she wondered how it was possible to miss a man so much. Most of her life had been spent away from Clint, but it had never hurt like this. Perhaps, she admitted quietly, because it had only been infatuation before. A wanting that had nothing to do with reality, but had sprung from her girlish daydreams about him. Daydreams that had gone up in smoke at the first touch of his mouth.

It wasn't infatuation anymore. She wanted him in a way that terrified her. Not just to sit and hero-worship, but to fight with, and work with, and love with for the rest of her life.

Her pale green eyes sought the horizon far in the distance. Where was he now? Who was he with? Was there a woman somewhere who could reach that proud, stubborn heart of his and make it throb with longing? She sighed, remembering the sultry look in his eyes when she'd yielded to him. She'd never seen that look on his face before, that dark, masculine triumph mingled with a hunger that was just as exciting in memory as it had been in reality. Clint had wanted her. But wanting wasn't loving. And she wondered miserably if Clint even knew the definition of love.

It was inevitable that she'd wind up by the little stream with its curtain of long, curling gray Spanish moss dangling lazily from the tall oak trees at the bank's edge.

With a sigh, her eyes went to the carpet of twigs and fallen leaves under that massive oak where Clint had . . .

Her eyes closed on the memory, hearing again the deep, soft voice in her ear, feeling the delicious crush of his arms, the slow, confident experience in the mouth that had taught hers what a kiss should be.

Her eyes misted with remembrance as she studied the leaf-covered ground that bore no trace of two enemies who had behaved almost like lovers here. If only. She sighed again, reaching up to touch the moss as her eyes followed the bubbling stream where it wound like a silver ribbon into the distance between the leafy trees. Oh, if only!

She had to leave. She knew it suddenly and surely. If she stayed here now, knowing the way she felt, she'd have no defense at all against him if he touched her again. Despite the promise she'd made to stay until Janna came, she'd have to leave. She was more vulnerable now than she'd ever been. And, she admitted to herself, Clint wouldn't hesitate to test that vulnerability. He'd always known—or thought he did— exactly how she felt about him. He seemed to enjoy the power he had over her. And now...

She turned back toward the house. She didn't have a choice anymore.

Surprisingly, almost as if Janna could read her mind, she called that night after supper.

"How's it going?" Janna asked, and Maggie could almost see the grin on her friend's face.

"How do you think it's going?" she asked. "Janna, I love you like a sister, but I'm going to poison you when I get back."

"Oh," she sighed. "I'd hoped from what Brent said..."

"You talked to Brent?" Maggie burst out. "But he's in Hong Kong...?"

"Hong Kong! Brent?"

Puzzle pieces whirled around in her mind. "But Clint said..."

"My sweet brother threatened to break his arms if he came back down there while you were in residence," Janna said triumphantly.

There was a long, static silence while Maggie tried to fit the puzzle pieces together into something that made sense. "I don't understand," she muttered absently.

"I do. You and Brent were always close, weren't you? Maggie, my dear," Janna said gently, "don't you know that my brother doesn't tolerate competition from anybody? If he wants something badly enough, he'll use some of the most ruthless methods in the book to get it. And apparently," she added with smug pleasure, "what he wants right now is you."

Boy, if you only knew, Maggie thought. "Been eating green toadstools again, huh, Janna?" she asked pleasantly. "The only thing going on between Clint and me is one everlasting argument, and this time we've very nearly come to blows. All I want is to go home. When are you coming down here?"

There was a wistful sigh on the other end of the line. "Saturday," came the reply. "Or maybe Friday night, I'm not sure. I had my vacation switched. If you're determined, we can go back to Columbus next week."

"Determined isn't the word. Oh, Janna, come protect me," she moaned. "I'm so tired of fighting..."

"Are you well, Maggie?" her friend asked. "You, tired of fighting Clint? That's got to be a first."

"It'll make all the record books, but I really am. Hurry, will you?"

"All right, since it's you asking. But, Maggie, why did Clint threaten to break both of Brent's arms?"

"Because we stole his rotor, tied bows on his cows' tails, and I filled the swimming pool with a box of bubble bath or two..."

"Never mind, and I thought it was something romantic. Can you stay out of trouble until I get there, Maggie?"

"Nothing easier," she laughed. "Clint's still gone, and all I have to do is keep out of his way until you get here."

It was late afternoon when Maggie delivered Emma's grocery list to Shorty, and she paused on the front porch to feast her eyes on the fiery sunset with its blazing fingers of color before she went inside. The city had nothing, she thought, to compare with this. The sweep of open land, the smell of country air laced with the smell of flowers, the sound of dogs barking in the distance, the peace of non-mechanical sounds. And Clint had called her a city girl. She shook her head as she went into the house. He didn't know her at all.

She walked into the study and, unexpectedly, he was there. It was like being hit in the stomach with a baseball bat. She felt her heart stop just at the sight of him. He looked as though he'd just gotten home, still dressed in a dark brown suit and a cream silk shirt. He turned and gazed at her, something dark and strange and violent flashing in his eyes at the sight of her standing there in the little yellow polka-dotted sundress she'd thrown on in a whim. He sketched her quietly, deliberately, pausing at the low bodice, the thin straps that left her round, smooth shoulders bare, her hair hanging silkily around them.

"H...hello," she stammered, captured by his narrow eyes.

"Hello," he replied. "Going somewhere?"

"Oh...the dress, you mean?" She shook her head. "I...it got hot."

"It's getting hotter by the minute," he mused, and his eyes went from her wavy dark hair to her sandals.

She swallowed nervously at the sensuous, masculine appreciation in his eyes. "How...how was your trip?"

His face seemed to go taut at the question. He turned away to light a cigarette and take a deep draw before he replied, "Not very pleasant, little girl. I swung by Austin to see Masterson."

"Duke?" She felt something dark stir inside her, something cold and ominous. "How was he?"

"I got there in time for the funeral," he said quietly.

The unexpected blow brought tears to her eyes as she remembered the big, dark man and ancient tombs and the lure of the past all at once in a jumble of thoughts. "Oh," she whispered brokenly.

He turned with a heavy sigh. "His plane crashed on the way back home," he told her. "In a way, it was a blessing. He was in a hell of a lot of pain. And to have to wait for it..."

She nodded silently, agreeing that it was best, while inside she felt as if something had been torn out of her. Tears ran unashamedly down her face.

His eyes darkened. "For God's sake, stop it!" he growled. "Masterson wouldn't want that. He wouldn't want you to grieve for him!"

She bit her lip, hating him for being so insensitive, so cold. "Excuse me," she said brokenly. "Caring is the number one sin in your book of rules, isn't it?"

She turned and started toward the door. He caught her before she went two steps, whipping her around into his hard arms, pressing her shaken, trembling body close against the warm strength of his.

"I can't bear to watch you cry," he murmured harshly against her temple. His fingers contracted in the cloud of hair at her nape.

The admission stunned her until she realized that, like most men, he couldn't stand tears from any source. She fought to regain her composure, to stop the hot tears from running down her face into the corners of her mouth.

"I liked him," she said unsteadily. "It was as if...as if I'd known him all my life."

"It happens that way sometimes." His arms contracted, and she felt one warm, lean hand against her bare back just above the line of her sundress, gently caressing the silky skin. Under her ear she could feel the sudden heavy sigh of his breath as his lips brushed against her forehead, and she stiffened involuntarily.

He drew back abruptly, his hand going to the inside pocket of his jacket. "Masterson had this in his pocket," he said, handing her an unsealed envelope. "It was addressed to you. His nephew asked me to deliver it."

She swallowed nervously, staring at the small white envelope in her hand, at the bold, black scrawl of her name and the ranch's address. "For me? What...what is it?"

"I don't know," he said, moving away from her to retrieve his smoking cigarette from the ashtray on his desk. "None of us felt we had the right to read it."

She fingered it with a sigh. She couldn't bring herself to open it here, now, with Clint only a few feet away. "I'll read it later. Clint, Janna called. She's coming Saturday."

He whirled on his heels, his eyes narrow, his face harsh. "Did you call for reinforcements?" he demanded hotly.

"No!" she flashed. "She called and said she was coming. What was I supposed to do? Tell her no, and that her brother...?"

"That her brother what?" he growled.

She turned away. "I left all your messages on the desk," she said quietly.

There was a long pause. "I bought some replacement heifers," he said finally, the iron control back in his deep voice. "And a couple of bulls to add to my breeding stock. We'll get those records out of the way tomorrow."

"Yes," she said in a whisper.

"Maggie."

She paused with her hand on the doorknob, but she didn't turn around to face him. "What?"

"Don't wear that dress again."

She was afraid to ask him why. The husky note in his voice was almost answer enough.

Upstairs, in the privacy of her room, she sat down in a chair by the darkened window and read her letter by the light of the small lamp.

Margaretta Leigh, it began in a thick, heavy masculine hand, *if I'd had more time to arrange it, I'd have sent you a ticket to Stonehenge instead. As it is, I was holding this one for a free week which, in all honesty, I'm not expecting to have. You'll find that all the expenses are covered, from the cruise to meals and lodging. I had to get home in a hurry, or I'd have twisted your arm and made you take this ticket.*

Maggie, please don't refuse it. Humor an old man who enjoyed a few of the happiest hours of his life in your company. It was almost like a homecoming. I don't know if you believe in déjà vu, the letter continued, and she shivered involuntarily, *but if such things happen, maybe we knew each other in some distant past and shared more than coffee and conversation. This lifetime wasn't for us. Maybe next time. With deep affection, Duke Masterson.*

Maybe next time... Her eyes closed as she folded the letter back around the ticket. When the tears passed, she read the letter over again and stared at the ticket. It was for a round trip passage to archaeological sites all over the Mediterranean, all expenses paid, on a cruise which was to begin the following Monday. She stared blankly at it. Could she really afford to go now, when she should be looking for a job...

Emma's voice calling her to supper stopped the confusing thoughts temporarily.

It plagued her, whether or not to go on the cruise. She wanted to, desperately. But she was torn between pleasure and the very real problem of a job to go to when she left the ranch. She hadn't told anybody about the ticket. It was safely put away in her purse, tucked in Duke's letter, and she kept it secretly like a prayer too precious to share with anyone. But she was troubled, and it showed.

She felt Clint's brooding eyes on her at breakfast the day before Janna was due home. He watched her like a hawk these days, she thought bitterly, even though he'd been careful to keep as far away from her as possible ever since he came back from his trip. The way he avoided her had even raised Emma's eyebrows, no mean feat. Maggie was at once hurt and relieved by it. At least she didn't have to fight any monstrous temptations. There weren't any.

"Why don't you talk about it," Clint growled finally when she'd finished picking at the eggs and bacon on her plate, "instead of sitting there with that damned crucified look on your face?"

Her eyes burned as her face jerked up. "Why don't you mind your own business?"

"You are my business," he said shortly.

"Not for much longer."

"Praise God!"

She threw down her napkin and stormed out past Emma who was just coming in with a plate full of ham. "Maggie...?" she called.

Clint went right out the door behind her, his jaw set, his eyes blazing.

"Clint...?" Emma murmured.

Neither one of them seemed to even hear her. With a sigh and a shrug, she took the ham back to the kitchen.

Clint caught up to Maggie on the front porch, jerking her around with a rough, cruel hand.

"Stop throwing tantrums," he said gruffly, "or I'll give you my cure for them."

She tossed her hair impatiently. "Please let go of my arm."

"Where are you going?"

"For a ride! Is that all right, or do I have to...?"

He pressed a long, gentle finger against her lips, reading the emotional storm that was tearing at her as he met her eyes.

"No more," he said softly. "Come riding with me. It'll help."

She gazed up at him helplessly, feeling the yielding start and hating it. "Aren't...aren't you busy?"

"Always, honey," he said with a kind smile.

"I...I can go alone," she murmured.

"I want to be with you," he said. His lean hand brushed some stray hairs away from her lips. "We haven't had much time together since I've been home."

"You wanted it that way," she replied, hiding her eyes from him.

"I know."

"Clint..." Her eyes went up to meet his, a question in them.

He shook his head. "Not now. Not yet." His dark brows drew together as he looked down at her, as if she made a puzzle he couldn't put together. "Damn it, woman...!"

Her lower lip trembled at the sudden anger. "What have I done now?" she grumbled.

He drew a sharp breath and turned away. "Never mind. Come on!"

They rode in a companionable silence for several minutes, and Maggie knew that she'd treasure this time with him like a hoard of gold when she left the ranch. Her eyes darted toward him when he wasn't looking at her, tracing the sharp profile, the powerful set of his shoulders, the straight back. The sight of him was like a cold drink in the desert. She wished she'd brought her camera, that she could have a picture of him to take home and... She sighed. She'd carry a picture of him in her heart until the day she died. That would be haunting enough.

"What are you thinking about?" he asked her after a while.

"The memories," she sighed, smiling at the sweep of open country as they reined up and sat quietly on their mounts, side by side. "So many of them. The meadow where Janna and I used to pick wildflowers, the pecan trees that had such delicious fat pecans on them in the fall, the..."

"The stream where I made love to you?"

She glared at him, blushing, her eyes on the brim of his hat, pulled low and shading his glittery eyes.

"Were you always that conceited, or did you have to work at it?" she returned.

"You make me conceited, little girl," he replied sharply. "My God, if you'd reacted to your poor fool of a fiancé the way you react to me physically, you'd still be engaged!"

She clamped her teeth together and ignored him.

He threw his leg over the pommel of his saddle while he lit a cigarette. He shoved the brim back over his eyes, and they burned into her face even at that distance, green and fiery and strange.

"How was it, Maggie?" he asked with a deep, low whip in his voice. "How did it feel to kiss me? You'd wanted it since you were sixteen. Was it worth the daydreaming?"

She studied her trembling hands on the reins, hardly believing the nightmare the ride had turned into.

He took a long draw from the cigarette. "No comeback? Maybe I disappointed you," he continued mercilessly, his eyes narrowing. "Infatuation doesn't stand up to the demands a man can make on a woman, does it, little one? Any more than dreams stand up to reality. What a hell of a pity you didn't realize that four summers ago."

"Amen," she whispered through her teeth. "Was that what..."

He laughed, and the harsh sound hurt more than the words had. "I couldn't think of a better way to cure you, honey. I'd had about all the hero worship I could stand. I did us both a favor."

"Thanks," she said in a pale whisper. "Coming on the heels of my broken engagement, it was just what I needed."

"You're breaking my heart."

"You don't have one!" she shot back, her eyes burning with unshed tears as she glared at him. "You wouldn't know what to do with it if you had one."

He shrugged, putting the cigarette back to his chiseled lips. "Maybe," he replied quietly. "But you'd better thank your lucky stars that I have a conscience, young lady," he added pointedly. "I could have had you."

It was the truth, and it hurt like hell, and she closed her eyes on the pain and the shame.

"Infatuation or not, you wanted me!" he growled, leashed fury in every line of his face.

"To my everlasting shame," she whispered brokenly. Her eyes when they met his were bright with tears and hurt.

His face went stone-hard, as if she'd slapped him.

"I'm leaving in the morning, Janna or no Janna," she whispered huskily. "I've been tortured by you enough for one lifetime!"

She whirled the mare and urged her into a gallop as she headed blindly back to the house, leaning forward in the saddle as if devils were in hot pursuit. But Clint wasn't following her. He was sitting frozen in his saddle, his eyes blank and unseeing as smoke trailed from the forgotten cigarette in his hand.

Supper was an ordeal, and Maggie wouldn't have felt the slightest twinge of conscience about missing it if it hadn't been for Emma.

She didn't look toward Clint at all through the meal, or speak to him. Emma, caught in the middle, tried to keep the conversation going with a monologue of comments about the weather, the government, and the Napoleonic Wars. But it was a lost cause. Neither of them even looked up.

Maggie helped clear the table while Clint stormed off into his den and closed the door behind him with a force that rattled windows.

"Is it because you're leaving tomorrow?" Emma asked as they washed up.

"I don't know." She dried a plate and set it aside. "We had an argument while we were out riding."

"You've had arguments since you were eight years old, missie, but he didn't ever slam doors before or leave good coffee sitting in his cup without even tasting it." Emma looked at her pleadingly. "Maggie, don't go. Not like this."

"You don't understand, Emma, I have to," she said miserably.

"Why? Because you're afraid he'll make you give in?"

Her face jerked up, astonishment in her pale eyes.

"Oh, yes, I know," Emma said gently. "It's written all over both of you. Don't you know why he got Brent away from here? Why he can't take his eyes off you lately?"

She lowered her eyes to the soapy water in the sink. "I can't give him what he wants."

"Do you know what he wants, Maggie? Does he?"

"Oh, yes," she replied bitterly. "He wants me to find someone else to 'hero-worship.'"

"Isn't that odd," Emma remarked, "when he never seemed to mind it before?"

Maggie attacked another plate with the drying cloth.

"Stay one more day," Emma coaxed. "Janna's going to be here in the morning and everything will be better. You'll see."

"Emma . . . !"

"Take him his coffee."

"And get my head snapped off?"

The older woman touched her hand gently. "Maggie, you can't let this drag on any longer. It's tearing you both apart. Take him his coffee, talk to him. I think . . . Maggie, I think he's hurt more than he's angry."

"You couldn't hurt him with a bomb. He's invulnerable," she growled.

"Go on."

She gave Emma a last resentful glance and, with a reluctant sigh, picked up the mug of hot coffee and took it into the study.

It was like facing a lion on his home ground, she thought, as she walked in after his gruff, "Come in!" She pushed the door shut behind her and carried the coffee to his big oak desk. He was standing outside on the patio, his shoulder against the doorjamb, a smoking cigarette in his hand.

He turned to watch her set the cup down, and she almost caught her breath at the sheer masculinity that seemed to radiate from his tall, powerful body. His shirt was unbuttoned against the heat, hanging loosely from his broad shoulders, revealing a thick mat of curling dark hair that made a wedge against the smooth bronze muscles of his chest and stomach. His thick hair was tousled, as if his fingers had restlessly worked in it. His eyes were narrow and solemn and darker than she'd ever seen them.

"I . . . Emma said to . . . to bring your coffee to you," she faltered, the words coming unsteadily as he shouldered away from the door and started toward her.

"Where's yours?" he asked quietly.

"Mine?"

"You could have had it with me."

"Oh." She studied the carpet. "I . . . I had mine in the kitchen."

He perched on the edge of the desk and crushed out the finished cigarette.

"I don't want it to be like this," she whispered miserably. "I don't want to leave here with you hating me . . . !"

"I don't hate you," he replied deeply.

No, she thought, because that required emotion and there wasn't any in him. He was simply indifferent.

She studied her shoes. "Anyway," she said quietly, "thanks for letting me come. I'm sorry to leave you without a secretary . . ."

"You aren't," he said coolly. "I ran into Lida while I was away. The marriage broke up overnight. She'll be here Monday." He smiled carelessly. "So you see, little girl, you picked a good time to go. No harm done."

She smiled brightly despite the throbbing ache in her heart. "No harm done," she echoed. "Well, I'll say goodnight . . ."

"Take this back with you." He drained the mug and handed it to her. But as their fingers touched, he felt the cold trembling of hers and something seemed to explode in his eyes.

"Cool as ice," he murmured through set lips. "But only on the outside." His hand whipped out and caught her by the shoulder, dragging her to him. In this half-sitting position, she was on an unnerving level with his jade eyes. "You don't like me to know just how much I affect you, do you, Irish?" he growled angrily.

"Don't . . ." she pleaded, all the fight gone out of her at the merciless fury she read in his eyes. "Clint, please, let me go, don't . . ."

"Don't what? Shame you?" he taunted. He snatched the cup out of her hands and tossed it onto the desk. His lean hands gripped her shoulders fiercely, slamming her against him.

"Clint, I'm sorry!" she whispered, realizing at last what was wrong. She'd stung his pride, and now he wanted revenge...

"You don't know what shame is," he growled, bending his head, "but I'm going to teach you."

"Clint...!" Her voice broke on the pleading cry, just as his hard mouth went down against hers and taught her what a punishment a kiss could be.

She tried to struggle against the merciless hard arms that held her, but she couldn't get loose, she couldn't breathe...yielding to the strength that was so much greater than her own.

Then, like magic, the crush of his muscular arms eased, cradling her now as gently as he'd hurt her before. The pressure of his mouth lessened, became soft and caressing, coaxing.

"Maggie," he whispered against her bruised lips, sliding his hands under the hem of her blouse to burn against the bare flesh of her back. "Maggie, you feel like silk."

Her fingers curled into the cotton of his shirt as she hung there, breathless, while he toyed with her mouth, taunting it with brief, biting kisses that kindled fires in her mind. His lean, warm hands pressed her even closer, rasping slightly as they brushed her smooth skin.

"Touch me," he murmured huskily. "Touch me, honey."

Involuntarily, her slender hands moved away from the cotton shirt onto the warm, bronzed muscles of his broad chest, tangling in the thick cushion of curling black hair as she caressed him blindly, feeling the sensuous masculinity of him, drowning in the tangy scent of his cologne as sensation after sensation washed over her.

"Like that, hellcat," he murmured, "that's it. Maggie, open your mouth, just a little. I want to taste it..."

Burning with the hunger he created in her, she yielded mindlessly as he opened her soft lips and drew her completely against the long, warm body, building the pressure until he heard the moan smothered under his mouth.

"Did that milksop fiancé of yours ever kiss you like this, Maggie?" he growled huskily. "Did he stir you until you moaned against his mouth?"

"Oh, don't," she pleaded dizzily, her slender hands making a halfhearted protest against the pleasure his were causing.

"Why not? You want it," he whispered. His mouth brushed lazily over hers, open and moist and deliberately sensuous. "You want my hands and my eyes on every inch of this sweet young body, don't you, Maggie? Answer me. *Don't you*!"

Her voice broke on a sob. "Yes!" she wept. "Damn you, yes!"

"Ask me nice and sweet, Maggie," he taunted. "Say, please Clint, say it, Irish. Whisper it . . ."

Her eyes opened slowly, bright with longing and love. "Please," she breathed against his hard, torturing mouth. "Please, Clint . . ."

His hands contracted on her waist as he suddenly thrust her roughly away. A cold, merciless smile tugged at his mouth. "And that, Miss Kirk, evens the score. You wanted something to be ashamed of. You've got it!"

It took seconds for her to realize what he'd said, what he'd done. Her face went red, then white. Deathly white. Ashamed of . . . even the score . . . She gaped at him numbly, feeling as though she'd been slammed with all the strength in that tanned, lean hand.

He lit a cigarette calmly, his narrow eyes flicking her stunned expression as he snapped the lighter shut and pocketed it. "You've been following me around like a damned pet dog since you were about eight years old," he remarked. "For future reference, I'm tired of it. I won't be a stand-in for a jilting fiancé, or a balm for a broken heart. From now on, if you want to be made love to, look in some other direction. I'm tired of giving you lessons."

Her face went, if possible, even whiter. Her mouth refused to form the words that would tell him how hateful she thought he was. Inside, she felt beaten, bruised. Tears misted on her long lashes, tears that she turned away to keep him from seeing. She went blindly toward the door.

"No comeback, Maggie?" he chided.

Her hand touched the doorknob.

"Would you like me to kiss you goodbye?" he persisted.

She opened the door and went out.

"Irish!"

She closed the door behind her and went blindly and quickly up the steps. Behind her she was vaguely aware of the door opening again, of eyes following her. But she didn't slow down or look back. Not once.

8

*

$\mathbf{M}$aggie sat in the chair by her bed in the dark for hours, aching with a hurt that went deeper than any pain. The deliberate cruelty was almost unbearable. He knew he'd hurt her. She'd seen the satisfaction in his jade eyes. And all because she'd stung his ego. For no other reason than that.

The tears hadn't stopped since she closed the door behind her into this womb of security that was darkness. Hadn't stopped, hadn't eased. Not when the knock came hesitantly on the door and Emma's voice called her name gently. Not when she heard two voices outside the locked room, one deep and slow and angry, the other soft and pleading.

When the first light of dawn filtered through the fluffy white curtains, she still hadn't moved from the chair, or slept. Her eyes were red-rimmed and dark shadowed, her face as white as it had been last night.

Automatically, she began to pack, quietly and efficiently stuffing clean and dirty clothes together in the single suitcase, gathering cosmetics from the chest of drawers, her toiletries from the bathroom. She didn't allow herself to think. Not about what she'd felt for Clint, not about what he'd done to her, not about the anguish of walking away from him for the rest of her life. She kept her mind on getting away and nothing else. Escape was the only important thing left in her life right now. She wanted to run.

Without pausing to drag a brush through her hair, she picked up the case and, without a backward glance, closed the door.

"Oh, there you are," Emma said in a strange, hesitant tone as Maggie reached the bottom of the staircase. "Ready for breakfast, missie? Surely you're not going to leave without breakfast?''

Maggie didn't answer, making do with a short, wordless shake of her head. She picked up the phone and calmly called a taxi, aware as she put the receiver down that Clint had come into the hall.

Emma exchanged a quick glance with him and left the hallway, quietly closing the kitchen door behind her with a soft click.

Maggie picked up her case and started for the front porch just as Clint moved, standing quietly in front of her, his hands jammed deep into the pockets of his jeans. His own eyes were bloodshot, his face haggard. She only spared him a brief, cold glance before she averted her eyes.

"Please get out of my way," she said in an uncommonly quiet tone.

"I want to talk to you, Maggie."

"Write me a letter," she said to her shoes. "If you try, you can probably come up with a few more insults by the time you mail it."

"Maggie!" he groaned, reaching out to touch her shoulder.

She flinched away from him as if he'd cut her to the bone, backing away with wide, burning eyes. "Don't ever do that again," she whispered unsteadily. "Don't ever touch me. I'm getting out of your life just as quickly as I can, Clint, isn't that enough?" Tears misted in her eyes. "What more do you want from me, blood?" she cried.

He drew a deep, slow breath. "My God, I never meant to hurt you . . ." he breathed huskily, something dark and somber in his eyes as they searched her face.

"No, you didn't, did you?" she asked bitterly. "You wanted to take the hide off Lida, but she wasn't here and I was. Maybe things will look up now, since she's coming back."

"Maggie, not like this, for God's sake!" he growled as she started for the door. "I want to tell you . . . !"

"The score's even, Clint, you said so," she told him from the porch, her eyes accusing. "There's nothing more you can say that I want to hear. You said it all last night."

His eyes narrowed as if in pain, his gaze searching, quiet, as if he'd never seen her before and couldn't get enough of her face. "No, honey," he said gently. "I didn't say enough. Maggie..."

A loud blare from a car horn coming up the driveway interrupted him, and she turned and started down the steps with a burst of relief that made her slender shoulders slump. "Tell Emma goodbye," she called over her shoulder, "and tell Janna I'll write!"

He didn't answer her, his face dark and still, his eyes riveted to the slender form as it crawled into the cab and the door closed. He watched her go, his eyes haunted and tortured as the cab slowly faded to a yellow speck in the distance.

Emma came out onto the porch behind him, drying her hands on the white apron.

"I've got breakfast," she said gently.

He didn't answer her, his eyes blank, his face drawn.

"You wanted her to go," Emma reminded him. "That's what you told me last night."

He turned and went into the house, into his den, closing the door behind him firmly. With a sigh, Emma went back to the kitchen, idly wondering how she was going to explain any of this to Janna.

Later, sitting wearily on the bus to Miami, Maggie read Duke Masterson's letter for the third time and said a silent thank you to the big dark man for this way out. She couldn't have borne going back to the apartment just yet, facing Janna and the inevitable questions. The wound was too raw, too new to be probed just now. In a few days, a few weeks... she gazed lovingly at the ticket that promised escape. It was a reprieve from too much hurting, too much pain. Philip, then Clint... especially Clint. She closed her eyes against the bitter memory. Would she ever forget how he'd humbled her; would she ever heal from the crippling blow her pride had suffered?

Her eyes turned to the window, to the palmettos and pines on the horizon, the occasional home tucked away in a nest of trees. Things were going to be awkward from now on. She wouldn't be able to spend holidays with Janna ever again if they meant the ranch and Clint. It would be worse when he flew into town on business and came to see his sister. She sighed wearily. Perhaps it would be better if she looked for a job in Atlanta and moved away from her childhood friend. That would be painful, too. But maybe, in the long run, it would be for the best.

She leaned her head back against the seat and closed her tired eyes. It seemed so long since she'd slept, since she'd felt any peace at all. Her mind was full of Clint, of the old days.

It seemed so long ago that she and Clint had sat on the porch swing together and talked about horses. Or went for long rides in the forest as she listened to his tales about the early days of Florida's exploration when canoes sailed down the Suwannee River on scouting trips.

He made the Sunshine State come alive for her. She could see the proud Spanish conquistadores tramping through the underbrush by the river. She could hear the drums of the proud, fierce Seminoles, who were never conquered by the United States government despite a series of three wars they fought between 1817 and 1858. She could picture the tall sailing ships that departed Florida's sandy coast, bound for the Indies or South America.

She sighed. Clint had liked her as a child. They'd been friends. But now he was an enemy, and all her tears wouldn't change that. Not after what he'd done to her. Her eyes closed with pain at the memory. Had that really been necessary, she wondered, the humiliation he'd caused? Why should it have upset him so, what she said while they were out riding, about being ashamed of what he could make her feel?

She shook her head idly. If he'd wanted to shame her, he'd accomplished that. But what puzzled her was the look on his face the next morning, the dark, hungry look in the green eyes that watched her leave the ranch. Had it been guilt in his eyes—or pain?

Her brows came together. She wondered what Janna would think when she got there; or would Clint even tell his sister the whole story? She hadn't mentioned that she was going to Miami. Nobody knew she had the cruise ticket. Clint and Emma had simply assumed that she was going home to Columbus.

Well, what difference did it make, she wondered, her eyes on the cloudy landscape outside the tinted bus window as the sunset made lovely flames in the sky. How quickly the day had passed, and soon the Miami skyline would come into view on the horizon. She shifted restlessly on the comfortable seat. Miami. Would any of them worry besides Emma and Janna? Well, she would mail Janna a postcard from Greece or Crete or wherever she landed. Janna and Emma, she corrected.

She got off the bus in Miami and took a cab to Miami Beach where Collins Avenue boasted almost wall to wall hotels. She gaped like a country girl at the sights and sounds of Miami Beach at night, drinking in the salt sea smell, the glorious fairyland colors of the night lights. There was no parking space available at the hotel she chose, so the driver let her out across the busy street and lifted out her suitcase.

"Watch the traffic, lady," he cautioned as he handed her the change from her fare.

She nodded and smiled. "Awesome, isn't it?" she laughed.

"Not after you've been here a while." He grinned as he drove away.

She lifted the suitcase, still smiling as she surveyed the bigness and richness of this man-made Mecca. In just hours, she'd be on that cruise ship heading out into the Atlantic. Leaving behind her worries, her heartaches, her obligations, just for a little while. She took a deep breath of warm sea air. Thank you, Duke Masterson, she said silently, feeling a twinge of sadness that the big, dark man wouldn't be somewhere in those ancient ruins waiting for her.

She started toward the hotel across the street, her mind far away, her eyes unseeing. She didn't notice the powerful car pulling away from the curb with a squealing of tires just a few meters away. Not until she felt the sudden impact and everything whirled down into a painful sickening blackness. . . .

Sound came and went in vague snatches, from a great distance.

"... Several ribs broken, internal injuries. She's not responding."

"She's got to! My God, do something, anything! I don't give a damn what it costs!"

"We're going to do all we can, of course. But...she's not trying, you see. To live, I mean. The will to live can make the difference in cases like these."

The voices faded away, and then one of them came back, deep and slow, and she was dimly aware of fingers curling around hers, holding them, caressing them.

"Running out on me?" the voice growled. "Is that what you're trying to do, Maggie, run some more?"

Her eyes fluttered, her brows contracted. Her head moved restlessly on the cool pillow.

"I...don't want...to," she whispered half-consciously.

"Don't want to what?"

"Live," she managed. "Hurts...too much."

"Dying's going to hurt more," came the short reply. "Because if you go, I'm coming, too. You won't escape me that way. So help me, God, I'll follow you! Do you hear me, Maggie?"

Her head tossed. "Leave me...alone!" she whispered painfully.

"Why the hell should I? You won't leave me alone."

The fingers tightened, and she felt or thought she felt a surge of emotion flowing through them, warming her, touching her, gently holding her to life.

She licked her dry, cracked lips. "Don't . . . let go," she murmured, clenching her hand around those strong fingers.

"I'll never let go, little girl. Hang on, sweetheart. Just hang on."

"Hang . . . on," she breathed, and the darkness came again.

The voices came and went again, now droning, now arguing. A feminine one joined in, pleading, soft. It was like a strange symphony of sound, mingled with the clanging of metallic objects, the coolness of sheets, the feel of warm water and cool hands. And that one voice . . .

"Don't give up now," it commanded, and she felt the strong fingers gripping hers. "You can do it if you try. Just hang on!"

She took short, sharp breaths and they hurt terribly. She grimaced with the effort. "Oh, it . . . hurts!" she moaned.

"I know. Oh, God, I know. But keep trying, Maggie. It'll get better. I promise."

So she kept trying, fading in and out of life until the sounds became familiar, until one day she opened her eyes and saw the white sheets and smelled the medicinal smell and saw sunlight filtered through the blinds across her bed.

Blinking, her lips raw, she looked up into a pale, haggard face with emerald green eyes and disheveled dark hair.

She frowned, numb from painkillers and sleep. "Hospital?" she managed weakly.

Clint drew a deep, heavy breath. "Hospital," he agreed. "Still hurt?"

She swallowed. "Could I . . . water?"

He got up from his chair and poured water and ice into a glass from the plastic pitcher by the bedside. He sat on the edge of the bed to lift her head so that she could sip the ice water.

"Oh, that's so good," she almost wept, "so good!"

"Your throat feels like sawdust, I imagine."

"Like...desert sand," she corrected, wincing as he laid her back on the pillows. "Am...am I broken somewhere?"

"A few ribs," he said.

The tone in his voice disturbed her. "What else?"

He ran a lean hand through his thick, dark hair. "You took a hell of a blow, Maggie," he said quietly.

"Clint, what else?" she cried.

"Your back, honey," he said gently.

With a feeling of horror she tried to move her legs...and couldn't.

"Oh, my God..." she whispered.

"Don't panic," Clint cautioned, brushing the damp hair away from her temples. "Don't panic. It isn't broken, just bruised. Your doctors say you'll be walking again in weeks."

Her eyes opened wide, searching his desperately. "You wouldn't...lie to me?"

His fingers brushed her cheek gently. "I'll never lie to you. It won't be easy, but you'll walk. All right?"

She relaxed. "All right."

"How did they...find you?" she asked.

A ghost of a smile touched his chiseled mouth. "Masterson's letter, in your purse. It had your name and the ranch's address on it, remember?"

She nodded, toying with the sheet. "I was...thinking about the cruise, when the car..."

"You might have told me where you were going," he remarked.

She flushed, turning her eyes away.

He drew a harsh breath. "On second thought," he said gruffly, "why the hell should you? God knows I didn't give you any reason to think I'd give a damn, did I, Maggie?"

She still couldn't answer him, the memories coming back full force now, hurting, hurting...!

"Don't," he said gently. "Maggie, don't look back. It's going to take every ounce of strength you've got to get back on your feet. Don't waste it on me."

She breathed unsteadily. "You're right about that," she murmured tightly. "It would be a waste."

"I'm glad you agree," he replied, without a trace of emotion in his deep, slow voice.

She studied her pale hands. "Why did you come?"

"Because Emma and Janna wouldn't rest until I did," he growled. "Why else?"

"Well, I'll live," she said bitterly. "And I'll walk. And I don't need any help from you, so why don't you go home?"

"Not without you."

She gaped at him, but there was no hint of expression on his dark face.

"The minute I leave," he mused, "you'd be up to your ears in self-pity."

"I wouldn't either!"

He reached out and caught her cold, nervous fingers in his. "I'll let you go the day you can walk away from me under your own power," he said. "That ought to give you some incentive, hellcat."

Hellcat. She remembered, without wanting to, the last time he'd called her that, pinning her down, holding her, hurting her, his hard mouth creating sensations that washed over her like fire.

"You're blushing, Maggie," he teased gently.

She jerked her hand away and her eyes with it. "I can go home...to the apartment," she faltered.

"Not on your life, honey," he said, and she recognized the willful, stubborn note in his voice. "Not if I have to tie you. Janna's home on vacation for the next three weeks, and I'll be damned if I'll leave you in an apartment alone and helpless."

"I'm not helpless!"

"No?" he taunted, his eyes sliding down her body.

She hit the covers with an impotent little fist. "I hate you!"

"As long as you're not indifferent," he chuckled. "Hatred can be exciting, little girl."

Her narrow, flashing pale eyes burned into his. "Just you wait until I get back on my feet!"

He only smiled, leaning back in the chair, the tautness, the age draining out of him with the action. "I'll try, baby."

Something in the way he said it made her blush.

Time passed quickly after that. The pain lingered on for a few days, especially when they cut down on the pain-killers, but Clint was always there, daring her to whimper about it. They gave her over to the physical therapists, and he was there too, watching, waiting, taunting. She worked twice as hard, focusing her weak muscles to do what she wanted them to, using the violent emotion she felt like a whip. She'd walk again. She would, if for no other reason than to prove to that jade-eyed devil she could!

Finally the day came when she was released from the hospital, when medical science had done all it could. She gazed over the back of the cab seat toward the fading sky-line of Miami as they reached the airport. And she'd never even gotten to see the cruise ship.

The flight home seemed to take no time at all. Clint relaxed as he flew the small single-engine plane, his eyes intent on the controls and landmarks of small towns and parks and farms and forests and herds of cattle as they flew above the misty landscape.

She glanced at Clint. Did he really want her to hate him, she wondered, or had he only said it to irritate her? She remembered her own forwardness in her teens, when she'd put him on a pedestal and done everything but worship him. That must have been unbearable for a man like Clint, being followed around like a pet dog, as he'd put it before she left the ranch.

Her eyes went back to the window, glancing out at the wispy clouds. If only she could live down that idiotic behavior, if only she could wipe the slate clean between them and start over and be...friends. The word almost choked her, but she realized belatedly that it was the only thing possible now. All the bridges were burned behind them. She'd done that all by herself.

Anyway, she thought with a chill, Lida would be back at the ranch waiting for him this time. She'd only seen the woman once, but that had been more than enough. It was going to make living at the ranch unbearable. It was why she'd fought so hard to go back to the apartment. But Clint, as usual, was going to have his way in spite of all her efforts to thwart him. Just like old times.

She stared down at her useless legs in the slacks she'd worn from Columbus on the bus. It seemed so long ago that Clint had swung her up behind him on the stallion.

It was the shock, the doctors had told her, that caused this temporary paralysis—the shock to her body, to her system, to her mind, and a good deal of bruising as well. At least she had the feeling back in them. But walking was going to be another matter altogether, and she shuddered mentally at what lay ahead. It was going to take a kind of determination she wasn't sure she possessed to make those muscles move again. What if she didn't have it? What if the doctors were wrong, and her spine had been damaged? What if...

"We're home!" Clint said above the engine noise, and nosed the small plane down toward the landing strip.

Janna met them with tears in her eyes, leaping from the big town car just as the propeller stopped spinning.

"Oh, Maggie, I'm so glad to see you," she wept, hugging her friend as though she'd come back from the dead instead of Miami.

Maggie forced herself to laugh as she patted Janna's shoulder. "I'm all right. I'm going to be fine. Ask Clint if you don't believe me. He insists!" she mumbled, glaring at him over Janna's shoulder.

He only grinned. "Move over, Janna, and let me get this load of potatoes in the car."

"I'm not a load of potatoes," Maggie protested as he slid his arms under and around her and carried her like a feather to the front seat of the car.

"You do have eyes," Janna remarked, tongue-in-cheek, as she opened the car door for Clint.

"And you do look fried," Clint seconded as he put her down gently on the seat. "Careful, Maggie, you'll singe yourself."

"You devil," she grumbled at him.

His eyes dropped deliberately to the soft curve of her mouth. "Daring me, honey?" he asked in a low voice as Janna went around the front of the car to get in.

"No!" she whispered back.

He smiled and closed the door. He went around the car, too, and opened the door on Janna. "Out," he said.

"But I can drive...!" she protested.

"Not my car, not with me in it. Out."

She gave a disgusted sigh and slid over next to Maggie. "I hate brothers," she muttered.

"That isn't what you always used to tell me," Maggie observed.

"Oh, do shut up," the younger girl moaned.

By night, Maggie was comfortably installed in the same guest bedroom she'd left, propped up with pillows, surrounded by books and magazines, pumped full of soup and sandwiches and hot coffee.

"But, Emma," she'd protested, "you'll spoil me."

"I'm just glad you're still around to be spoiled," came the reply as the housekeeper went out the door.

Janna sat down in the chair by the bed, laughing. "You might as well give up. You know that, don't you?"

Maggie smiled in surrender. "I ought to, I guess. Janna..."

"What?"

She looked down at her hands. "Is Lida here yet?"

Janna gaped at her. "What did you say?"

"Well...Clint said that Lida was coming back."

"The fool!" Janna got up and went to the window. A hard, angry sigh passed her lips. "He'll never learn, never! Why does he want her back here now, of all times? And when did he tell you she was coming?"

"Why...the Monday after I left here," she said.

"Well, she didn't show up. Thank God," Janna added angrily. "Hasn't he learned yet? My gosh, she went off and married that rich old man . . . is she leaving him already?"

"That's what Clint said."

"He'd be better off alone for the rest of his life. Oh, Maggie, why are men so stupid?" she moaned.

Maggie had to smile at the sincerity in her friend's soft voice. "I guess God made them that way so they'd be vulnerable to women."

"The only women my brother's vulnerable to are glorified streetwalkers," Janna grumbled. She eyed the oval face on the pillow with the cloudy tangle of wavy hair framing it. "Why hasn't he ever noticed you?"

Maggie reached for her coffee to try and keep Janna from seeing the color that surged in her cheeks. "I'm like his kid sister, you know that," she hedged.

"Well, it isn't due to a lack of effort on my part," Janna admitted. She sighed. "Well, can I get you anything?"

Maggie shook her head. "I'm spoiled enough, thanks. Don't let me keep you up. It's late."

Janna leaned down to hug her. "I'm so glad you're all right."

"So am I. I'm just sorry I missed the cruise. I would have enjoyed it so much . . . even if only because Duke wanted me to."

Janna smiled. "I liked that big man, too. Goodnight, my friend."

"Goodnight."

The door closed behind Janna, and the room seemed to shrink. She picked up a magazine and began to read, but the words blurred. With the silence and solitude, her mind began to work, weighing possibilities, worrying about her legs . . .

"So much for leaving you on your own," Clint said from the doorway, his eyes narrow as they studied her frowning face. "Wallowing again?"

She made a face at him. "I'm just reading this stupid magazine, is that all right?"

He folded his arms across his chest and leaned back against the door, just watching her. "Were you reading? Or were you worrying?"

She sighed. "Both."

He moved forward, taking the magazine away. "Lie down," he said, jerking a pillow from behind her head so that she could lie flat.

"You awful bully...!" she fussed.

"That and more. Here." He pulled up the covers and tucked them in around her chin. "Now go to sleep and stop torturing yourself. All you have to remember is that you're going to walk again."

Her eyes, wide and a little frightened, looked up into his. "I will, won't I, Clint?" she asked softly, letting the barriers down just long enough to seek reassurance.

"Yes," he said quietly, and with certainty.

She relaxed against the pillows. "Is...is Lida coming soon?" she murmured, avoiding his eyes.

"Lida?"

"Yes. You know, you said..."

"God, I forgot," he said heavily. "She called just after I left for Miami and gave Emma some spiel about changing her mind and going to Majorca instead. It didn't even register at the time Emma told me." His jade eyes glared down at her. "You've given me a hell of a bad time, Irish."

"Sorry," she said softly.

"Show me," he murmured deeply, bending to her mouth.

She stared at him, shaken, not knowing how to take this gentle assault, not knowing if she dared to take him seriously.

His long finger traced the soft tremulous curve of her mouth. "You don't trust me, do you?" he asked quietly.

She shook her head. Without words, her eyes showed the hurt, the memory of why she'd left here.

He tilted her face just a little and his mouth brushed against hers softly, slowly, in a kiss so tender, so exquisitely caring that it brought tears misting into her eyes.

He drew back and searched her face with darkening, intense eyes. "I've got a hard head," he murmured absently, "and sometimes it takes a hell of a knock to get through to me. But I learn fast, little girl, and I don't make the same mistakes twice."

She lowered her eyes as the words got through to her. He meant that he wasn't playing any more, that he wasn't going to encourage her to lose her head. It should have made her happy. Instead, there was a king-sized lump in her throat.

"I'm . . . I'm so tired, Clint," she murmured.

"No doubt." He smoothed her hair with a gentle hand. "I'm safe, Maggie. I'm not going for your throat any more. We'll keep things at a friendly level from now on. Is that what you want?"

"Oh, yes," she breathed, and didn't look up in time to see the tiny flinch of his eyelids.

"Sleep well," he said in a strange tone, and tugging playfully at a strand of her hair, he turned and left her there.

She snuggled down into the pillows. At least, she thought miserably, they'd be friends for once in their lives. Maybe that would ease the hurt a little. And maybe all wolves would suddenly become vegetarians.

9

Is that the best you can do, Irish?'' Clint taunted as she pulled herself along the parallel bars in the makeshift gym he'd had equipped for her.

She glared at him, painstakingly dragging her weak legs along behind her as she let her arms take her weight. "You try it!" she panted. "Do you think you could do any better?"

"Sure," he chuckled.

She stopped to catch her breath. "You," she told him, "are a slave driver."

"I'll have you back on your feet in two more weeks," he said smugly. "If," he added darkly, "you stop cheating. Use your legs, Maggie, not your arms. Stand up, dammit!"

Her lower lip trembled. Tears formed in her eyes. "Don't you think I'm trying to?" she cried.

He came forward, lifting her up in his arms like a tearful child. He carried her to an armchair by the window and sank down in it, holding her on his lap until the cloudburst was past. He passed a handkerchief into her hand and sat back, watching her mop and sniff away the evidence.

"I'm sorry," she mumbled.

"You're human," he told her. "So am I, although I don't think you like to believe it. I don't want to browbeat you, but you'll never get on your feet again unless you try to walk. Dragging won't cut it, baby."

She thumped her small fist against his broad chest under the deep gray shirt. "I'm trying!"

"Try harder."

She glared at him with all the pent-up rage she felt. "I'd like to hit you!" she said hotly.

His eyes narrowed. "All that sweet, wild emotion," he whispered, "and no way to let it out, is that it? Let me help you..."

He caught her face in both hands and brought it up to his mouth, kissing her suddenly, violently, with a force that made her clutch at his shoulders to steady herself. She felt the wildness in her own blood reaching out to him, burning him back, in a release that was better than tears. With a hard moan, her arms went around his neck, her mouth opened hungrily under his, and she gave him back the kiss with every bit of strength in her body and all the longing she had felt for him since her teens.

Suddenly he drew away, his eyes burning, his breath jerking as he managed to catch it. "My God," he breathed unsteadily, and his hands bit into her upper arms like steel clasps. "What are you trying to do to me?"

Dazed, vaguely embarrassed at her passionate response, she dragged her eyes down to the hard pulse at his brown throat. "You...started it," she accused shakily.

"It's all I can do to keep from finishing it, you little fool," he said deeply. He stood up abruptly, met her eyes as he placed her hands on the bars, probing them in a silence that simmered between them.

"The sooner I get you out of here, the better," he said in a goaded tone. "Now, stand up, dammit!"

Whipped by the anger in his voice, the admission that he wanted to be rid of her, she forced her body to go erect, forced the screaming muscles in her legs to move.

"I'm going to walk if it kills me," she told him.

"Don't tell me," he replied. "Show me."

"Stand back and watch, then." And she moved her legs, for the first time.

From that first step, it was on to a second, a third, and finally as many as it took to go the length of the parallel bars. It was the greatest feeling of accomplishment Maggie had ever known, and better than any medicine. She could walk again. She could walk alone. She could walk away from Clint for good.

Not that it seemed to bother Clint. Once he had her moving alone, he seemed to vanish, leaving her with Emma and Janna for moral support while he went about his business. He kept his distance except at meals, and then he made sure the conversation was kept on general topics. To Maggie he was courteous and polite, nothing more. It was worse than the old days, when he fought with her. It hurt.

Janna was sitting with her one night, when Clint passed by the open door with little more than a glance and a nod. Maggie muttered something under her breath and Janna got up and closed the door.

She turned, eyeing Maggie curiously. "Do you hate him so much?" she asked gently.

Maggie pushed a strand of hair out of her eyes. "I'm indifferent," she lied. "Numb, I guess. I don't think there's enough emotion left in me for hate."

"Serves him right, I guess." The smaller girl sighed. "All the hearts he's broken over the years, it was poetic justice."

Maggie's heart jumped and ran away, but the excitement never touched her composed expression. "What do you mean?"

"If you'd seen his face when he got that call about the accident you were in, you wouldn't have to ask." Janna sighed as she sank back down in the chair by Maggie's bed. "He went whiter than any sheet. I've never seen anything upset Clint like that, not in all my life. He went straight to the airstrip without even packing. And when he got to Miami, he never left you except to sleep, and not for long at that." Janna studied her fingernails. "The doctors told him you weren't going to make it, that you weren't trying to live. He wouldn't accept that. He sat and held your hand and talked to you...I stayed for two days, then he made me come home when he saw you were going to be all right." She smiled. "He said somebody had to run the ranch while he was gone."

Maggie stared at her for a long time before she spoke. "I don't remember anything...." She sighed. "Oh, Janna, I'm so sorry I worried everyone. It was such a stupid..."

"It could have happened to any of us. All I wanted to do was make you understand that Clint cares."

Maggie smiled wistfully. "It's guilt, Janna, not caring," she corrected gently. "He . . . he said some very cruel things to me the night before I left the ranch for Miami. I don't think either one of us will ever forget. God help me," she said, her eyes closing on the memories, "I don't think I can forget or forgive him, ever, for what he did to me that night."

There was such a deathly silence in the room that Maggie quickly opened her eyes—and found Clint standing just inside the door, his face frozen, his gaze dark and quiet and faintly violent. That he'd heard those words was evident.

"I wanted to remind you that Jones is bringing that bull tomorrow morning," Clint told Janna, without bothering to spare Maggie another glance. "I've got a meeting in Atlanta, so I won't be back until late. Have the boys put him in that new pen and get the vet out here."

"I will," Janna said uncomfortably. "Are you going in the morning?"

He nodded. "Goodnight."

He was gone, and Janna met Maggie's wounded eyes in the silence that followed. "Maggie, what happened?" she asked gently.

But Maggie shook her head with a tearful smile. It didn't bear telling. Not to anyone.

It was late, and the house was long asleep, but Maggie couldn't even close her eyes. With a quiet sigh, she finally gave up and got out of bed, painstakingly pulling on her long jade green robe and making her way into the dark hall and down the stairs.

Her legs were still sluggish, but by taking her time, she made it to the kitchen without stumbling. A cup of hot chocolate, she thought, just might put her to sleep. Failing that, she was ready to try a sledgehammer.

While the milk was heating, she got down a heavy mug and filled it sparingly with a tablespoon of sugar and one of cocoa. And all the while, she hated her own tongue for the words Clint had heard. After everything he'd done for her, and she had to throw it out like that, and he had to hear it. Her eyes closed on the pain. And she hadn't really meant it at all.

She poured the hot milk into the mug on top of the sugar and cocoa. The sudden opening of the door startled her so that she almost dropped the pot. She whirled to find Clint standing just inside the doorway.

"What the hell do you think you're doing?" he asked quietly. His dark hair was rumpled, his shirt half undone, his dark face heavily lined as if he'd tried to sleep and couldn't.

"I...just wanted to have a cup of hot chocolate," she murmured, as she placed the pot in the sink and ran water in it.

"Who told you to get out of bed and start climbing up and down stairs in the dark?" he persisted.

She flashed a glance at him. "The President, both houses of Congress and my senator," she said with a hint of her old spirit.

"You left out your representative," he mused, and for just an instant a smile touched his hard mouth. "You ought to be in bed, honey."

Amazing what the soft endearment could do to her nerves, she thought, sitting quickly down at the table in front of her hot chocolate before her legs gave way. "I'll go back up in just a minute."

"Stubborn little mule," he accused. "All right, I'll have a glass of tea and wait for you. How about some cheese and bread?"

Her eyebrows went up. "Hoop cheese?" she asked hopefully.

"If I can find where Emma hides it. Aha!" He pulled it out of the refrigerator, sliced some of it, and put it on a saucer. "Would you rather have crackers or bread?"

"Crackers!"

He laughed softly as he poured himself a glass of tea and plopped ice cubes into it. "Same here."

Seconds later, he put the cheese and crackers on the table between them and relaxed in the chair next to hers, drinking his tea thirstily.

"Couldn't you sleep?" she asked, suddenly shy of him.

"No," he replied quietly.

She shrugged. "Neither could I." She munched on a piece of cheese.

He finished off his part of the cheese and crackers and leaned back in his chair to study her. "Look at me," he said suddenly.

She met his level gaze, startled, and as quickly looked away from it.

"The robe matches your eyes," he remarked.

She smiled. "That's why Janna gave it to me, or so she said."

"Legs hurt?" he asked.

She shook her head. "I took my time coming down the steps. After all," she reminded him, "you were the one who said I needed more exercise."

He drained his glass. "I said too damned much," he replied. "Hurry up, honey, I'm not leaving you down here alone."

She finished her hot chocolate and got up to put the cup in the sink. As she turned away from the sink, she found herself being lifted into a pair of steely, warm arms and carried out of the kitchen.

"Oh, don't," she protested gently, pushing at his shoulder. "Clint, I'm too heavy...!"

He flicked off the light switch in the kitchen as he carried her out into the hall and up the staircase. His eyes, dark and strange, looked deep into hers. "You don't weigh anything, little girl. It's like carrying an armload of soft, warm velvet."

"If you're going to make fun of me, just put me down and I'll walk!" she said defensively, stirred by the sensations being this close to him was causing.

"Oh, hell no, you won't," he replied imperturbably, and tightened his hold on her.

"You awful bully!"

"You little shrew."

She drew a deep, hard breath and glared up at him with her green eyes blazing. "It's like arguing with a stone wall!" she growled.

He chuckled softly. "See how simple life is when you stop struggling, Irish?"

Her lips pursed in a sulking pout. "I won't even dignify that remark with an answer."

"You'd hate it if you could fight me and win, Irish," he said gently.

She lowered her eyes to his open collar, where the bronzed flesh with its covering of dark hair was tantalizingly visible. She could feel the hardness of that broad chest where she was pressed against it, and she wanted suddenly to reach out and touch that warm rough skin. A tremor went lightly through her body.

He looked down when he felt it and caught her eyes, held them, and searched them with an intensity that made her heart race.

He drew a deep, harsh breath and kept walking. He carried her into her room and laid her on the bed as quickly as if she'd been an armload of burning straw.

"This time, stay put," he growled, and his eyes were blazing as they looked down into hers.

She glared up at him. Her breath came in irregular gasps, from the proximity she'd endured, from the hunger of loving him. "Must you always growl at me?" she whispered.

"Do you have to be told what I'd rather do?" he asked flatly, and his eyes slid over her like a warm caress, from her lovely flushed face in its wild tangle of dark, wavy long hair down to her slender body. "I want you to the point where it's like having an arm cut off, does that make you feel better, hellcat?" he asked harshly.

The admission stunned her. He'd said something like that before, but she always thought it was part of the humiliation he'd thrown at her. She lay there quietly, staring up at him like a curious young cat, her eyes asking questions as they met his.

"That's all you know anything about—wanting," she said quietly, her eyes accusing.

"What should I believe in?" he asked. "Love? It's a myth, little girl. An illusion that doesn't last past the marriage vows."

"How do you know?"

He studied her mouth with a mocking smile. "How do you?" He bent forward, leaning on the arms that pinioned her on either side. "I've always been able to read you like a book," he murmured, holding her eyes. "No, I'm not guilt-ridden, and don't you believe that I am. There are a thousand reasons why I came to Miami after you, but guilt wasn't one of them."

She stared up at him, curious but afraid to voice the question.

"You know one of them," he whispered deeply, studying her mouth. "But I'm not going to offer you marriage, Maggie. Not now, not ever."

She swallowed nervously. "I won't be your mistress," she said unsteadily. "I won't, Clint."

"Could you feel with another man what you feel with me?" he challenged roughly.

She shifted restlessly on the pillow. "There are other things."

"Name one."

"Children!" she shot at him, feeling vulnerable under those cutting green eyes.

Something came and went in his face. He studied her for a long time before he spoke, weighing what she'd said with the soft light in her eyes.

"You want children?" he said.

"Of course."

"There's not any 'of course' about it, little girl," he said solemnly. "Lida couldn't bear the thought of them. I can't

remember another woman I've been around who even considered them as part of a relationship.''

"That doesn't come as any surprise to me," she said
flatly.

He ignored the sarcasm. "Do you know, Maggie," he
told her gently, "I've never thought about children?"

She toyed with the pillowcase. "Why should you?" she
murmured. "You don't need anybody. You never have."

His fingers tugged hers away from the pillowcase to
swallow them gently, firmly. "I'm human," he said, his face
solemn. "We all need someone from time to time, Maggie."

"I can't picture you being lonely," she murmured. "What
with all the women following you around like..." She was
going to say pet dogs, but with the memory came pain and
her face went white.

"Don't, for God's sake!" he growled huskily. He slid his
hands under her and lifted her up against his hard, warm
chest, rocking her gently, his face buried in her dark hair, his
hand tangling in the smoky tresses so hard it hurt.

"Clint, I want to go home," she whispered shakily, her
eyes closing as she yielded against him, glorying in the feel
of him, the tangy scent of his cologne mingling with the
spicy soap he used.

"Why?" he asked at her ear.

"Because I've got to find a job," she said weakly. "I can't
stay here..." It was hard to think this close to him. She remembered too well the feel of his hard mouth against her
own, and she wanted it so... Her nails bit into his shoulders involuntarily as she fought to keep that hunger from
being betrayed by her own body.

"Stay with me," he whispered softly, and she felt his lips
moving in her hair, against her cheek, the corner of her
mouth. His hands came up to cup her face and hold it up to
his narrow, glittering eyes. "Be my woman, Maggie."

Her lips trembled as they formed an answer, but his
mouth whispered across them, his tongue tracing gently the

soft curve of her upper lip. "I like the way you taste, Margaretta Leigh," he murmured sensuously.

"You . . . you just like women," she whispered unsteadily, and tried to draw back.

"Honey, I don't want anybody else," he said matter-of-factly. "I haven't for a long time."

She couldn't find a way to answer him, and that seemed to amuse him. He watched her with eyes that were as patient as they were calculating.

"Caught in my own web," he mused, and mischief danced in his dark green eyes. "Doomed to a lifetime of frustrated desire for the one woman I can't have. My God, I wonder if I'm too old for the French Foreign Legion?"

Her eyes lit up. She laughed, her eyes glowing like liquid emeralds, her face flushed and soft and radiant with laughter, her hair like a dark halo framing her face. Clint caught his breath at the picture she made, at the color and animation in that sad little face.

"Think it's funny, do you?" he growled in mock anger, roughly cradling her against him. He bent and kissed her savagely, his mouth demanding and getting a response from her lips. He drew back just far enough to see the eagerness in her eyes. "Now laugh, hellcat," he murmured deeply.

She reached up and touched his mouth with slender, cool fingers. "Barbarian," she whispered.

He smiled. "Did you like it?" he taunted.

She dragged her eyes down to his brown neck. "A lady never admits such things."

"Lady, hell." He brought her mouth up to his and cherished it softly, slowly, with such tender ardor that she gasped. "You're a woman," he whispered huskily. "All woman. My woman. You belong to me, little cat."

She pushed against his chest and sank down on the pillows with a wistful sigh. "No," she told him quietly, and tears brightened her sad eyes. "Not that way."

He drew a deep, short breath and stood up, moving away from the bed to light a cigarette. He took a long draw before he spoke. "Is that final, Maggie?" he asked.

"Yes," she whispered. "I'm sorry."

"The world's full of women, Maggie." He laughed shortly, and threw a mocking glance at her just before he left the room.

Clint was already gone when she got downstairs the next morning. Janna was waiting for her at the table.

"It's about time," she teased. "I thought you were going to sleep all day."

"I thought about it," Maggie replied with a wan smile. She pushed away the plate at her place, ignored the bacon and scrambled eggs and toast on the table, and settled for a cup of black coffee.

"Okay, you might as well tell me what happened," Janna grumbled. "Clint did the same thing. He wouldn't eat in spite of all Emma's coaxing, and he looked like a thundercloud when he went out the door. Was it another argument?"

Maggie lowered her eyes to the reflection of the light in her coffee. "You might say that."

"It's like trying to coax a clam open. Maggie . . . !"

"He wants me to be his mistress," she replied impatiently, meeting Janna's gaping stare calmly. "And I said no. That's all."

"That's all, she says!" Janna gasped. "You mean you finally stopped fighting long enough to get involved with each other!"

"We're not . . . involved. At least, not that way." Maggie sipped her coffee. Tears formed in her eyes and she bit at her lip to keep them from falling, but she felt the betraying trickle down her face. "Oh, Janna, what am I going to do?" she whispered brokenly. "I love him so!"

Janna got to her feet and wrapped her thin arms around the older girl, hugging her quietly until the flood of tears showed signs of slowing.

"I'm sorry," Janna murmured. "I feel responsible, sending you down here when you didn't want to come. Oh, Maggie, why didn't you tell me?" she wailed. "I'd never have insisted . . . !"

"It's all right, it's not your fault," she replied soothingly. "You can't help it that you've got a hardheaded, half-savage beast for a brother. I just don't understand why. . . . One day he'd tease me, the next he'd kiss me, the next he'd act as if he hated me . . . Oh, Janna, I'm so confused."

"He wants you," Janna said, with an ear-to-ear grin.

"Of course he wants me, for all that he spent the first week I was here denying it," she sighed, wiping at her red eyes. "But that's all there is. He told me that he didn't even believe in love, Janna, and that he'd never marry. He wants me, but I can't settle for that kind of relationship. As much as I love him, I can't."

"He wanted Lida, you know," the younger girl reminded her gently. "But he wouldn't have rushed to her bedside, or spent weeks helping her to walk again."

"Wouldn't he?" Maggie asked wistfully. "How do you know that? No," she shook her head. "It's only a physical kind of caring that he feels for me. And it's not enough."

Janna nodded miserably. "What will you do?"

"What can I do? I'll go home." She finished her coffee. "Temporarily, at least. Janna, don't look like that," she pleaded when she saw the crestfallen expression on her friend's face. "You know I wouldn't be able to bear it. He'd call you, like he always has. When he comes to town, he'll come to see you. Do you think I could bear that?"

"How will I bear being without you?" Janna murmured unsteadily. "All these years, and growing up together, and sharing the apartment . . . Oh, Maggie, I'll go with you!"

"You haven't heard a word I've said," Maggie groaned.

Janna sighed. "Yes, I have. Oh, darn Clint, anyway! Why did he have to bring things to a head? You could have gone on hating each other for years!"

That brought a smile to the pale green eyes. "Oh, Janna, you're so comforting!" she laughed weakly. "Come on up and help me pack. I want to be long gone when Clint gets back."

"I'll go with you!"

"You will not. You're on vacation, and he is your brother," she said firmly. "Besides, isn't your mother due home soon?"

"Yes," came the grudging reply.

"Then that's settled. Everything will work out," she added gently. "I promise you, everything will work out. Now stop pouting and come help me pack."

Atlanta was exciting and new, and Maggie's job with a firm of corporation lawyers kept her energies focussed on coping with a different routine.

Day by day it was getting easier to let the past rest. Janna had argued, when she returned from vacation, that if Maggie would just give it a little time, everything would be different. But Maggie was adamant. She'd already found a job, and an apartment downtown, and was in the process of moving when Janna walked in the door.

"He's changed, you know," Janna told her quietly during a lull in packing. "When he isn't working himself into a coma, he just...sits. Mama came home and even *she* couldn't get through to him. It's like he's...grieving."

"For me?" Maggie scoffed. "That'll be the day. If anything, he was glad to see the last of me. All I ever did was irritate him."

"Are you really over him, already?" Janna asked quietly.

Maggie turned away and went back to the mountain of clothes she'd stacked on her bed. "Sit down and let me tell you all about my new job!" she said brightly.

One of her new bosses was young and single, and he reminded her vaguely of Brent. They seemed to gravitate together, and it was no time before she was going out with him. But with the understanding that it was going to be strictly a friendship on her part.

"That suits me." Jack Kasey grinned from his superior height. "Even though she can't marry me, Sophia Loren gets so *jealous*!"

"Are you sane?" Maggie teased.

He tossed his blond head arrogantly. "Madam, how dare you?" he demanded.

"Well, excuse me!"

"I should think so!" he replied, unruffled. He reached in his pocket and held out his hand, palm up. There was nothing in it. "Want one?" he asked.

"One what?" She blinked.

"Funny, that's just what my psychiatrist always asks."

"Oh, good heavens," she laughed. "You're the living end!"

"But of course! And I'm loaded, too," he said in a stage whisper. "How about a steak tomorrow night?"

"I'd love it!"

"Great. I know this little restaurant . . ."

After the little restaurant, there was another little disco place, and then an all-night bar. It was after two o'clock in the morning when she got back to her apartment.

"Sorry to keep you up so late," Jack apologized as he walked with her from the elevator to her apartment door. "Next time, I'll try to remember that we're both working stiffs."

"I enjoyed it, though," she said, laughing.

"So did I." He grinned. "Well, goodnight, fair lady, my dragon awaits without."

"Don't ride him too hard, now," she cautioned. "You know how nasty dragons can get when they're overworked!"

"I'll remember!" he called as the elevator door shut.

With a sigh, she fit her key into the lock and walked in. There was a light on in the living room, and she hadn't remembered leaving it on. The carpet muffled her footsteps as she moved cautiously forward. The lock was strong, surely no thief had been able to...

She came silently to the doorway and froze there. Clint was sitting in an armchair facing the hall, his eyes quiet and dark in the distance, his face solemn.

"Wha...how...how did you get in here?" she asked hoarsely.

"Never mind how," he said in a voice tight with anger. "Who the hell were you with, and where have you been half the night?"

She threw her evening bag down on the coffee table and glared at him, the color of her emerald green dress making her eyes even more vivid.

"None of your business, Clint," she replied with a calm she was far from feeling. "I don't owe you any answers."

He lit a cigarette, his eyes never leaving hers. "I asked you a question. I can get an answer in any number of ways. One," he remarked quietly, "would be to lay you out on that sofa."

She flushed at the insinuation. "I thought you were tired of giving me lessons," she said tightly.

He started to get up.

"All right!" she said quickly. "I...I was out with one of the lawyers in the firm I work for. Just...just a friendly date, Clint. He's very much like Brent."

He sank back against the cushion, with a heavy sigh. "Maggie, is that the kind of man who really appeals to you?" he asked wearily.

She studied her evening shoes. "What kind of man are you talking about?"

"Clowns. Boys."

"They don't make demands," she said on a sigh.

"No," he agreed. "They don't. Why are you afraid of a man who would? Do you feel that inadequate, little girl?"

"Yes," she said, in what was little more than a whisper.

"Why?"

She shook her head and perched on the arm of the sofa, her eyes avoiding his.

She heard him get up, heard the muffled thud of his footsteps as he came to her. His lean hands caught her shoulders and forced her to look up at him.

"Because of what that excuse for a fiancé said to you?" he asked quietly. "Or because of what I did to you?"

"A little of ... both," she murmured, hating the weakness he could cause with only an impersonal touch like this.

He let her go and moved away, smoking his cigarette quietly, standing in front of the window to watch with blank eyes the colorful glow of the city stretching to the horizon.

"Please," she murmured, "why are you here? Is everyone all right at home ... ?"

"Everyone," he agreed wearily. "Except me."

She studied his straight back. "What's wrong?" she asked gently.

"I love you, Maggie."

She felt the words. Actually felt them, like a blinding surge of electric current that made her tremble.

He turned, and she saw the truth in his eyes, in the deep lines of his face.

"Have I shocked you?" he asked harshly. "God knows, I've shocked myself. I didn't think I could feel that for a woman. I didn't think I was capable of it." He took a long draw from his cigarette, and his eyes gazed at every inch of her from head to toe. "Do you want to know what it felt like when you left? Do you want to know how many nights I've spent sitting in the chair by my bed staring out into the darkness, missing you? My God, I have hurt until it feels like I've been cut in two."

Her lips parted tremulously, but she couldn't speak. It was too new, too incredible. Was she asleep and dreaming it all?

He put out the cigarette and came toward her like a cat, all muscle and grace and vibrant masculinity. He reached down and swung her up into his arms.

"You don't believe me, do you?" he asked quietly. "Let me prove it to you, Margaretta Leigh. Let me show you what I feel."

His arms brought her sensuously close and his mouth burned down into hers, opening it, tasting it, devouring it with a hunger that was fierce and blistering.

He dropped down onto the couch, holding her across his lap, touching every soft line of her face with his lips, tenderly smoothing away the tears that his gentleness brought from her closed eyes.

"Clint...!" she whispered brokenly, clinging to him.

"What do you feel, when I kiss you?" he asked against her soft mouth, his breath coming quick and heavy.

"As if I'm...being burned...alive," she wept, and her fingers went trembling to his cheek, the silvery hair at his temples. "I love you so much," she breathed. "I love you so...!"

"Show me," he challenged, bending his head. "Sweet little enemy, show me how much!"

She brought her mouth down onto his and kissed him slowly, hungrily, her nails digging into his back, her lips parting sensuously under his.

He drew back a breath, his eyes almost black with what he was feeling, his heavy heartbeat shaking her. He studied her flushed face, her misty, yielding eyes, and with a tender deliberation, his lean hand slid up her body over the soft, young curves until he felt her tremble.

"Do you like this?" he whispered gently.

She nodded, choked with the force of her own emotions so that even a word was impossible.

"So do I, little innocent," he said tenderly. He bent and kissed her gently, and his lips curved in a smile against the soft moan that broke from her throat as his hand moved again.

Her head fell back into the crook of his arm and she looked up at him with eyes that held all of heaven.

"I've fought this until I thought it was going to kill me," he said, and she could see the seriousness in his eyes. "Honey, I want more from you than a night in my bed. I want children with you. I want to be there when you hurt so I can hold you until the tears go away. I want to stand between you and the world and keep you safe. God, Maggie, I can't bear to live without you!" he whispered torturously. "Marry me, Irish. Live with me. Love me."

Tears were flowing down her cheeks. "Yes," she whispered, and found herself drowning in his ardor almost before she could get the word out.

Minutes later, he tore himself away from her and stood up, smoothing his ruffled hair, fastening the buttons of his shirt.

"We'd better settle for a civil ceremony," he said huskily, "and soon."

She nodded, straightening her clothes and her hair while her heart threatened to storm through her chest.

"When did you know?" she asked, moving into the kitchen and starting a pot of coffee.

He stood in the doorway watching her with a smoking cigarette in his hand, looking so attractive, it took all her willpower not to throw herself at him.

"The summer you were seventeen," he said gently, smiling.

She gaped at him.

"I wanted you," he said. "I couldn't get you away from the ranch fast enough, I wanted you so. From that day on, it was a losing battle. I used every excuse I could think of to keep you away from the ranch, to avoid you when you were there. My God, I'd never felt like that about a woman, any woman. And you were little more than a child." He shook his head with a wistful sigh. "I thought it would eventually go away. Right up to the day you called and told Emma you were engaged." He laughed shortly. "I went into a black sulk for days. I got drunk out of my mind. Two of my men threatened to quit because I rode them so hard. And nobody knew why, except me. But even then I wouldn't admit it."

"And then I came for the summer," she said.

"And I went over the edge." He reached out and touched her cheek. "Oh, baby, you'll never know how I fought to keep my hands off you. Until that day by the stream, when

I finally let myself go...and every second of it was like a dark, heady wine. If you'd touched me the way I wanted you to..." He broke off with a deep, short breath. "I tried to stay away from you, and it got harder all the time. That last night...it was either make you hate me or carry you upstairs. I hated what I did, even while I was doing it. But at that time, I still didn't think I wanted marriage." His eyes closed. "I found out how much I wanted it when they called me from Miami. I damned near crashed the plane getting to you, and I swore if you made it I wouldn't waste a day getting you to the altar. Then you started recovering and when you remembered what I'd done, you hated me. I couldn't seem to get close to you again until we had that midnight snack in the kitchen. That was another close call. And then I began to have doubts all over again. I knew you wanted me. But I wasn't sure you loved me. You'd been infatuated with me for so long, I couldn't be sure...in a way, I was testing you that night. If I'd been able to make you say yes with no offer of marriage...I thought it would prove that you really did love me. But you said no. And I got my back up and left without saying goodbye. Then you left, and I was too damned proud to go after you."

She met his eyes and smiled. "Why did you come tonight?"

His finger traced her mouth. "Because Janna told me you loved me," he said softly, "and put me out of my misery."

She moved into his arms and pressed close. Her eyes closed as he drew her up against him.

"Are...are you sure you want to marry me?" she asked.

He chuckled deeply. "I don't see any alternatives. We can't very well have a family any other way."

"I hope they're all boys, and they look just like you."

"I want one little girl with dark hair and green eyes."

Her lips brushed his chin. "I'll see what I can do."

He kissed her gently. "Let's call Janna," he said with a grin. "And mother. And especially," he added with a glint in his eyes, "Brent."

"You were jealous!" she gasped.

"Hell, yes! And angry. He kept getting in my way. That night in the pool ... Oh, that night," he whispered against her mouth, "Maggie, I could feel your hands on me for days, do you know that? That was when I began to suspect what I really felt."

She toyed with a button on his shirt. "Does that mean," she asked, "that I can't tie ribbons on the cows' tails anymore?"

He glared down at her. "Maggie..." he began warningly.

She reached up and linked her arms around his neck. "Let's call Janna," she murmured contentedly, "and tell her we've decided to become very friendly enemies."

He smiled down into her eyes. "Sweet enemy," he whispered, "show me how friendly you want to be."

And she did.

*   *   *   *   *

LOVE ON
TRIAL

1

*

The little coffee shop was crowded, its spotless white linen tablecloths and tempting aromas drawing a maximum crowd, but the two stubborn young women weren't discouraged. They managed to find one empty table and collapsed into the dainty chairs, spilling their packages onto the floor with weary sighs.

"I thought you said the stores would all be empty on a day this hot," Marty reminded her friend with a glare over the single rose in its ceramic budvase.

The slender young blonde only smiled, her amber eyes sparkling. "I didn't say empty of what," she laughed.

"Oh, Siri," her friend moaned, "you're just impossible!"

Cyrene Jamesson studied the oversized menu with silent amusement, warming to the sound of her nickname. No one called her Cyrene except Mark; but, then, her conservative-minded boyfriend never called anyone by a nickname.

She put the menu aside after making an instant decision, and watched Marty frown uncertainly over the varieties of coffee and pastries.

"Why not close your eyes and point at one?" Siri suggested helpfully.

"That's easy for you to say," came the reply. "You don't have to watch your weight."

She sighed. "At the speed I move, it's impossible to gain weight."

"You didn't have to be a reporter, you know," Marty reminded her.

Siri looked thunderstruck. "You mean," she said in mock astonishment, "there are other professions that cater to crazy people?"

"You're not crazy."

"No," Siri agreed. "Most people run river races in inner tubes, hang out of airplanes with 35 mm cameras, lie down behind cars while police tear-gas snipers, and chase bank robbers down back streets."

Marty closed her eyes. "Deliver me," she whispered.

Seconds later, a young, harried waitress darted toward them with her order book in hand, almost panting with the effort. "Sorry I took so long," she apologized. "We're swamped today!"

"Only because the coffee's so good." Siri smiled.

The waitress beamed and took their order, darting off again in a flurry of ruffled apron.

"Miss Diplomacy strikes again," Marty laughed, tossing her dark hair.

"It doesn't cost anything to be nice to people," Siri reminded her.

"Reporters are supposed to be hard, uncompromising and stubborn," Marty remarked. "Aren't they?"

"That's only a stereotype. You can't lump people into groups and label them anymore, it's too complicated."

"Thanks for the benefit of that priceless bit of wisdom from Psychology 102," Marty laughed.

"Wait till we get the pastries and coffee," Siri threatened, "and I'll treat you to a lecture on Glasser's theories."

"Please, we don't all share your fascination with abnormal psychology," came a moan from the other side of the table. "How does your poor old Dad stand it?"

"He likes it."

"He would," Marty grumbled. "Does Hawke?"

The light went out of Siri's rosy complexioned face.

"Don't mention that savage to me," Siri growled.

"Siri, what's wrong with you?" her friend wondered. "Half the women in the country would give their eye-teeth just to meet that gorgeous man. And there he is, your father's partner, one of the most famous criminal lawyers alive, and you don't even like him!''

"Hawke doesn't go out of his way to be likeable," she replied quietly. "He thinks all women should be locked up in harems and only let out once a year to have their hair trimmed."

"While you, my dotty friend, are the world's foremost libber."

"Guilty as charged." Siri smiled. "Hawke's too *macho* for my taste. We've always knocked sparks from each other, ever since Dad took him on seven years ago."

"Not all the time, though." Marty grinned. "I've seen a few pictures of the two of you together at parties."

"He can be pleasant enough. There are times when I feel almost comfortable with him. And the very next minute, he'll say something to get my back up and laugh when I lose my temper." Siri shook her head. "It's never dull, I'll give you that."

Siri got a brief respite while the waitress set two cups of *Kaffee mit Schlag* in dainty wineglasses before them, along with delicate French cream cakes.

"Two thousand calories a bite," Marty moaned.

"Only," Siri remarked, "if you eat it. Why not just sit there and gaze at it lovingly?"

Marty glared at her and dug into the cream cake with a vengeance.

"That was delightful," Siri sighed as she finished the last drop of her strong coffee. "This is the best day off I've had in months."

"Naturally. It's the only day off you've had in months. How did you manage it?"

Siri laughed. "Because of the Devolg murder case."

Marty blinked at her. "Huh?"

"You've heard of it? The young boy who was accused of the knife murder of Justin Devolg?"

The brunette's mouth flew open. "You mean the case that's been on the front page..."

"The same. Hawke's counsel for the defense," she added.

"I still don't get it. Why did that get you a day off?"

"Because," Siri said calmly, "Bill Daeton wants me to go to Panama City with Hawke to track down a witness in the case."

"Oh, you lucky little devil." Marty smiled. "Panama City, all expenses paid, and Hawke Grayson!"

"Hold it right there. I said Bill wants me to go, not that I plan to do it."

Marty lifted her eyes. "And why, pray tell, aren't you going? Doesn't Hawke want you along?"

"You're getting warmer. Bill asked Dad to approach him about it," Siri explained, "because he knew I'd refuse. So Dad asked him."

Marty leaned forward earnestly, moving the budvase aside. "So?"

"Hawke told Dad he had enough to do without playing chaperone to an adolescent."

"Adolescent! Siri, you're twenty-one years old!"

"To a man of Hawke's advanced years," the blonde said maliciously, "I probably do seem underaged."

"I thought he was in his middle thirties."

"Late thirties," Siri corrected, "or early forties. I've never asked. He's too old for me, and that's a fact. Anyway, he said it was fine if Bill wanted to send a male reporter along, as long as Hawke had some control over the story to make sure the facts were presented accurately. How do you like that? A male reporter was welcome, but I can go hang."

"What did Bill say?"

"I don't know, I haven't asked him." She fished in her purse for a five dollar bill. "Hawke really burns me up. It isn't that I wanted to have to go with him, it's just the principle of the thing. I guess it's just as well, though, you know how Mark is."

"Don't I just?" Marty said venomously. "That pompous little...!"

"Now, Marty."

"Don't you 'now, Marty' me!" the other girl grumbled. "Why you put up with him is beyond me."

"Because he's good company most of the time, and he doesn't make demands," Siri said quietly. "I don't have to fight him off, and we do enjoy each other's company."

"How exciting!"

"I don't want excitement in my private life," Siri said. "I get enough of that during the day running from fires to murder scenes."

"I'm waiting," Marty said.

"For what?"

"For that old 'eyes and ears' of John Q. Public routine," she laughed. "Honestly, Siri, I think you bleed ink!"

"Of course!" she replied with a smile. "It's required."

She took the Marta bus to the corner of Peachtree and 10th Street, and got off there. It was such a pretty day, she felt like walking the rest of the way to her father's law office. She sighed, studying the Atlanta skyline, the new construction, and the mingling of old architecture with modern innovation. It was difficult to picture what this great city must have been like in 1864 when it was ravaged by Sherman's army. For an urban area, it was strangely small-townish. There was a community feeling among the people who lived in the old elegant apartment houses along the wide street, among the merchants who ran small shops there. Siri always felt comfortable in this stretch of the city, despite the alarming crime rate. Of course, she had the good sense not to venture out alone at night.

She turned into the office building where her father had his practice, and took the elevator to the 10th floor, which was occupied by the law firm of Jamesson, Grayson, Peafowler, Dinkham, and Guystetter.

Her father's middle-aged secretary, Nadine, greeted her with a smile.

"He's here," she said before Siri could ask. "Shall I warn him, or do you prefer to have the element of surprise?"

Siri smiled from ear to ear. She liked the trim, little brunette who was so like her late mother. If only Jared Jamesson would notice what a jewel of a woman his secretary was... Siri shrugged mentally.

"I think it might be safer if you announce me," Siri told her with a wink. "I'll know if I'm in the doghouse before I walk in."

Nadine nodded and pressed the buzzer. "Mr. Jamesson, your daughter's here to see you. Shall I send her in?"

"You're mistaken, Miss Green," came the deep, sharp reply, "I don't have a daughter. My daughter wouldn't let herself be shoved aside from a juicy assignment like the Devolg murder case."

Siri leaned over the intercom. "She would if Hawke Grayson has his way," she said into it. "You can't argue with a brick wall, Papa dear."

There was a deep chuckle in the background, joined by her father's muffled laugh.

"Come on in, Siri. I think I've convinced the brick wall for you."

Siri straightened with an apprehensive look at Nadine. "Is Hawke in there?" she asked with irritation.

"If I say yes, are you planning to dive for the elevator?" Nadine asked.

Siri shook her head. "I wouldn't give him the satisfaction," she replied. She straightened her shoulders and opened the door to her father's plush office.

Jared Jamesson was stretched back in the swivel chair behind his desk, with his elbows jutting out to either side behind his head. Hawke was perched on the edge of the big oak desk, looking, as usual, dark and formidable.

"Do you still want to go to Panama City?" Jared asked his daughter, swinging forward to rest his forearms flat on the desk.

Siri shrugged. "Not if it's going to mean giving up my bubble gum and my Barbie doll," she said with a pointed glance in Hawke's direction.

She could see the tiny dark flames that began to smoulder in her target's eyes, as he folded his arms across his massive chest and raised an eyebrow. He didn't smile at the dig. But, then, Hawke almost never smiled.

"Someday, sparrow," he told her, "I'm going to make up for a noticeable omission in your upbringing. Jared ruined you."

She tossed her thick blond hair, making a face at the nickname. "No, he didn't," she defended her parent, "every good father gives his children champagne for lunch and takes them to girlie shows at night."

"Siri!" Jared burst out, horrified.

She laughed. "It's okay, Dad, I didn't mean it. Hawke, we never had champagne for lunch; only for supper," she added, and ignored Jared's groan.

"No wonder your father's hair is gray," Hawke remarked in that deep, resonant voice that carried so well in a courtroom. "Well, do you want to go with me, or don't you?"

She didn't but she'd have died rather than admit it. She really wasn't prepared to find an explanation.

"I thought you hated reporters," she recalled. Her fingers tightened around the full shopping bag and her purse.

"Only certain unscrupulous ones," he corrected. "In this case, if I give you an exclusive, at least I can be sure the facts you release are accurate. And," he added, reaching for a cigarette, "you won't be able to print a word of it until I say so."

"Or what?" she challenged.

He lit the cigarette before he replied. "I'll sue the hell out of your paper. And I'll win."

That wasn't conceit. It was a statement of fact, just as if he'd made a comment on the weather, and she knew it. His deep, slow voice sent shivers down her spine.

"Does Bill Daeton know you get the final word on the release date on my copy?" she asked.

He blew out a cloud of smoke. "What do you think?"

She glanced toward her father, who was listening to the exchange with amusement sparkling in the amber eyes that his daughter had inherited from him.

"Do you want to go or not, Siri?" Hawke asked pointedly.

"Well, if I can get somebody to take my assignments for a few days," she mumbled. "I've got that interview with..."

"Excuses?" Hawke prodded. "Or is it that Holland doesn't approve?"

She bristled at the sarcastic reference to her boyfriend. "Mark does have some say in what I do."

"Why should he?" came the harsh reply. "Do you tell him how to do his job at the accounting agency, or where he can travel in connection with it?"

"You don't understand, Hawke...!"

"The hell I don't!" he growled.

"Now, now, world tensions are bad enough without World War III erupting between you two," Jared remarked, moving to stand between them. "And I don't have time to referee."

Siri and Hawke exchanged glares, but her eyes fell first. He always managed to back her down, and it burned her up inside that she yielded so easily.

"All right, I'll go home and pack," she grumbled, turning away.

"I won't be able to get away before Thursday," Hawke said coolly. "Criminal court's in session all week, and I've got two clients to represent. If the jury doesn't get deadlocked, I should be able to leave Friday morning. Check with me later in the week."

She nodded. "See you at home, Dad," she called over her shoulder.

"Don't trip over your mouth on the way out," her parent called after her.

"You should have gone into comedy instead of court," she called back, and closed the door behind her with a flair.

"How'd it go?" Nadine asked as she headed toward the elevator.

Siri paused, thought for a minute, and smiled. "I lost."

"You have to stay home?"

Siri shook her head. "I have to go." She grinned.

The smile faded when she was in the elevator, alone, going down to street level. How in the world was she going to explain to Mark, who didn't trust her past his heel, that she was going away for a week with the most notorious man in local legal circles? From one battle to another, she thought resignedly. But at least with Mark, she'd have a chance of winning, which was more than she'd ever had with Hawke Grayson.

2
*

Siri fumed around the house like a steaming clam, and every time she saw that arrogant dark head, she fumed even more. The trouble with Hawke, she told herself, was that he was too used to feminine adulation. He was accustomed to getting his own way about everything. But, even so... why did she always yield?

"He makes me feel like a spoiled brat," she grumbled, as she headed for the shower. "That's why I don't like him!"

Not that she was spoiled. Jared had seen to that. When her mother died, just before Siri's sixth birthday, he'd made sure she had enough love to make up for both parents. But he hadn't indulged her to any great extent. His law practice took up a great deal of his time, and Siri had to settle for odd moments of togetherness. Jared didn't spoil her; he forced her to fight her battles on all fronts. Even now, he only interfered when things got blazing hot between Hawke and his daughter. Which was another curious thing, Siri thought as she undressed and stepped under the spray of warm water.

She wasn't naturally antagonistic toward anyone, except her father's famous partner. It had been that way from the beginning, as if she'd sensed in Hawke an adversary the first time she saw him. There had been the occasional pleasant time, as Marty had hinted earlier. But even those fleeting moments of affinity had been laced with tension, because she could never relax completely with Hawke. No matter how congenial he was on the surface, she always felt the tingle of deep fires burning just under his impassive exterior.

She stepped out of the shower refreshed, and was on her way to change when the phone caught her.

"County morgue," she droned into the receiver, expecting to hear Marty's voice on the other end.

There was a brief pause, followed by an irritated masculine sigh. "Must you answer the phone that way, Cyrene? What if it had been mother, or your editor?"

She raised her eyes heavenward. "Mark," she explained patiently, "I'm a reporter, remember? This is the way I am."

"So you keep telling me. Never mind. We're having dinner at the Magnolia Inn. I'll pick you up at six."

"I know," she reminded him. "You told me yesterday."

"Yes," he said in a long-suffering tone. "But you tend to forget dates you make with me as you move from fire to murder."

"It was only once," she defended herself. "And you know it was one of the very biggest fires in the city."

"And that's another thing," he grumbled, "always hanging around with men; firemen, policemen, civil defense..."

"It's my job, Mark," she reminded him.

"But, Siri, the way it looks..."

Her temper boiled over. "That's it," she said tightly, "if you can't bring yourself to accept me the way I am, you can jolly well go chase yourself!" With that, she slammed the receiver down.

She didn't get two steps before the phone rang again. She jerked it up. "Yes?" she asked impatiently.

"I'm sorry," he said. "It's been a long day, and I'm in a rotten mood. Come out with me and cheer me up."

Out of habit, or weariness, she gave in. After all, she wasn't any more perfect than he was.

They went to a popular restaurant on the outskirts of the city, and business was booming.

Without bothering to ask if the cigarette smoke would bother her, Mark led her straight to the smoking section of the plush, carpeted restaurant and seated her. She barely had time to scan the extensive and appetizing menu before the waitress was asking for her order. She ordered a steak, wild rice and a tossed salad bypassing the delicious but horribly fattening strawberry shortcake with its foot-high topping of whipped cream. The waitress returned a few moments later with trays laden with steaming, fragrant dishes.

She thanked the girl—who looked as if she could press 200 pounds without any effort from the way she was handling those heavy trays—and froze as she looked past the girl's frilly apron.

Hawke and his current girlfriend, a darkly elegant brunette in a dress cut almost to the waist, were seated just across the way. Siri carefully rearranged her chair so that her back was slightly toward them, and hoped Hawke wouldn't notice her.

"It's been a rotten day," Mark sighed as he attacked his steak. "One of my clients had to go downtown for an audit with the tax people, and they found a mistake. My secretary," he groaned, "typed the right numbers, but in the wrong places. So instead of getting the refund he expected, my client wound up owing money."

"How awful," Siri said automatically.

"Amen. I caught it from both sides." He reached for his soft drink, grimacing at the steaming cup of black coffee at Siri's right. "How can you drink that stuff?"

She shrugged. "Habit, I guess. Dad and I always have it for breakfast and dinner—with every meal."

There was the sudden interruption of loud conversation just behind her, and she caught the familiar sound of a rival reporter's voice.

"I hear there's some new evidence in the Devolg case, Mr. Grayson," Sandy Cudor was probing in his pleasant voice. "Anything to the rumors?"

"You'll find out in the courtroom, Sandy," came the deep, equally pleasant reply.

"In other words, you aren't talking," the reporter interpreted, and Siri knew there would be a smile on the young man's face.

"Exactly."

"Well, have a nice evening," Sandy said, and Siri instinctively leaned down to pick up the napkin she dropped on purpose, so that her colleague wouldn't see her. It worked.

"Disgusting," Mark was grumbling.

"What is?" she asked.

"Reporters," he replied with a glare after Cudor's retreating back. "And grandstanding lawyers," he added for a good measure.

"Just hold it right there," she told him icily. "If there's any grandstanding, it's usually done by young lawyers trying to make reputations. Hawke's a long way past the struggling stage. And Sandy may be impetuous, but he's young and learning, and bound to be a little overeager."

"I didn't think you cared a fig about either one of them," Mark recalled, his own voice cool.

"I don't," she agreed. "But then you aren't attacking personalities, you're attacking two professions that I know intimately."

He drew a harsh sigh and tossed down the rest of his soft drink. "You don't even have to work," he said unpleasantly. "I don't know why you insist on pursuing that job—"

"Because I like it!" she shot back.

"You like associating with all those men, and showing your legs," he retorted.

"You go to hell," she said in a furious whisper, her amber eyes shooting flames toward him, as she crumpled her napkin and threw it down to the right side of her plate.

"I didn't think it was so easy to keep secrets in a newsroom," Hawke remarked from behind her.

She turned, flushed with anger, to meet the taunting light in his dark eyes as he paused beside their table with the impatient brunette on his arm.

"It isn't," Siri managed, irritated at the breathless tone of her usually steady voice, hating the effect Hawke always had on her nerves. "I don't suppose Bill's told any of them yet."

"If he does, you'd better check under your hood every afternoon before you leave there," came the cool reply. "Hello, Holland," he added, finally acknowledging the younger man's presence.

"Hello," Mark grumbled. His eyes speared Siri. "What's all this about?"

"Siri hasn't told you?" Hawke asked, and even though he didn't smile, the mocking amusement was there in those unfathomable eyes. "She's going with me to Panama City for a week to research some new evidence in the Devolg case."

Mark's thin face flushed red. "Is she? It's news to me!" He glared at Siri. "Does your father know?"

"I'm twenty-one years old, almost twenty-two," she replied. "I don't need Daddy's permission!"

"My God, how am I going to explain it to mother?" he groaned.

"No dessert?" Hawke remarked, noticing Siri's barely touched dinner. "You're thin enough, aren't you?"

"She's just fine the way she is, thanks. I don't want her to look like a cow," Mark replied hotly, with a speaking glance at the well-endowed brunette beside Hawke, who bristled visibly at the insult.

Hawke didn't say anything, but his eyebrows went up as if the remark astonished him.

"Enjoy your dinner," Hawke said pleasantly, and escorted the brunette out of the spacious dining room.

"I don't like that man," Mark grumbled, glaring at the retreating broad back. "What business is it of his how you look or what you eat? And what the devil did he mean about you going with him to Panama City?"

"Just what he said," Siri replied coolly. "You don't own me, Mark. Not now, not ever, and I can't think how you've convinced yourself that you did. I don't have to apologize to you for the job I do. And that's precisely what the trip concerns—my job. I won't be sharing Hawke's bed, if that's what you're wondering."

The way he averted his eyes told her what he'd thought.

"I should think you'd be too young to interest a man like that anyway," he finally said. "He must be at least forty."

That bothered her for some reason, but she bit her lip to keep from making a reply. "Hawke's got all the women he needs, I imagine," she said finally.

"I don't doubt it." He laughed humorlessly. "Wasn't his father a shipbuilder, or owned a fleet of ships or something in Charleston?"

"Something like that."

"And his mother was an heiress. There was some horrible scandal before he left there." Mark frowned, trying to remember.

"Was there? I don't keep tails on Hawke, I never have. He's Dad's partner, not mine, and I like it that way," she said harshly.

"If you dislike him so much," he protested, "why do you start changing color the minute you see him?"

"Do I?" She searched in her purse for her compact and lipstick. "Temper, probably. He's always telling me how inferior a woman reporter is, and this afternoon was no exception. Dad had to separate us."

There was a long pause while she put on her lipstick. "Siri, I'm sorry," he said finally. "It's just that I don't trust him around you. You're so...naive."

She almost laughed. Mark, who'd never even tried to touch her, or intimately kiss her, telling her she was naive.

"To Hawke, I'm still the teenager he used to bring to football games when I was a cheerleader. He doesn't think of me as a woman." And, boy, am I glad, she almost added. She'd never seen Hawke in action, but she'd have bet her typewriter that there wasn't a woman alive he couldn't get with that dark, sensual charm. She didn't really want to find out if she could resist it. Besides, she told herself silently, he was almost twice her age. Far too old to even dream about.

"Can we go now?" Siri asked, putting away her cosmetics. "I'm really tired."

"Of course. Just let me finish this cigarette," he said, lighting one up. "Won't be a minute."

It was ten, and she felt like screaming before he finally stubbed it out and took her home.

"Siri, got a minute?" Bill Daeton called from the doorway of his office.

She left the half-finished story on her desk and joined him. "What's up?"

"Look, I know you don't do family news," he said, anticipating an argument, "but I've got a great feature story on my desk and no cameraman to shoot it. Can you spare an hour from that burglary wrap-up to take some pictures of an art exhibit at the museum? There are a couple of paintings by Jacques Lavelle in it—you know, our local talent who does those exquisite portraits in pastels?"

She glared at him without speaking.

"Think of the class that story will give the paper," he coaxed, "an international exhibit, right here in our city, and a local artist included in it, along with some of the old masters. The arts council will love it. So will old Sumerson. Remember that? He owns 65% of the stock in our publishing company? Pays both our salaries? Siri, dammit, I haven't got a photog. Everyone's out on assignment, and I've got to have those shots today!"

She saw a chance for some bargaining and grinned. "Remember that opinion poll you wanted me to conduct in my spare time to see how local people felt on the gun control issue? Well, if you'll make Sandy do it instead, I'll just be purely tickled to cover your art exhibit!"

"Blackmailer!" he burst out.

"It's no worse than what you did to me," she replied. "A week in Panama City with Hawke Grayson...one or both of us will be in shreds by the time we come home, and it'll be all your fault. You knew I didn't want to go."

"Who else was there to send?"

She sighed. "Do we have a deal?"

"Sandy," he reminded her, "already has it in for you. I told him this morning about the Devolg case."

"He's young," she said soothingly. "He'll get over it. And if he won't, send him instead!" She grinned.

"Can't. I've already got him assigned to the lottery investigation."

"City editors," she said with vigor, "were invented by God to torment the ignorant."

"Thanks." He grinned. "Now get out of here and get those pictures. And don't forget, I'm still searching for somebody to take over the 'Dear Mother Jones' column permanently."

"Sadist," she mumbled as she walked away.

The art exhibit was delightful to shoot. The lighting was good, the subject matter was fascinating, and, best of all, it got her out of the office. She sat down on one of the brocade benches, clutching the camera, and stared blankly at a charcoal sketch. The really wonderful thing about reporting was that it didn't tie you to a desk for eight hours. You could get out into the city, meet people, and visit exciting places, without having to belong to any elite crowd. It was always exciting, even a little dangerous at times. Most of the women she knew would rather have suffered torture than trade jobs with her. But she knew with a certainty, that she couldn't have endured being a secretary or a receptionist. She was only alive with a pad and pen and camera in her hands.

"I might have known I'd find you here," Hawke said suddenly, and she whirled on the bench to find him leaning carelessly against one of the big round columns, his hands in his pockets, just watching her.

Her heart flew up in her chest, but it was just the unexpected surprise of seeing him, she told herself.

"I . . . Bill bribed me," she stammered.

"Did he have to twist your arm that hard?" he asked. "You love these damned things."

"Guilty," she admitted with a tiny smile, slinging her collar length blond hair away from her face. "But he didn't know that. I got out of doing an opinion poll."

"Witch. Sometimes I think you cast spells."

"So does Mark," she sighed. Her eyes brushed the beauty of the canvasses on the high walls. "You got me into a devil of a mess last night. I was going to wait until he was in a better mood to break the news to him."

"I've never seen him in a good mood. He's a whiner, sparrow. The world's full of them...complainers without the guts to change the things they complain about."

"People can't help being what they are, Hawke," she said quietly, avoiding those piercing dark eyes. "You can't go around trying to change people to suit your own taste."

"At least your father taught you that," he replied. "Where do you go from here?"

"I thought I'd go steal bread crumbs from the pigeons in the park," she replied.

"You look like that's what you do for lunch every day," he said with an unappreciative glare at her slender figure. "Come on."

"Where are we going?" she asked, grasping her camera and purse as she tried to keep up with his long, quick strides.

"To Kebo's. I'm going to feed you."

She drew back. "Oh, no, not today. It's Wednesday," she told him.

"So, what the hell does that have to do with it?" he demanded, his face leonine and faintly dangerous.

"Middle of the week, and I owe my soul to a mechanic on Peachtree Street for repairs on the VW," she said in a breathless rush. "I simply can't afford Kebo's. You'll have to take me to the Krystal instead."

His eyes narrowed, and his square jaw locked stubbornly. "You damned little independent mule," he growled softly. "I said I was taking you to lunch, and I can afford Kebo's. Now come on."

"Yes, sir!' she replied smartly, and had to skip to keep up with him.

It wasn't until they were inside the plush restaurant enjoying roast beef au jus and perfectly cooked scalloped potatoes with a salad, that she began to wonder how Hawke had known where to find her.

"I wasn't looking for you," he replied when she asked the question. "I stopped by to see Lavelle's part of the exhibit. I represented him in a libel case several years ago. His art impressed me then. It still does."

"It's surrealistic," Siri commented.

One dark, heavy eyebrow went up. "Yes, it is."

Her lower lip pouted as she added a touch of the thick cream to her coffee and stirred it. "I'm not completely ignorant when it comes to things like art."

"I never said you were. I thought your taste ran to Renoir and Degas."

"It does, but I..." She sighed. "I just like art. I don't know all that much about it, really, but I like beautiful things."

"Remind me to show you my African wood carvings someday," he said. He leaned back in the comfortable semicircular padded chair and lit a cigarette. "Or don't you like art that exotic?"

"I have several African pieces of my own," she told him. "Although I'm sure mine aren't as expensive as yours."

"Stop that," he said coldly. "I don't care for snobbery, inverted or not."

She bit back a retort, busying herself instead with her coffee. The lunch had been perfect, and she shouldn't have attacked him. A twinge of color dotted her cheeks, and she let herself relax.

"I'm sorry," she said quietly.

The waiter came back before he could reply and while he was ordering strawberry shortcake for them, she studied him absently. He was, she thought, a striking man. Not exactly handsome. His brow was too jutting, his face too leonine, his jaw too square. It was a strong face, not a pretty one. His build was equally strong—husky as a wrestler, and narrow-hipped with powerful legs. He wasn't overly tall, but he didn't need to be. There was such raw power in his big body that he was as intimidating as any man two heads taller would have been. He really was quite attractive. Darkly, sensuously attractive. Her eyes rested briefly on the wide, chiseled perfection of his mouth, and she allowed herself to wonder, just for one mad instant, how it would feel to kiss him....

"Are you trying to memorize me?" Hawke asked quietly, as he caught her staring at him.

She blushed red as a cherry. "Sorry. I wasn't really looking at you," she lied glibly. "I was thinking about an assignment...."

"Was that it?" he asked, unconvinced. He caught her restless eyes and held them with an intensity that made her heart race. He'd never looked at her like that—not with that fiery, expressionless look that burned in his eyes. He held her gaze for so long, and with such raw power, that she was visibly shaken when she managed to drag her eyes down towards her coffee cup. She lifted it unsteadily to her lips.

"I . . . I don't really need dessert," she said softly.

"Yes, you do." He took a long draw from the cigarette. "What did Holland say about the trip? Has he convinced you that I'm going to ravish you the first night?"

She felt the color pour into her face. "Actually," she said huskily, "he thought you were a little too old to think of me in that respect."

"Well, I'll be damned," he said. "How old does he think I am, for God's sake, sixty?"

"Close," she remarked, avoiding his piercing eyes.

"How old do you think I am?" he asked suddenly.

She shrugged. "I've never thought about it."

"Liar." He took a swallow of his coffee and suddenly reached out to catch her cold, nervous hand in his, forcing her to look up into those threatening eyes.

"I'm seventeen years older than you, sparrow," he said in a deep, quiet tone. "But if I wanted you, those seventeen years wouldn't make a damned bit of difference to me. Or to you."

She felt her heart beating her to death from the inside. He'd never spoken to her like this, and it was devastating. Frightened, she drew her hand away from his and leaned back.

"What the hell difference does it make to Holland's mother if you go to Panama City with me?" he asked suddenly, harshly. "Are you engaged?"

She shifted uncomfortably. "He's asked me."

"And?"

"I don't want marriage," she replied. "Not now, not ever."

"Why?"

"Don't cross-examine me, Hawke, I'm not on the stand!" she cried.

"God, you're a puzzle," he remarked. He leaned one big arm over the back of his chair. He was wearing a light jacket over a pale blue shirt. The fabric stretched over the massive muscles of his chest. Under it, she could see the shadow of a mass of black, curling hair. Why did he have to be so masculine, so...

"I have to go..." she began weakly.

"Not yet," he said, gesturing toward the approaching waiter. "Not until I get a little more flesh on those bird bones."

"I'm not skinny!" she hissed at him as the waiter was walking away.

He dug into the massive dish of fresh strawberries and cream on their cake base, lifting an eyebrow as his eyes went pointedly to the soft rise and fall of her rounded breasts under the thin white blouse.

"Parts of you aren't," he corrected.

"Don't!" she whispered, attempting to give her entire concentration to the dessert.

"Doesn't Holland ever touch you, little one?" he asked gently.

She moved her thin shoulders as if trying to twist out from under the question. "Mark's a gentleman."

"Mark's a boy, Siri," he corrected.

"He suits me very well," she countered, savoring the sweet taste of the whipped cream. Her tongue came out to whisk it off her upper lip, and Hawke's eyes narrowed on the tiny movement. The deliberate scrutiny confused her, and she put the coffee cup quickly to her lips.

"Should I bring the camera?" she asked, trying to sound cool and professional.

"Only if you're planning to do a speculation piece on the 'Miracle Strip' for some travel magazine," he replied, "or photos for your album."

"Maybe," she said thoughtfully, "I could hire one of the hotel employees to pour beet juice over your head while I take pictures."

"I wouldn't advise it, honey," he said, mildly amused. "You might not like the way I'd reciprocate."

"You wouldn't hit that hard." She smiled.

His eyes travelled over her face, from the crown of golden hair to the amber eyes, the soft curve of her mouth. His gaze lingered there until her lips parted under the scrutiny that was as potent as a caress.

"Siri," he said in a deep, sensual tone, "if I ever lift my hand to you, it won't be to hit you."

The look in his eyes said much more than the words. It haunted her all the way back to the office.

3

*

That lunch marked a turning point for Siri. Suddenly, the thought of Panama City, of being with Hawke for the better part of a week, was unbearable. And she knew when she reached her office that she wasn't going to go. No matter what, even if Bill fired her, she wasn't going. She took a deep breath and walked into his office.

"You're *what*?" Daeton exploded.

She stood her ground. "I'm not going with Hawke."

"Why, for God's sake?"

Now there, she thought miserably, was a good question. What could she tell him? I'm afraid of Hawke because of a look he gave me across a table?

She swallowed. "My . . . boyfriend doesn't like the idea," she said finally, digging up the only excuse he might find acceptable.

He threw down his pencil and leaned back in his chair. "Siri, there just isn't anybody else I can send," he explained. "Nobody. And even if there was, Hawke told your father that it was you or no one. This is one hell of a hot story. I don't want to blow it because your boyfriend's got a bad case of jealousy."

She stared at the cluttered top of his desk. "I'm sorry," she muttered, turning to open the door.

"Siri, if you do this to me," Bill Daeton threatened quietly, "I'll take you off the police beat and switch you to the garden club circuit for the next ten years."

She shrugged fatalistically. "I like flowers," she said over her shoulder, and closed the door.

If Daeton was disbelieving, her father was dumbstruck. He gaped at her over the dinner table, his face blank.

"Do you realize," he said quietly, "how long it took me to convince Hawke to let you go?"

She smiled. "Five minutes?" she guessed.

"Four." He shook his head, toying with the brussel sprouts. "Want to tell me why you changed your mind?" he pursued.

"I'll sound silly."

"Oh, I'm already convinced of that. Tell me anyway."

She wrapped her cold fingers around her coffee cup. "It's kind of hard to put into words," she began.

Jared spread his fingers behind his head and leaned back lazily. "I've got all night."

"I thought you were taking Nadine to that new night club."

"Don't change the subject."

She shrugged. Of all people, she couldn't lie to her father. "I'm afraid of Hawke," she said miserably.

He didn't seem in the least surprised. "You've spent the past five years being alternately fascinated and terrified by him. Did you realize that you start backing away the minute he comes near you?" he asked with a patient smile.

She took the napkin from her lap and folded it. "Isn't this where I get the lecture about the evils of running away?" she asked.

"Just about." He leaned forward on his elbows. "He took you to lunch, didn't he?"

She nodded, dazed.

"Well, did he try to seduce you at the table?" he persisted.

"Of course not!"

"You needn't sound so indignant. I know Hawke," he laughed. "He isn't even vaguely subtle when he wants something, and that includes women."

"I didn't know he was such a playboy," she observed, wrapping both cold hands around her coffee cup.

"He isn't." He picked at a speck of lint on the sleeve of his jacket. "Oh, he's got money. But that can be a two-edged sword, my girl, didn't you know? I don't think he's ever been really sure if women want him or what he can give them.''

"It wouldn't make a bit of difference if he didn't have a dime,'' she said without thinking.

Jared's grin went from ear to ear. "I didn't know you thought he was so attractive,'' he remarked, noting the sudden color in her cheeks.

"Even if he is a generation ahead of me, I can notice him,'' she said defensively.

"Age isn't everything, you know.''

"It is to him,'' she grumbled absently. "Any day now, I expect him to offer to buy me a balloon or an ice cream cone. Even now, with an award of merit under my belt for investigative reporting, he's still giving me the 'helpless little Siri' looks.''

"You could change his mind if you tried,'' her father said gently.

"Why in the world would I want to?'' she asked, aghast. "My gosh, dad, he's almost twice my age, and you know we don't get along at all. We never have!''

"Do you get along all that well with Holland?'' he probed. "Honestly?''

She glowered at him. "I can handle Mark.''

"That's probably the only reason you let him hang around, too,'' he said flatly. "And someday you'll accidentally marry him if you don't open your eyes!''

"I don't want to marry anybody,'' she muttered.

"It can still happen. Go with Hawke, Siri,'' he said, more solemn than she'd ever seen him. "Face it. Will you do that, for me?''

He didn't make sense, but at the suggestion, she gave way to a twinge of panic. She stood up, shaking her head stubbornly. "I'm sorry. I love you very much,'' she said, "but not enough for that. The story can go hang. I'm fresh out of sacrificial urges.''

"Siri...!''

But she was already halfway up the staircase, running for privacy.

She knew her father wouldn't be back until late, so she threw on a deep blue caftan and stretched out in the living room on the couch with a book and put on a stack of easy listening records. The book should have taken her mind off the problem of Panama City, but she opened it and couldn't get past the front page.

It was almost a relief when the doorbell rang an hour later. Expecting that her father had lost his keys again, she threw open the door with a smile and a quip on her mouth and froze when she saw who was standing there.

"Oh!" she murmured.

Hawke raised an eyebrow at her, his dark eyes taking in every inch of her body outlined under the clinging blue fabric. He was obviously on his way home from a date, still dressed in his dark evening clothes. He had on a white ruffled shirt that was anything but effeminate, making his complexion seem even darker. His hand was propped against the door facing, and ruby cuff links gleamed rich and red in the light.

"Yes, 'oh', " he said. His eyes narrowed. "What the hell do you mean, you're not going with me?"

She swallowed hard, hating her nerve for deserting her as she stepped back to let him in the house. "I . . . well . . . you know. . . ."

"I don't know. That's why I'm here. I ran into your father and Nadine downtown, Siri, so help me, sometimes I think you belong back in high school instead of in a newspaper office!" he growled.

She stared at the carpet, unaware of the picture she made with her blond hair curling delicately around her flushed face, her long lashes hiding the expression in her amber eyes.

"It's kind of hard to explain," she mumbled.

"Then let's do it over a nightcap." He took her arm firmly and propelled her back into the living room, while she tried desperately not to let him see how much his touch affected her.

He poured two drinks at the bar, handing her a sherry while he fixed himself a scotch on the rocks.

"I like scotch, too," she protested, glaring down at the pale red liquid in her glass.

"I like you sober. You cry when you're drunk," he taunted.

"Only that once!" she defended herself.

"Once was enough. Or have you forgotten...?"

"I'm sure trying to, if you'll let me!" she flashed back, embarrassed at the memory of how she'd clung to him in the car that night she overdid it at the senior prom, and he had to rescue her because Jared had been out of town.

He smiled down at her, something he rarely did, but there was a boldness in the dark eyes as he gazed over the clinging caftan again.

"I like you in blue," he said.

"Thanks," she murmured. She sipped the sherry nervously.

"Now tell me why you don't want to go."

She shifted restlessly. "Hawke, you know how Mark feels..."

"All I know is what a damned possessive jackass he is," he said shortly, the smile disappearing at the mention of her boyfriend. "I don't like the way he treats you. I never have."

"You don't understand!" she protested.

"The hell I don't!" His eyes narrowed into a piercing glare. Hers fell before their onslaught, and she clutched the glass like a shield.

He studied her downcast face for a long time, pausing to light a cigarette and take a long draw from it. "Now tell me the real reason, Siri," he said firmly. "You're afraid of me, aren't you?"

She couldn't meet his eyes, but she wasn't going to lie about it. She drew a slow breath. "Yes," she admitted.

A smile tugged at the corner of his chiseled mouth. "Why?"

She shook her head. "I don't know."

He took a draw from the cigarette. "Don't you?" he asked.

She lifted her eyes only to the top button of his shirt, quickly dropping them again.

"Hell, I don't know whether to be flattered or insulted," he said. "My God, Siri, you're still wet behind the ears."

She clenched her teeth. "I didn't mean it that way!"

"What other way is there? And look at me, dammit!"

Her eyes jerked up. She flushed at the intent, totally adult look he was giving her.

"You...you said...in the restaurant..." she grasped for words.

"I said what?" he growled. "That those seventeen years didn't matter? What the hell did you think I was talking about? Siri, if I meant to seduce you, I wouldn't have to take you all the way to Panama City!"

There it was, out in the open, and she'd never felt quite so stupid. She closed her eyes. "I... I feel pretty dumb."

"You're just young, sparrow," he said, kindly. "I understand you very well. Come with me."

She nodded. "All right."

"Holland will get over it," he assured her. "Tell him we'll send a joint postcard."

"He won't like it," she said with a wistful smile.

"Why the hell does it matter?"

"Because he's my—"

"Your what?" he shot at her. "Your lover?"

She glared at him. "No!"

"That I can believe." His dark eyes traced the supple lines of her body, and a musing smile touched his mouth. "He hasn't left a mark on you."

"What do you do? Brand your women?" she fired back.

He considered that for a minute, studying her through a thin veil of gray smoke. "Honey, if I'd had you, everybody who came in contact with you would see it written all over you," he replied flatly.

"In dollar signs?" she said venomously.

He smiled involuntarily. "Is my money my only attraction, little girl?"

She sighed loudly. "You ought to know it isn't," she said reluctantly. "Women follow you around like puppies."

"Children like me, too, don't you?" he retaliated.

"Ooooh!" she groaned, stamping her foot on the soft pile of the carpet. "Hawke Grayson, you make me so mad!"

"And your eyes burn like fiery topaz," he told her. Something wild and untamable flamed in his eyes for just an instant as they held hers. "Holland isn't man enough to kindle any fires in you, little bird, much less put them out."

"He suits me just fine, thanks."

"He wasn't suiting you at that restaurant the other night, was he?" he asked with a confident smile, as he threw down the last swallow of his drink. "It sounded like a down-home brawl from where I was sitting."

"You and the scarlet lady, that is," she returned with a defiant glance in his direction.

One heavy eyebrow went up. "Scarlet lady?" he probed. "Gessie? She types my letters, little girl, and answers the phone."

"Excuse me," she apologized. "I didn't know she could do all that on her back."

He burst out laughing. "You little brat! What the hell business is it of yours if I keep a mistress?"

She didn't want to think about that. "None at all. And Mark isn't any of yours, either," she said stubbornly.

"We'll have to have a long talk about that someday."

"My love life . . . !" she began.

"What love life?" he countered pointedly. "You'd faint if he started to make love to you."

"Mark," she said harshly, "is a gentleman!"

"God help him," he said with feeling. "What do you think men are made of, you little blond mule, ice water and spirits?"

"All of them aren't like you," she countered, feeling strangely out of her depth.

"Oh, to be twenty again, and so wise." He sighed heavily. "I appreciate the sentiment, little one, but with the amoral and licentious life I lead, it's hard to remember the innocent days of my youth.''

"I doubt you were ever innocent," she muttered darkly.

"I was until my fourteenth birthday," he said, and smiled amusedly at the flush that burned her cheeks.

"Why don't you go home?" she asked hotly.

"I might as well," he remarked, studying his empty glass and her angry face. "If you were waiting up for your father, you'd better sleep light. He and Nadine were going strong at the disco when I left."

"You, at a disco?" she said insultingly.

"How good are you?" he challenged.

"I'm young," she countered, "remember? We youths adjust to new steps better than you old people."

"By God, I ought to take you over my knee," he threatened.

She backed away, grinning. "Remember your blood pressure," she cautioned. "We wouldn't want you to have a stroke or anything."

His eyes kindled with amusement. "You damned little cat," he said.

"Flattery will get you nowhere, Mr. Grayson. Anyway, it's way past my bedtime, and you interrupted me right in the middle of *The Three Bears*."

He returned his empty glass to the bar, stubbed out his finished cigarette, and started toward the front door.

"Remind me to send you a copy of the unedited version," he told her with a wry smile.

"Dirty old man," she said, blissfully unaware that she was flirting with him, or that it was the first time she ever had.

"Little brat," he countered. He turned as he started out the door. "Better start packing, Siri. I'm planning to fly down to Panama City in the morning. I'll call you in time to get breakfast before we leave."

"Okay. Hawke?"

He turned. "Yes?"

She shrugged apologetically. "I'm sorry I acted my age."

"You haven't, yet." He tugged at a strand of her wispy blond hair. "I don't think you know how."

"How to what?" she asked curiously.

"Goodnight, honey." He went down the steps two at a time without bothering to answer her.

The next morning, sitting beside Hawke in the big Cessna he co-owned with her father, she wondered why she'd been so terrified of this trip. The weather was sunny, the plane was comfortable, and Hawke was actually being pleasant for once and not his usual sarcastic self. In fact, she was enjoying every minute of the flight.

Her one regret was that Mark hadn't accepted her decision to make the trip. She'd finally had to hang up on him on her way to the airport, amid ultimatums that he'd never see her again if she went. And while Jared might understand his daughter's sudden change of mind, Bill Daeton was still scratching his gray head trying to figure out his police reporter's strange behavior.

Siri sighed pleasantly and closed her eyes. For the next week, she wasn't going to let herself look backwards. She was going to enjoy the sand and the sun and the surf, and do her job, trying not to get in Hawke's way.

She glanced at him, noticing the hard, dark face that never seemed to relax, the rigid lines of his chin and mouth. They hallmarked the uncompromising personality of the man. Womanlike, she wondered if there was any tenderness under that stony exterior. No more of that, my girl, she warned herself firmly. Hawke was safe only so long as she thought of him as a big brother, a friend. She had a feeling he'd be totally devastating in a romantic role, and she was wary enough not to want to find out. With such a man, there'd be no freedom at all. It wouldn't be the way it was with Mark—a relationship that was comfortable, that made no demands, that left her to live as she pleased. Oh, no, Hawke would make demands. He'd want a woman who could match his own fierce spirit, who'd be as much a part of him as his own soul. He wouldn't settle for any easy-going relationship. She didn't know how she knew that, but she was sure she was not mistaken.

They landed in Panama City, and Hawke reached up to lift her to the ground from the metal step. It seemed almost as if he deliberately let her slender body slide slowly against his before he finally eased her feet to the pavement. His dark eyes held hers disturbingly the whole time, reading the effect on her flushed face.

"There's a restaurant here," he said as he released her. "Do you want to stop for a cup of coffee or go straight to the hotel?"

She took a deep breath of the hot, sea-smelling air. "I'd kind of like to get to the beach," she admitted, trying to disguise the childlike eagerness to wet her feet in the surf.

He only chuckled, as if he could pick the thoughts out of her mind. "All right. I'll get a cab."

It was her first time in Panama City, and her eyes digested the atmosphere of it as they made the short trip from the airport to the hotel. The 'Miracle Strip' gave a sweeping impression of blinding white sand and scruffy palm trees, beautiful modern hotels, and, most of all, traffic. It was noisy with the impatient sound of horns and voices calling back and forth, drowning out the distant sound of waves breaking against the beach. The predominant smell at the moment was not tangy sea air, but exhaust fumes from the tangle of automobiles.

"Disappointed?" Hawke asked beside her.

She flicked a glance at him, quick enough not to be caught by those wise, dark eyes. "A little," she admitted. "It's going to be terribly crowded."

"You're a reporter, remember?" he taunted. "Crowds, and the people that compose them, are supposed to be your stock-in-trade."

"I get sick of people sometimes," she said absently, her eyes on the colorful, skimpy dress of tourists pouring from the motels on the wide highway. "I have to deal with them all day long, every day. Even when I get home at night, the phone always rings, and very rarely because of an emergency," she laughed. "Once I had a lady call me about putting an ad in a rival paper—at 11:30 at night, yet."

"Where would you be without those people?" he asked with a trace of a smile.

"Sleeping peacefully at night like everybody else," she quickly responded. Her eyes went to a flaming red hibiscus blooming against the brick wall of a motel they were passing, and she smiled involuntarily. "I don't know how I got to be a reporter in the first place," she mused, almost talking to herself. "Crowds terrify me. I rarely even go to parties because I wind up sitting tucked away behind a potted plant with a glass frozen to my hands." She glanced at him. "Do you mind crowds? I don't suppose you could, being surrounded by them all the time."

"It goes with the job, honey," he replied. "A lawyer gets used to it."

"But do you really like it?" she persisted, meeting his eyes at last.

He reached out a big hand and twisted a strand of her soft hair around his fingers. The touch made her pulse race. "I like what I do. The kind of life my father preferred would have been the death of me."

"He . . . he built ships, didn't he?" she asked.

He caressed the strand of hair absently. "He was in shipping, Siri, when he wasn't frequenting casinos or sailing on the Aegean with some new playmate. Mother ran the business."

She dropped her eyes to the steady rise and fall of his chest. "Is she still alive?"

His eyes shifted to the white shoreline in the distance. "Both my parents are dead," he said flatly, and in a tone that didn't encourage her to pursue the subject.

"I don't mean to pry," she said gently. "I'm so used to asking questions . . . I suppose I ask too many sometimes."

He drew a deep breath and lit a cigarette. His dark eyes glanced at her. "Two different worlds, Siri," he remarked quietly. "I'm used to keeping secrets, while you're conditioned to revealing them. I'm a solitary man, little girl. Privacy is sacred to me."

She shrugged. "I thought I'd apologized," she said in a small voice, turning her attention out the window. She felt vaguely like a scolded child.

"For God's sake, don't pout!" he shot at her.

She flinched at the tone. "I'm not," she managed.

There was a brief silence. She wanted to sink right through the floorboard. He was angry with her, and she couldn't understand why. But it was like being a little bruised. Tears misted in her eyes, and she couldn't understand that, either.

"Siri," he said gently.

She kept her eyes averted, not answering him. The lump in her throat hurt.

"Siri," he repeated, and his big hand went out to force her chin up so that he could see her face. "Oh, damn!" he breathed when he saw the unshed tears.

"Will you just leave me alone?" she fired at him, jerking away from his hand.

A deep, harsh sigh came from the other side of the cab. He moved, catching her by the nape of her neck to press her face against the lightweight fabric of his summer suit jacket. "Let it out," he said at her temple. His arm circled around her shoulders, bringing her closer. "Let it out, Siri."

She fought the flood of tears, but they spilled over silently, running hot down her cheeks, onto the pale blue fabric. Her small hands clenched on his massive chest, as she relaxed against him with a choking sigh.

He pulled out a handkerchief and mopped her red face. "You don't even cry like a normal woman," he said softly.

"I never cry," she whispered, embarrassed, drawing away from him. "It wasn't allowed when I was growing up."

He brushed the damp hair away from her cheek. "Why?"

She shook her head. "Mother hated the sound of it. That's all I remember about her. I remember how she punished me for crying."

"What brought this particular cloudburst on?" he asked softly. His eyes narrowed dangerously. "Did you speak to Holland before we left?"

"Yes."

"What did he say?"

She lifted her face proudly. "That's my business, Hawke."

He reached out and touched her soft mouth with a dark, gentle finger, tracing its full outline. "I didn't mean to snap at you. There was a woman once, Siri. She used to blow up and pout if I looked at her sideways. You brought back a memory that sets fire to my temper."

"I didn't think a woman lived who could get that close to you," she remarked, as she mopped away the last traces of tears with the once-white handkerchief now stained with lipstick and mascara.

A mocking smile touched his hard mouth. "There was one until I found out she liked my money more than she liked me. The curse of being rich is that you never know whether people prefer the man or the wallet."

"Cynic," she accused. She shifted on the seat to hand the handkerchief back to him. "If the money bothers you that much, why not donate it to charity?"

"To what charity?"

She grinned at him. "The Lonely Hearts society?" she suggested.

He chuckled softly at her impudence. "I'm not that lonely."

"Of course not. You probably have to lift the mattress every night to chase out the women," she agreed.

"What makes you think I keep women, you little innocent?" he challenged.

She studied the big masculine form beside her, the darkness of his face, the sensuality of his chiseled mouth, the massive chest that strained against the open shirt, where a nest of hair was just visible. . . .

"Don't you?" she replied.

He caught her eyes and held them, just as he had that day in the restaurant, and something in the look made her blush.

He leaned forward, allowing the hand holding his cigarette to rest against the back of the seat while he caught her cheek with the other hand, turning her face toward him. His thumb passed gently over her lips, parting them, pressing harder now, caressing the pearly hardness of her teeth. She tasted the faint tartness of tobacco on that tough skin, and felt her pulse whipping her at the touch that was openly seductive. His eyes dropped to the inviting young softness of her mouth.

Before either of them could move, or speak, the cab pulled up in front of the hotel and stopped. The moment of intimacy shattered into a thousand shimmering pieces, and was lost amid the subsequent routine of gathering possessions and getting settled into new lodgings.

Hawke's secretary had booked them a suite with bedrooms leading off opposite sides of a huge sitting room. It was practical, but knowing Gessie's diabolical train of thought, Siri took offense at the insinuation of it. Gessie knew that Hawke wouldn't think of taking advantage of his partner's daughter. But she also knew how compromising the arrangement would look to all concerned, especially to Mark Holland. Siri flushed with anger as she studied the suite.

4

*

Don't be such a damned little prude!'' Hawke growled irritably, reading the expression on her face. "I imagine your door has a lock, if you're that unnerved about sharing a suite with me.''

"I didn't say a word,'' she countered, following him into the plush bedroom with its double bed where he set her case on the floor.

"You were thinking it,'' he said flatly. He studied her through narrowed eyelids.

"I was thinking what a trouble-making busybody your secretary is,'' she threw at him, eyes blazing. "How is this going to look if Mark finds out—and I'll bet you she'll find a way to make sure he's told!''

"I don't give a damn what he thinks,'' he said calmly.

"I do!''

He drew a deep, angry breath. "I came down here to work, Siri, not to have a running battle with you. Get your bathing suit on and we'll go down to the beach. Maybe the cold water will douse some of that hot temper before it triggers mine,'' he added roughly.

She shook back her hair. "I'm not trying to start an argument,'' she said apologetically. "Please, let's not quarrel.''

"Why? Are you admitting that you're outgunned?'' he asked.

Her eyes blazed. "Never!''

A wisp of a smile touched his hard mouth. "I play to win, Siri,'' he said as he went out the door.

"If it's going to be war, you'll have to fly me to Fort Sumter,'' she called after him.

"So you can fire off the cannon?" he replied. He chuckled softly. "I think I'll take you to Charleston one day, and let you see the size of those old cannons."

"Gessie wouldn't like that," she said cattily.

He looked back at her from the doorway. "Push a little harder," he invited softly, "and I'll put you on the first charter flight leaving for Atlanta."

She glared at him. "We just got here!"

"Then behave, if you want to stay," he threatened, his eyes glittering.

She dropped her eyes to the carpet. "I'm not a child," she muttered.

"That," he replied heavily, "is the problem. Get your bathing suit on." And he left her standing there as he closed the door firmly.

It was her first bikini, although not her first two-piece bathing suit. But the thought of Hawke seeing her in the wispy, aqua bits of string-tied fabric made her uneasy. It would have been different with Mark, she thought, as she gathered her towel and started into the sitting room. Mark had a habit of never noticing what she wore. But Hawke's dark eyes spoke volumes when he saw her in anything particularly feminine. She wondered for an instant why she'd packed the bikini in the first place. It had been a last-minute whim, one that she regretted as she opened the door and walked into the sitting room.

Hawke was wearing a green, and blue patterned shirt unbuttoned over his bronzed chest, with a pair of white swimming trunks that left his powerful thighs bare. He had a towel over one shoulder and a lit cigarette in his hand. When he heard her door open, he turned from the window, his eyes openly interested, quiet, speculative as they traced deliberately every soft line and curve of her body in a silence that literally smouldered.

"God!" he breathed.

She blushed, feeling vaguely undressed by the look he was giving her. "I . . . I'm not used to this much bare skin," she murmured, trying to keep her own eyes off that hard, husky body with its taut brown skin and its covering of black, curling hair.

"That makes two of us," he said tightly. "Have you got a beach jacket?" he added harshly.

"Yes, but . . ."

"Then go get the damned thing and put it on!" he growled, turning back to the window.

"Yes, *sir*!" she breathed venomously. She went back into her room and shouldered into a thigh-length white terry cloth jacket, buttoning it up to her chin. She marched back into the sitting room with a towel held in a strangling grip.

"I'm ready when you are," she called over her shoulder, opening the door to march down the corridor, not caring whether or not he was following.

It was like being five again and having her father sling orders at her, she thought, feeling quite embarrassed. She found one bare spot on the beach, ignoring the blistering heat of the sand on her tender feet, and spread her big beach towel a few yards from the noisy surf. She slammed herself down onto it on her belly, pulling her dark glasses down to cover the hurt in her eyes. She didn't notice the children playing around her, building sandcastles and hunting sand crabs, or the couples wandering up and down in the surf. She felt crushed inside.

A movement beside her attracted her attention. Hawke spread down his own towel and lazily stretched out on his back, sunglasses hiding the expression in his eyes.

"Are you through having a tantrum?" he asked.

"Not quite," she replied tightly, pushing up on an elbow and facing him.

"When you are, you might consider taking off that jacket so the sun can get to you," he observed.

"You were the one who insisted I put it on," she reminded him sweetly.

He rolled over on his side, and she felt his eyes burning her. His hand went out to the top button of her beach jacket, undoing it with a deftness and sensuality that made her pulse race. Her breath was coming in quick and unsteady bursts.

"Do you have any idea," he asked softly, undoing the second button, "what it does to a man to look at a sweet young body and know that it's never been touched before?"

She felt the blush run the length of her as he finished the last button and leaned over to ease it off her shoulder. His fingers lingered for a moment on the creamy skin at her collarbone.

"I'm not immune to you, little virgin," he said in a deep, soft tone. "I may be over the hill in your young eyes, but my instincts are in excellent condition, and I still respond like a healthy male. Don't trust those seventeen years to keep you chaste, Siri. I can lose my head just like any other man. Especially," he added quietly, "when you encourage me to lose it."

"I don't know what you mean!" she whispered unsteadily.

"Yes, you do." He rolled over onto his back. "You put that bikini on deliberately, sparrow."

She closed her eyes and lay back down on her stomach. She wanted to deny it, but he'd have seen through the lie, and she knew it.

"It's perfectly normal, Siri," he murmured lazily. "You're young enough to want to test your ability to attract men. Just don't test it on me."

"I'm sorry," she said in a strangled tone. "I think I must be going crazy."

"You're only growing up, little girl," he replied, "and it's about time. Stop brooding about it."

"I'm not brooding, I'm embarrassed," she admitted tightly.

He reached out and caught her hand where it lay on the towel, pressing it gently. "Nothing you could do would embarrass me. But if you try to seduce me, I'll put you over my knee. I think too much of Jared to play fast and loose with his daughter."

"You aren't mad at me?" she asked hesitantly.

He smiled. "No, honey." He let go of her hand, shifting as two little boys leapt over his legs. "Watch out," he warned her with a chuckle.

She dodged the little feet just in time. "I was afraid somebody was going to walk on me," she murmured.

"It's human nature," he remarked.

"What is?"

"The urge to step on people when they lie down and ask for it," he replied, amusement in his deep voice.

"You'll probably never feel it," she remarked, studying the size and powerful masculinity of his husky form. His legs were broad and powerful. He had a natural bronze tan that had nothing to do with sunlight. Muscular, masculine, he drew a woman's eyes like a magnet. He was vividly exciting in swimming trunks, especially compared with the skinny white bodies of most of the other men on the beach.

"You're staring, baby," he said suddenly, and she turned her face away with a flush of embarrassment.

"I was thinking," she corrected hotly.

"You must think a hell of a lot these days," came the bland reply.

She shifted restlessly on her towel. "Where do we start looking for your witness?" she asked, attempting to change the subject.

"In the hotel bar," he replied lazily. "I hope you've got your driver's license with you. Right now you look about sixteen."

"Is that a compliment or an insult?" she muttered.

"A little bit of both, sparrow." He stretched his big arms above his head and sighed. "God, I needed this! I can't remember a rougher week."

"I know what you mean," she replied. "Remember that controversy about the ambulance service not answering a call, when that teenager almost bled to death? Bill sent me to get the story."

"Did they fry you?" he asked.

"With onions," she sighed. "I felt two inches high when I walked out. It wasn't one of the regular ambulance service technicians who answered the call and refused to make it; it was a cocky young rookie who only signed on for a few weeks during a break in his schedule. He was fired the day after the incident. But nobody told us that." She again sighed wearily. "I hate this stinking business sometimes. Those men care, Hawke. Most of them really care, and they don't make fortunes, either. They do a thankless job and the only publicity they ever get is when something like this happens. They get crucified for their mistakes, by well-meaning people like me."

"If you didn't do it, who would?" he asked quietly, slanting a glance in her direction. "The taxpayers are entitled to know how their funds are being spent or misspent. That's what your job is all about, Siri, observing and reporting, not judging. And for objectivity, on a scale of ten, I'd give you a nine plus."

That made her smile. "Thanks. But I still feel like a 14K creep." She sat up on the towel, folding her arms around her raised knees, leaning her chin on them. "Hawke, who are we looking for?"

"No notebook?" he commented drily. He then watched her dig in her beach bag and produce a small pad and a pen.

"Okay, shoot," she said smugly.

He smiled as he lit a cigarette and blew out a cloud of smoke. "Do you carry it into the tub?" he asked.

"Sure!"

He raised an eyebrow. "As to who we're looking for, remember when the landlady was rousted out of bed at three in the morning to open the door to Devolg's room for that 'concerned friend'?"

"The one who mysteriously disappeared when the landlady got the door open and found Devolg, lying on his bed stabbed to death?" she replied.

"The same."

"Hawke, is that who we're looking for?" she asked excitedly.

"Let's just say I've got a hunch who the man was, and I've a contact here who may be able to unravel the mystery for me," he said solemnly. He took another draw from his cigarette. "If I'm right," he mused with a dark smile, "it's going to blow one big hole in the prosecution's case."

"You think the boy is innocent?" she asked.

"My God, Siri, would I have taken the case if I thought he wasn't?" he asked harshly.

"I never try to second-guess you," she replied. "It's not worth the wear and tear on my nerves. Are you going to give me a name?"

"What do you think, honey?" he asked nonchalantly.

"I think hell will freeze over first."

"Shrewd perception."

"If you're not going to tell me anything, why did you agree to let me come along?" she asked, peering at him over the top of her pad.

His head turned toward her, but she couldn't see his eyes through the dark lenses of his sunglasses. He didn't say a word, but she felt vaguely uneasy.

"Hawke, what will you do if the prosecution gets to your mystery man first?"

Both dark eyebrows went up. "What do you think they'd do, bump him off? Honest to God, Jared needs to take those detective novels away from you."

She shrugged. "James Bond..." she began.

"...is a remarkable piece of fiction, but fiction, nevertheless. Why," he asked himself, "*did* I bring you along?"

"Because you promised Dad." A mischievous smile touched her pink bow of a mouth. "Hawke, can I play in the sand now? Will you buy me a bucket and a shovel?"

His chiseled lips made a thin line as his head turned once again in her direction. "Aren't you a little old for these kind of games?" he asked shortly.

She felt whipped. "Can't I even tease you, for Pete's sake?" she asked irritably.

"Not that kind of teasing, no!" he growled.

"You're as touchy as a sunburned water moccasin," she grumbled.

"I thought you came out here to sunbathe," he remarked.

She stretched out on her towel with an irritated sigh. "So I did," she murmured, but she was talking to herself.

Supper in the hotel restaurant was the best she'd ever had, perhaps because her swim in the Gulf had whetted her appetite, or maybe because Hawke was in a better mood. He seemed more relaxed, as if the delicious meal had taken the edge off the black humor he'd been in most of the day.

She liked the way he looked in his cinnamon colored silk shirt, worn with a lightweight beige suit that made him stand out from the crowd. He was, she thought miserably, such a handsome man; not in the conventional sense, but in a rugged, very masculine way that made her fingers want to reach out and touch him. It was a feeling she'd never experienced before. It puzzled and frightened her, all at once.

She concentrated on her coffee. "When do we go to the bar?" she asked.

"In," he studied the watch strapped in the curling dark hair on his wrist, "ten minutes. I contacted my informant by phone." His dark eyes met hers across the table. "You'll have to pretend to be invisible, sparrow. I don't want anyone in that bar, especially the man I'm meeting there, to believe you're anything other than my date. It's a dangerous game, hunting a murderer. In that respect, your precious mystery writers have a valid point."

"But, Hawke..." she protested.

"My terms, Siri," he reminded her. "And you agreed to them. I want you kept out of this as much as possible. I'll tell you what I want you to know, when the time is right."

"Male chauvinist," she grumbled. "I can take care of myself."

"I'm going to let you prove that one of these days. But for now, you'll do what I tell you," he said darkly.

"Yes, Uncle Hawke," she said in her best juvenile voice. "Will you buy me an ice cream soda?"

His eyes narrowed. "Keep digging me, and you'll wish to God I *was* your uncle."

She made a face at him. "Honestly, you and my father...!"

"Do you think I want to find your body washed up on some godforsaken stretch of beach because you flirted with danger one time too many?" he demanded hotly. "I'd give blood if Bill Daeton would take you off that police beat. You like the risk just a little too much for my peace of mind."

"You're not my keeper!" she flung at him.

His eyes narrowed, sliding boldly over the bodice of her beige dress, and it was almost as if he was touching her.

"Do you burn like that with a man, Siri?" he asked in a soft, low voice. "Has Holland ever tapped those deep fires?"

She felt herself flushing. "I'd like to go now."

"Afraid to talk about it with me?" he taunted.

"The lobster was delicious," she replied as she rose.

He chuckled softly, walking behind her to the cashier. There was something almost predatory in the sound of his soft laughter.

She didn't believe for a minute that she might wind up being washed in on a wave with her throat cut, but Hawke was so doggedly protective of her that it made her uneasy. He seated her in a booth in the darkened bar where the jukebox blared like an orchestra in a closet, deafening and brassy. He ordered her a sherry, ignoring the dirty look she gave him.

"Stay put," he said, leaning over to growl in her ear so that he could make her hear him over the music. "I'll be at the bar."

"Hawke, why are you being so..."

He caught her soft throat with one big hand and pressed her head back against the cold leather of the booth, his mouth hovering just above hers. He held her eyes for a long, static moment. His hand moved, testing the effect of the look with a finger at the stampeding pulse in her throat.

The noise, laughter and flickering candlelight faded away and there was only Hawke, bending over her, with his eyes appearing almost black under those darkly knit brows as he studied her. His fingers lifted to her mouth, touching her lips, whispering across them, making them part as her breath whispered frantically past them.

His thumb gently pressed down on her lower lip as he bent. Dazed, her eyes dwelt on the chiseled perfection of his mouth as it opened slightly just before he leisurely fitted it to hers. It was a tantalizing kiss, so brief and light and teasing that it felt more like a fleeting breeze. But the effect it had on her was evident in her trembling pulse, the breathless sigh that passed her lips, the slender young hand that involuntarily lifted in protest when he drew away.

His forefinger pressed against her mouth for an instant, and he smiled at her with a quiet, tender warmth that made lightning spark in her mind.

Siri gazed after him, helplessly. Of course, he'd planned it, it was part of the charade. But his mouth had been hard, and tasted of tobacco and mint, and she ached for something more violent than that whisper of promise. What would it be like, she wondered dazedly, to let him kiss her the way he must kiss Gessie; to feel the hunger and rough passion in that eager mouth, to let him touch her....

She jerked her mind back into place as the waitress brought the mild drink he'd ordered for her. She took a long, deep swallow of it and willed her strung nerves to relax. She couldn't afford to think about him like that. Hawke wasn't a manageable boy like Mark. He was a man, and he didn't play games. The chaste kisses she was used to wouldn't come near to satisfying someone like Hawke; she knew that without being told. And, for her, anything deeper was out of the question. She couldn't make that kind of commitment.

Her eyes involuntarily sought him out. He was talking to someone now; a tall, skinny blond man with a mustache.

Their conversation was intent, and Hawke frequently nodded. The blond man finished his drink and left the bar.
Hawke came back to the booth, carrying a tumbler of what
was obviously scotch and water on the rocks.

"Well?" she asked loudly, hoping that her nervousness
wouldn't show.

He finished the drink in one swallow. "We've got to talk.
Let's go upstairs."

She gathered up her purse and followed him, away from
the shuddering impact of the music. She didn't want to go
back to that lonely suite with him. Not yet, not feeling this
kind of longing when he could read her expressions like the
weather report. But, there was no hope for it. And she was
curious about what had happened to make him look so solemn.

Going down the hall, Siri sidestepped to keep from col-
liding with another couple and heard Hawke's sudden, deep,
"Well, I'll be damned!"

"That depends on how good you are between now and
the day your number's up," came the laughing reply from
the tall, blond man who grabbed Hawke's outstretched hand
and shook it heartily. "Hawke Grayson! God, it's been
years! The only time I see you now is on the news or in the
papers. You remember Kitty, don't you?"

Hawke grinned down at the petite little blonde hanging on
to the tall man's sleeve. "How could I ever forget your
wife?" he asked. "Just as pretty as ever, too."

"You lawyers are all alike," Kitty said through a blush,
smiling shyly at the husky, dark man.

"Randy, Kitty, this is my partner's daughter, Cyrene
Jamesson," Hawke said, introducing the couple to his puzzled companion. "Siri, these are the Hallers. Randy and I
went through law school together. Our families were neigh-
bors in Charleston."

"I'm very glad to meet you," Siri said politely.

"Ah, that's because you don't know us yet," Randy told
her with a twinkling smile.

"Honestly, Randy," Kitty muttered. "Siri, you'll have to excuse him, it's spending so much time around crazy people that does this to him."

Siri grinned back. "I know all about crazy people."

"Amen," Hawke said with a long-suffering expression. "Meet the poor man's Lois Lane. Siri," he explained, "is a police reporter."

"So you report policemen." Randy smiled blankly. "Good for you. Who do you report them to?"

"It runs in his family, you know," Kitty said in a conspiratorial tone. "His grandfather was a ballet dancer."

"My God, why did you have to shame me like that?" Randy groaned. "Conjuring up images of an old man parading in a pink ruffled tutu."

"How would you like to come up to our suite for coffee?" Kitty asked quickly. "If you're not in a hurry...."

Hawke took Siri's arm. "No hurry," he replied. "We'd enjoy it."

"Of course," Siri seconded, but her mind was on what Hawke had discovered in the bar.

Siri liked the Hallers. Randy possessed not only a keen wit, but an inquiring mind to go with it; a fact that became quickly apparent the minute he and Hawke began discussing law. Kitty was open and friendly and simply loveable. She and Siri found an instant rapport and spent the rest of the evening comparing notes on art, music and books, leaping from one subject to the next, fired by the rapid exchange of viewpoints.

"Ladies, I hate to break this up," Hawke said finally, "but it's past this youngster's bedtime." Ignoring her outraged look, he reached down and pulled her up from the sofa with a firm hand.

"Yes, Uncle Hawke," she muttered with a false pout, and Randy's laughter burst the silence.

"That's a new role for you, Hawke," Randy observed.

"Yes, it is," came the deep, drawled reply, while the hard glance that went Siri's way along with it promised early retribution. "Come on, Miss Pain-in-the-neck, we've got a long day ahead of us tomorrow."

"Not all of it, I hope," Kitty said. "We're going to that marine world place down the road, and we were going to invite the two of you along."

Hawke glanced down at Siri. "Want to?" he asked.

She smiled at Kitty. "I've never been to one before."

"We'll leave here about ten in the morning," Randy said with a grin, "if that's not too early."

"Not at all," Hawke replied. "And before you start getting ideas, Siri and I are working on a case, not each other. She's spoken for," he added.

Randy seemed to flush, but he recovered quickly. "I have to admit, I wondered, even though she is a little younger than your normal... That is... Oh, hell, we'll see you in the morning."

Hawke nodded with a wispy smile. "Goodnight." He drew Siri along with him, leaving her to call her goodbyes over her shoulder.

He unlocked the door to their suite and let her in, locking it firmly behind him as he faced her with angry dark eyes.

5

*

"Now," he began in a low, quiet tone, "what's this 'Uncle Hawke' business."

"Why did you have to make such an issue out of it being strictly business in front of the Hallers?" she countered, still feeling the embarrassment. "I'm sure they weren't thinking anything of the sort! Look at the age difference!"

His eyes went slowly up and down her body. "I'm looking," he replied quietly. "And I'll remind you that it didn't seem to matter to you in the bar. You wanted more."

She felt herself turning red. Her lips parted, but she couldn't make a sound. She turned away, folding her arms across her slender body, feeling again the hunger, the newness of passion.

"Remind me at some appropriate time," he said shortly, "to give you a brief lecture on the danger of provocation."

She felt her heart pounding under her ribs. "I . . . wasn't trying to provoke you."

"Smart girl," he replied. She felt his eyes on her. "Just keep in mind that I'm past the age of hand holding and chaste kisses. If I ever start making love to you, I won't stop."

She felt the color burning in her cheeks, and she whirled to face him with her eyes widening in something between disbelief and outrage. "I . . . I wouldn't let you!"

"Yes, you would; because I'd know how to make you." He paused to light a cigarette, but his eyes never left hers. "You react to me in a way that makes my blood splinter, little girl. You may think it's carefully hidden, but I don't miss much." His eyes darkened. "I could rouse you to a kind of passion you never dreamed existed, and in minutes

I could make you give me what you've never given any man.''

"You couldn't!" she whispered huskily.

One dark eyebrow went up with a corner of his mouth. "Would you like me to prove it, Siri?" he asked gently.

Her eyes widened. Just the thought of it made her tremble. She knew he could, it was written all over her. But it wouldn't mean anything to him, except a new conquest, and she knew that, too. With a sound resembling a sob, she turned away, opening the sliding glass doors to walk out onto the cool balcony. In the distance, she could see the chain reaction of the waves as they hit the beach in a watery white rhythm, with a sound that was violent yet strangely soothing.

She heard his step behind her, and smelled the tang of cigarette smoke in the semi-darkness.

"Did I wound you, sparrow?" he asked calmly.

She rubbed her hands over the chill on her arms. "I'm not bleeding," she replied coolly. "I'm tough enough, Hawke. My line of work requires it as much as yours does."

There was a deep sigh behind her. "Randy's known me for a lot of years. This is the first time he's ever seen me with a woman in a hotel when it was innocent. I didn't want either of them thinking you were the kind of woman I usually carry around with me."

The statement made her turn to face him, her eyes wide and curious. "But they'd probably never see me again...?"

He didn't say anything, but his eyes were intent on her face, and she saw his jaw clench as she looked up at him.

She dropped her eyes. "I'm sorry," she murmured. "I've been touchy this week. It's my fault. I...I don't know why."

"I do," he said softly. "But there isn't a damned thing I can do about it." Before she could pick up on that, he moved to the balcony railing. "Siri, I've got a good lead, but it's going to mean leaving you here for a day or so while I run it down."

"Tomorrow?"

"The day after. Can you amuse yourself until I get back?"

"Of course. But can't I come along?" she asked.

She saw the white flash of teeth as he grinned. "If you want to share a bed with me. I'll be staying in a friend's apartment."

She knew without being told that the friend in question was female. She felt vaguely betrayed and angry.

"I didn't think it was ethical to get information that way," she said tightly.

"What way?" he asked imperturbably.

"Well, it's a woman, isn't it?" she asked.

"Yes."

"Then . . ."

"You'd better quit while you're ahead," he remarked with patient amusement. "I might get the impression that you're jealous."

"Me? Jealous? Of you? The idea!" she exclaimed.

He chuckled softly, dangerously. "If you were a few years older, or only a little more sophisticated, I'd take you to bed and teach you what being a woman is all about."

"You . . . you . . . how . . . !" she sputtered. Before she let her temper get the best of her at his merciless teasing, she ran back into the suite, into her bedroom, and locked the door loudly behind her. Of all the maddening men in the world, Hawke Grayson was definitely at the top of the list! In the distance, she heard again the soft, dangerous sound of his deep laughter.

The taunting left its mark on her. She was withdrawn the next morning as she and Hawke rode along the white satin coast with Randy and Kitty. She was thankful for Randy's chatter which made it unnecessary for her to carry on a conversation.

It seemed like no time at all before they got to the marine world complex, an enormous circular building with people streaming in and out. Even though it was crowded, Siri re-acted to it with the same eager curiosity that had led her into reporting. Everything here was new, exciting, and she felt like a child in a candy store.

The dolphins in the aquarium outside were beautiful and sleek, looking so delicately gentle for all their size that she felt a sudden surge of compassion for them. It was sad that animals of such remarkable intelligence that they could save men in the sea, and communicate with each other in their own unique language, were reduced to the level of performing dogs.

"Aren't they beautiful?" Kitty sighed, smiling as the trainer held a fish over the tank, which the dolphin leapt up to take gently out of his hand.

"In the open sea, yes," Siri said vaguely. "Here, imprisoned..."

"It beats having them slaughtered by Japanese fishermen," Hawke remarked, watching her closely.

She nodded as she met his probing eyes, amazed at the way he had of reading her mind.

"She doesn't like zoos, either," Hawke told their two companions with a half smile. He caught Siri by the hand and pulled her along with him. "I'll take her downstairs to see the turtles."

"Do people eat sea turtles?" Siri asked as they went down the steps to the darker level of the building.

"Yes, honey, they do. But not these," he added. "God, you're a little crusader."

"I can't help it if I don't like to see things caged," she muttered.

He turned her to him by the wall, out of the way of other tourists, and looked down into her flushed face. "Including people?"

"Including people," she said reluctantly. "I...I don't like being a possession," she added uneasily.

His big hands moved caressingly to her shoulders. "How would you know, little girl," he asked in a deep, slow voice, "when you've never been possessed?"

She blushed, meeting the teasing look in his eyes. "You don't know that."

"Don't I, sparrow?" he asked softly. He drew her slowly against his broad, hard body, feeling her stiffen even at the light contact. The implied intimacy of the action, as she felt his broad thighs touch her own, caused her to draw back as if she'd been burned.

"Coward," he murmured. "What could I do to you here?"

She pulled gently away from him and concentrated on the shell exhibits all around the well-lit room. Inside, she was trembling with the newness of that note in Hawke's deep voice, from the unfamiliar fire in his eyes when he'd looked at her.

"Don't panic," he said at her shoulder, "I was only teasing, Siri."

"I...I'd like it if you wouldn't," she replied tightly. "You said yourself once that I was still wet behind the ears. I know I am, but it hurts to have you make fun of it."

His hands touched her waist lightly, and she felt his breath in her hair. "God knows I'm not making fun of you, sparrow," he said quietly.

"Then why do you..."

"God, baby, what can I do?" he asked huskily.

"I don't understand."

But before she could turn around, or he could answer, Randy and Kitty joined them and the rest of the afternoon went by quickly as they discovered one tourist attraction after another. It was at the last one, the snake palace, that Siri balked.

"Oh, no," she said quickly, hanging back as the other three started toward the enclosed building with its gaudy pictures of vicious-looking reptiles. "I'd rather bleed to death than walk in there."

"Are you afraid of snakes?" Kitty asked gently.

"Oh, no," Siri denied, "I'm terrified of them!"

"You two go ahead," Hawke told them. "I'll keep Siri company."

"You don't have to do that," Siri protested quickly, and the snakes began to look better and better to her. "I can..."

"Hawke? Hawke!" came a sultry, surprised voice from behind them.

They turned, just in time to see a dark, petite little brunette throw herself into Hawke's arms and pull his head down to kiss him feverishly. Siri turned away from the sight, which went through her like a flaming lance.

"Oh, Hawke!" the brunette cooed softly, with more than a trace of Spanish accent, "what a wonderful surprise to find you here! Can you come back with Renaldo and me for a drink?"

"I'm with friends, Angel," he replied with a smile.

"*No importa,*" Angel said breezily, "bring them, too! I've got a villa near here, with miles and miles of beach. And Renaldo would love to talk over old times with you."

"Where is your brother?" he asked, puncturing Siri's vain hope that the missing "Renaldo" might be the woman's husband.

"Back there. Rey...Rey!" Angel called, and a strikingly tall, dark man came wandering up to join the small group. His eyes swept over Siri's slender body.

"You remember Hawke, don't you?" Angel asked with a flash of white teeth.

"Most assuredly," Rey said. "A pleasure. And this is...?" he asked, swinging without warning to face Siri, his eyes level and plainly interested.

"My partner's daughter, Siri Jamesson," Hawke replied with a curtness in his tone that was lost on Rey.

"A pleasure," the Latin repeated, and lifted Siri's hand to his lips.

Hawke introduced Randy and Kitty, and Angel persisted until she got her way and had them back in the rented car headed for her villa. Oh, well, Siri thought wearily, at least she had escaped the snakes.

But when they got to the hacienda-style villa with its seemingly acres of untouched beach, Siri wondered if the snakes just might not have been better. Between Angel's openly seductive manner toward Hawke and Rey's dead-tilt efforts to catch Siri's wary eye, it was like being caged with tigers.

The worst of it was the familiarity between Hawke and the little brunette. They were more than just old friends, and it showed. Why it should have mattered so much, Siri didn't know. But it mattered. She wanted to get out, to run, to go home. She couldn't bear the way his dark eyes played on Angel's face, and she didn't understand her own indignation.

"What do you do, Miss Jamesson?" Rey asked politely, perching himself comfortably on the arm of the massive chair she was sitting in. "Are you an attorney like your father?"

"I'm a reporter."

"A reporter!" His eyes brightened with interest.

Siri laughed. "I work for a daily newspaper, but I cover the police beat; fires, wrecks, murders, those kind of stories. And believe me, there's nothing funny about that."

"A woman involved in such tragic work?" he exclaimed. "You must have nerves of iron!"

"Not really," Siri admitted, sipping the rum punch in her tall glass. "What do you do?"

He shrugged. "Not much of anything," he admitted. He grinned. "I have, fortunately, the means to pursue a life of pleasure."

"How nice," she murmured appropriately.

"Yes, it is."

She glanced at him, mentally comparing him with Hawke, who also had the means to pursue a life of pleasure, but preferred useful work that also had its dangers. Hawke didn't seem to care for Angel's brother, and she wondered if he didn't remind him of his own father; a pleasure seeker, uninvolved and uncaring except for his own idle pursuits. It didn't sound like much of a life, but she kept quiet. To each his own, she thought.

"I wish I had not promised to join my friends for a cruise," Rey said. "I would much prefer to spend the time with you."

"Unfortunately," she smiled, "I have very little time to spend on pleasure. I'm a working girl, and I'm here on assignment. I have to account for my days."

"You are not . . . how you say . . . Hawke's woman?" he asked.

She glared at him. "I have a steady boyfriend back home who suits me very well," she said with ice in her tone. "I'm here working on a story, of which Hawke is part. That's all. Period. I am not available for fun and games for bored playboys!"

"Please, Siri, you misunderstand . . . !" Rey began quickly, his face going rather white at the tone of her voice.

"I don't think so," she told him, rising. She moved back to where Kitty was sitting and squeezed in beside her, leaving the stunned Latin behind her.

Hawke glanced toward her, then toward the glass she was holding, and she read the amusement in his dark eyes. It made her flush uncomfortably. I'm not tipsy, she wanted to yell at him. In defiance, she lifted the glass to her lips again.

"Having trouble, honey?" Kitty whispered, squeezing her hand.

"Not any more," she replied smugly, and finished the rum punch while the others sailed forth on the subject of ships.

Rey left soon afterwards with a really wounded look about him. Siri half regretted what she'd said, but not that she'd said it. She didn't have time to fight off an amorous Latin in whom she wasn't really interested.

If she'd been hoping for an early departure, her hopes were doomed to disappointment. Angel insisted that the small group stay for a meal. She had her combination housekeeper-cook busy in the kitchen before anyone could protest.

Siri hated the ordeal of watching Angel smother Hawke. She hated even more the fact that he didn't seem to mind her attentions. It went from bad to worse when the little Spanish woman turned on her expensive stereo system and flooded the room with soft, seductive music. She threw back the carpet and invited the others to dance, pointedly ignoring the fact that Siri didn't have a partner as she glued herself to Hawke's broad body.

Randy, a gentleman from the shoes up, asked Siri to dance, but she quickly shook her head with a convincing smile.

"Oh, I don't dance," she said quickly, "but thanks all the same."

She dodged the incredulous look Hawke threw her over Angel's bare shoulder and curled up on the sofa with a magazine about the latest fashions. Did Angel have to dance that close to him, she wondered, darting a green glance their way. Did she have to press so close, and tangle her hands in that softly curling hair at the nape of his broad neck? Did she have to look so bloody content?

As soon as it was humanly possible, she promised herself that she was going to get out of that room and make herself scarce until supper. She'd never felt more suffocated. She had the oddest feeling that Angel found her threatening, and it puzzled her. There wasn't anything between her and Hawke, wasn't it obvious? After all, Siri sighed, remembering her nose that was too short, her eyes that were too big, her hair that was too silvery to be a true blonde—she was no competition for that spicy Latin. So why was Angel throwing her the icy looks?

While she was working that out, she failed to hear the phone ring, or see the housekeeper motioning to Angel. She missed the sudden intent look in Hawke's dark eyes as he started toward her. She felt him catch her hand, and she gasped with surprise. She hadn't realized he was so close.

"Dance with me, sparrow," he said quietly.

She let him pull her to her feet and lead her out onto the bare wood floor. His big arms enveloped her close against his broad, husky body until air could barely have gotten between them. She felt the tremor go through her slender body and wondered at the strength and newness of what she was feeling.

The sun was just beginning to go down outside the huge picture window, darkening the room gently, intimately. The slow, sultry pace of the music made the atmosphere all that much more intimate, and Randy and his young wife were already oblivious to their surroundings as they danced a few feet away.

Drowning in new sensations, Siri moved closer to Hawke. Obeying an instinct as old as time, her hands slid up over his broad chest to tangle gently in the thick hair that curled just slightly at the nape of his powerful neck.

"Siri…" he warned softly, something tight and odd in his tone as his big hands contracted bruisingly at her waist.

She nestled her head against his chest with a sigh, letting the music and the nearness wash over her as the amber glow of a setting sun added to the magic of being close against Hawke like this, making her feel reckless.

Her fingers caressed the back of his head slowly, gently. Against her slenderness, she could feel the heavy, driving beat of his heart through the thin fabric of his shirt. The blazing warmth of his chest caressed her cheek.

"Do you know what you're doing to me?" he asked gruffly, his grip tightening painfully.

"You didn't grumble when Angel did it," she murmured drowsily.

"Angel wouldn't mind the consequences. You would," he said flatly.

She moved closer. "Are you sure?" she whispered softly.

His big hands moved up to the back of her head, forcing her face up to his dark, blazing eyes. "You'd better be," he warned huskily.

Something in the way he was looking at her made her blood run wild through her veins. Her fingers reached up and touched his mouth gently, sensually. "Oh, Hawke…" she whispered, her eyes soft with faint pleading as they met his.

"Watch the table!" Kitty called, but it was too late. Siri hit it with her hip, and it was just bruising enough to break the spell.

She drew slightly away from Hawke, gingerly touching her bruised hip, then suddenly remembering what she'd been doing. She glanced at him just once and turned quickly away. Her nervous fingers opened the sliding doors of the picture window where steps led down to the beach.

"Excuse me," she murmured over her shoulder, "I think I need some air."

She darted down the steps, embarrassed, and onto the gritty sand of the beach, feeling it fill her sandals as she started running along the shoreline. The sun hovered low on the horizon, and the breeze felt good in her face, cool and sobering. Her hair lifted from her hot neck, cooling the dampness, bringing her swaying mind slowly back into focus.

She was so lost in sensation that she didn't notice how deserted the surroundings were or that a sand dune hid the lonely stretch of beach from the house. She didn't even hear the heavy thud of footsteps behind her, or see the husky, very angry man who was every bit as quick as she was.

He caught up with her at the water's edge, throwing her off-balance so that she fell heavily to the wet sand beside him. He turned, pinning her down, his strong hands pushing her wrists into the sand while the surf lathered around them, cold and wet.

"Hawke...the water," she stammered. He was dynamite at close range. This man who was so familiar was at once strange and dangerous and wickedly exciting. She gaped up at him with the shock she was feeling plain in her amber eyes, a little unnerved by the feel of his massive chest bruising the softness of hers, the way that mat of curling dark hair where his shirt was unbuttoned felt against the skin her low-cut top left revealed. His eyes were like slate now, dark and glittering, narrowing slightly as he looked down at his captive.

"Did you think you were going to get away with it?" he demanded roughly. "My God, Siri, you can't incite a man like that and expect to walk away untouched!"

"I didn't...I didn't mean to, Hawke," she breathed. "It must have been the rum, and I'm not used to it. I'm sorry...!"

His fingers tightened on her wrists as his head bent. "So am I," he said in a deep, tight voice. "But I can't turn it on and off. Just be still, little girl. Don't make it worse by fighting me."

She caught her breath when she saw his eyes drop to her mouth. "Hawke, don't..." she pleaded half-heartedly.

"Haven't you ever wondered," he whispered roughly as his warm, hard mouth brushed against hers in the dim reddish sunlight, "what it would be like with me?"

She tried to answer him, but her blood was singing from the slow, brief, expert kisses he was whispering across her trembling lips.

Her fingers hesitantly touched the dark face above hers, exploring his forehead, his cheek rough with its day's shadow of beard, his chiseled mouth—liberties she'd never have dared to take before, but he didn't seem to mind.

"Your hands are cold," he murmured.

"I...I'm nervous," she admitted.

His lips brushed against her closed eyelids. "It's a public beach," he reminded her. "This is hardly the place for what you're afraid I'm going to do to you."

"I know."

His teeth nipped at her lower lip. "Then why these little tremors I can feel going through you?" he asked in a deep, slow whisper.

"Hawke..."

His big hands slid beneath her shoulders, bringing her body sensuously up against him while his fingers caressed the softness of her back under the thin blouse.

"Stop talking," he murmured. "Touch me."

She relaxed unsteadily, pressing her small hands against his hard, cool chest, enjoying the masculine feel of it against the palms of her hands. His mouth explored hers very gently, coaxing, rather than forcing, her lips to part under the eager pressure of his.

"Hawke...the water," she whispered, feeling it dampen the back of her head.

"To hell with the water." His lips brushed against hers more insistently, pressing them apart until he could fit his mouth precisely to hers in a leisurely, ardent kiss that made a moan break from her throat.

His big hands slid up to her head, cradling it from the water, as his mouth grew hard and bruising and intimate in its assault on her soft lips.

"Don't..." she protested weakly, trying to escape his mouth as he began to deepen the kiss, to arouse feelings beyond her slight experience.

He drew back a breath to look down into her wide, amber eyes. "Why not?" he asked quietly.

"I...I've never kissed anyone...like that," she faltered.

"You're going to kiss me like that. Just relax," he whispered, tenderly smoothing the wild, damp hair away from her flushed face as he bent again. "There's a first time for everything, sparrow," he murmured against her mouth. "It's part of growing up, of being a woman. I want to be the one to teach you. Here, Siri. Now..." He forced her head back against his big hands, coaxing, tantalizing, teasing her soft mouth until he made her want it, need it, until her lips parted for him without protest and she sank down into the sand under the staggering wave of emotion that swept over her. A sound—half surprised gasp, half sob—wrenched from her.

"Does it make you ache, baby?" he whispered against her mouth.

"Yes!" she moaned, her nails biting into his shoulders as his body shifted slowly, sensuously against hers.

"Now you know how I felt in the beach house, you damned little tease!" he growled.

All at once, he rolled away from her and got to his feet. He stood facing the ocean, fumbling in his shirt pocket for a cigarette and match, and she thought just for an instant that she saw a shudder run through his big, husky body.

The blazing orange colors on the horizon danced around them, in a silence made noisy by the watery crash of the surf. The fiery glow gave Hawke a satanic look, emphasizing his darkness in a silhouette of power and strength against the horizon.

Siri sat up, aware of the dampness of her hair and back, and the bruised ache of her body from the fierce pressure of his. She tasted blood on her lips as she touched the inside of them with her tongue. The taste of him was there as well— a smoky, masculine taste that brought the color into her cheeks when she remembered how intimately she'd let him kiss her. As if that hadn't been bad enough, she'd revealed what his touch could do to her. She felt vaguely ashamed of herself, humiliated. If the name of the game was get even, he'd done a good job.

She got to her feet, still dazed. "I...I'm going back to the beach house," she managed weakly.

"You might as well, honey, the lesson's over," he said with a cutting edge on his deep voice. "I'm a little old to be tutoring curious teenagers, Siri. From now on, you'll have to let Holland teach you what you want to know. I'm not going to let you get to me like that again."

Get to him? Lessons? She felt all the color drain out of her face as she looked at him.

6

He turned, as if he sensed her puzzlement, and she could feel his eyes touching her. His cigarette glowed orange in the fading light. "Isn't that clear enough?" he asked harshly. "Get out of my sight, you little hypocrite! Whatever the game is, I'm damned well not playing!"

Her hand went to her cheek, feeling as if he'd slapped her. She turned and started back toward the beach house alone.

With her heart pounding in her ears, she joined the others, trying not to let the turmoil of her emotions show. Her amber eyes had an unnatural brightness, and her hair was damp in back from the surf and disheveled from Hawke's rough fingers. But she managed to keep her voice calm, her hands steady.

"Where is Hawke?" Angel asked with venomous curiosity. "He followed you out."

"I don't know," Siri replied innocently. "He passed me on the beach and kept right on walking."

"I'll bet that did a lot for your ego," Kitty teased lightly.

Siri smiled. "It's not like that at all. Hawke's years too old for me. Goodness, he used to drive me to cheerleading practice when I was barely in my teens." She laughed, and saw some of the suspicion and tension drain out of Angel's delicately boned face.

"We will wait for him," the little Latin woman said. "In the meantime, let us have another drink."

Siri welcomed the rum punch as never before. Perhaps she could recover before...

Even as the thought formed in her mind, Hawke came in the door, looking as imperturbable as ever and just a little dangerous. His eyes darted toward Siri for just an instant before he joined Angel at the bar and after a while, the din of conversation dispelled some of Siri's tension. Not that the meal had much taste when they sat down to eat it. It might have been cardboard for all she knew. She kept her eyes on her plate and carried bites of food automatically to her mouth, pausing only to murmur appropriate responses to Kitty's bubbly remarks. The evening passed agonizingly slowly, a mingling of soft music and conversation that seemed to go on forever.

Finally, Randy announced that he and Kitty had to get back to their hotel. Siri was right behind them, hoping that Hawke might decide to remain with Angel. But he didn't. Parrying aside her invitation to spend the day with her tomorrow, he explained that he'd be leaving town in the morning, adding that he'd look her up the next time he was passing through.

Siri followed the Hallers outside, while Angel took her sweet time saying goodbye to Hawke. Oh, why couldn't he have stayed? She didn't want to have to go back to that lonely suite with him, to be taunted anymore, to be shamed anymore. She just wanted to go back to Atlanta, and her father, and the newspaper. This was like being left in an unescapable cage with a lion.

Driving back to Panama City was the most uncomfortable thing in Siri's recent memory. She sat as far away from Hawke as possible, and her face was turned toward the darkness outside, with its sparse highlights of neon signs and colored lights as the "Miracle Strip" stretched out before them. The other two made casual conversation, but Hawke's replies were clipped and terse.

If only, Siri thought unhappily, they'd gone to see the awful snakes. She'd have had nightmares, but perhaps they wouldn't have been so painful. In her mind, she could see those dark, narrowed eyes looking down at her, feel the angry crush of his mouth, the bruising strength of his big body pressing hers relentlessly into the soft, damp sand.

She trembled just at the memory, wrapping her arms tight around her body to contain the shudder of shame that racked her. Why did she have to drink the rum? Why did she have to tease him like that while they were dancing? For all that she'd dreamed with a juvenile curiosity what it would be like to kiss him, it hadn't in any way prepared her for what had actually happened. She hadn't known that a man could be so demanding, that her own strength was nothing when compared with a man's superior force. She hadn't realized that a kiss could be so intimate, or that she could want it so much. Her eyes closed in embarrassment. He'd made her want it deliberately, but not because he wanted it to be a beautifully shared emotion. He had only wanted to pay her back for dancing a little too close.

They were at the hotel before she realized it. She stuck to Kitty like glue, finding one excuse after the other to keep her talking about art, about recipes, about anything. When the Hallers invited them in for a nightcap, Siri refused quickly. Pleading a headache, she asked Hawke if she could have the key; only to be shattered when he remarked casually that he'd go along, too. He silenced her protest with a look that knocked the resistance right out of her.

Meekly, she said her goodnights and followed him along to the suite they shared, waiting silently while he unlocked the door. She went in past him and reached for the doorknob at her bedroom.

"Siri." Just one word, just her name, but it was enough to freeze her where she stood.

She kept her eyes on the brass metal knob. "Please, just let me go to bed," she said in a voice totally unlike her normal tone. "You can't possibly make me feel any more ashamed than I already do."

"Did I hurt you?" he asked quietly.

She shook her head, flushing at the intimacy of the question, determined not to let him see the tears that were collecting in her eyes.

He took a long, agitated breath. "Since you're too afraid to listen to me, when you get home, ask Jared what that kind of provocation does to a man. It might surprise you. Goodnight, Siri."

She stayed where she was until she heard the door open and close. She went quickly into her bedroom and locked the door behind her.

"Goodnight, Hawke," she whispered to the empty room.

The next morning, Siri found a note propped up on the coffee table written in Hawke's broad, scrawling hand.

"Siri," it began, "if you need to contact me for any reason, I'll be at this number," and it gave an unfamiliar set of digits. "I should be back by Thursday. Behave yourself. Hawke."

She sighed, reading it. That last remark was just like him. Behave yourself, indeed! And just who did he think he was, anyway? Her keeper?

She stormed out of the suite and down to the beach. Well, she asked herself, what did she expect, a love letter? She blushed at the memory of that scene on the beach. It was a blessing not to have to face him for a few days. The wound was still too raw for the sting she'd feel every time she met those dark, knowing eyes. Only a few more days, she told herself. Only a few more days, and she could go back to her old familiar routine and pick up the pieces. But those pieces wouldn't include Mark. Not now. After what she'd discovered in Hawke's arms, it would be impossible to let Mark touch her ever again. She wondered miserably if she'd ever be able to feel that kind of emotion with anyone else.

Hawke was suddenly a stranger; a mature, very capable man who possessed a hidden fire she'd only dreamed he might conceal under the restrained impassive mask he wore. The man who'd wrestled her to the sand and kissed her with such bruising hunger—had that really been the Hawke who had brought her souvenirs from his travels and helped her with her homework? The idea took a lot of getting used to, She'd never experienced Hawke in any kind of real physical sense until now. She had a feeling she'd never quite get over it. He'd only been gone a few hours, and already she felt as if part of her had gone with him. That, too, was new—the feeling of being cut in two parts without someone.

Why did she miss him so much? Why couldn't she remember only the harsh words, the accusations he'd made, instead of the feel of that hard, sensual mouth as he'd made her yield to him? Was he really investigating a case, or was he using the case as an excuse to spend a few days with one of his women?

She dived into the waves and relished the feel of the cold water on her burning skin. She simply wouldn't think about it anymore. She wouldn't allow it!

Kitty came to see her that night, moaning that Randy had gone out somewhere with one of his friends and left her there all alone. Over coffee, they compared notes about Panama City and the delights of the beach.

"Will you get mad at me if I ask you what was wrong with Hawke last night?" Kitty asked suddenly, cupping her hands around the mug filled with steaming black coffee.

Siri looked down at her lap. "We . . . had an argument."

"Which Hawke started, no doubt." Kitty smiled. "I know Hawke very well. He was engaged to a friend of mine back in Charleston, just before he went into partnership with your father. I'm afraid she left him with a bad opinion of women in general. People tried to tell him that Nita liked to collect men, but . . ." She sighed softly, meeting Siri's intent, curious gaze. "Nita was just eighteen when she and Hawke started going together; a very young eighteen. She was very pretty, and I always felt she was flattered by the attentions of a man as masculine and mature as Hawke. But while he wanted commitment, she wanted variety and fun. What happened was inevitable."

Siri was sitting on the edge of her seat. "What did happen?" she asked.

"To make a long story short, Hawke caught her out with a boy just a year older than she was. He broke the engagement, but I don't think he ever really got over it. And then, to have his mother found dead in her lover's apartment barely two weeks later . . ." Kitty shook her head. "He hasn't had an easy life. He had to let his law practice go while he straightened out the family finances. His father was too busy with women to be of much help.''

Siri was taking it all in with wide, astonished eyes. She'd known Hawke for so long, and not really known anything at all about him, it seemed.

"You didn't know, did you?" Kitty probed gently.

Siri shook her head. "Hawke's very tight-lipped about his private life. I doubt even Dad knows very much about him." She sipped her coffee. "The girl he was engaged to...did he love her?"

"He was besotted with her, to use an old phrase. Nita was a gorgeous girl, and she wasn't ever intentionally cruel, just thoughtless. But even though I liked her, I wasn't blind to her faults. She was a born flirt, and she liked rich men. Hawke was good-looking, and had more money than even she could plow through very fast."

"Did she marry the boy?" Siri asked.

"Yes. As a matter of fact, she's gone through three husbands since, and I hear she's on the prowl for number four right now." Kitty shook her head. "Hawke had a lucky escape. I'm glad he left Charleston when he did. Nita wasn't quite what he needs in a wife," she added bitterly.

"He doesn't need a wife now," Siri said with a knowing smile. "Not as long as he's got women like Gessie and Angel following him around. Angel was lovely, wasn't she?"

"If you thought she was so pretty," Kitty asked slyly, "why did you spend so much time glaring at her?"

Siri shifted uncomfortably. "Her brother irritated me."

"He irritated Hawke, too." Kitty set down her cup and looked at the other girl intently. "Siri, I told you about Nita for a reason. He was so bitter about it, I don't think he'll let another woman get close. But he might hurt one very badly out of that bitterness. I've come to know you these past few days. I wouldn't like to see you hurt."

Siri felt the words go through her and fought to keep calm. "You're very kind, Kitty, but I told you..."

"You told me one thing," came the wise reply, "but I watched you dancing with Hawke at Angel's house. Siri, it's very hard to hide when you care that much."

"I'd had a lot to drink," she protested.

"Not that much. Siri," she said gently, leaning forward to cover the younger woman's trembling hands with her own, "didn't you know that you were in love with him?"

Those words haunted her through the night. "Didn't you know you were in love with him?" The question returned like a painted horse on a merry-go-round, passing in front of her over and over again as she lay awake in her bed.

That couldn't be true, could it? Not Hawke, of all people, not after all this time! After all, you didn't go around falling in love with people who were like part of the family. And besides, he was years too old for her; too old, too set in his ways, and far too possessive.

She'd laughed off Kitty's probing remark convincingly enough at the time but it wasn't so easy to laugh it off in the darkness. To be with him, to touch him, to listen quietly as he talked with her father—when had such commonplace things become so important? And why hadn't she seen it coming? Why hadn't she realized what was happening while there might have been time to do something about it?

One thing was certain; Hawke didn't feel that way about her. She could still see the fury in his eyes, hear the whip-lash of his voice as he accused her of provoking him into kissing her. Had she, really? Or, perhaps, had he wanted to...?

She drew a deep, unsteady breath. That, she told herself, was pure conceit. A man like Hawke wouldn't look twice at a girl as young and innocent as she was. He liked women like Angel—sleek, sophisticated, women who weren't afraid of the consequences of their flirting.

It was unsettling to realize just how deeply Hawke's absence was beginning to affect her. The next day, she barely touched food. She alternated between lying on the beach and swimming. Later, she contemplated her miserable state on the balcony when the sun went down. She and Kitty visited some of the nearby restaurants just for a change, and pored over shells and souvenirs in the little gift shops. But nothing took her mind off Hawke for very long. She hated her own helplessness. She'd never been vulnerable before, never been dependent on a man for happiness. She hated that new vulnerability. She wished with all her heart that she'd stuck to her guns in the first place and stayed home. She could be working on a fire right now, or some controversy in the police department. She could be where the action was, instead of stuck here on a beach littered with tourists. She could be doing something else beside mooning over Hawke.

The second night, she forced herself to sit in the living room of the lonely suite with her small portable typewriter on the coffee table. Without much success, she tried to concoct a presentable summary of the Devolg murder.

She studied her notes without any real enthusiasm. In a city that was notorious for homicide, another murder wasn't that sensational. Not that she'd become hardened to the extent that she didn't feel compassion for the families of victims, but she'd covered so many.

As she stared at her notes, she came across the original news story she'd done on the murder. Datelined Atlanta, it read: *Justin Devolg, 49, of Oak Street, Atlanta, was found dead in his apartment this morning from stab wounds.*

Her eyes scanned the page, resting on the paragraph that read: *Inspector Long stated that no motive for the killing was readily apparent. The dead man had a large sum of cash in his wallet, but it was untouched. He was wearing a diamond ring with an estimated value of $2,000 at the time of his death, and the ring was still on his finger when police arrived on the scene.*

A search is still pending for the unidentified man who fled when the body was discovered. Police have arrested a fifteen year old juvenile for questioning in connection with the murder, but no further information was available. The

murder is still under investigation by local police and the
FBI. Some pieces of evidence have already been sent to the
state crime lab for inspection, and an early wrap-up of the
case is expected by law enforcement officials.

Siri frowned. Of course, the update would confirm stab
wounds as the cause of death, but they also would include
the arrest of Hawke's young client in connection with the
murder. The sensational nature of the case made it a natural for front page treatment.

She was searching her brain for a good, strong lead, when
the door opened unexpectedly and Hawke walked in. She
gaped at him, as if she were looking at a ghost, her mind still
on the murder.

"Have you eaten?" he asked quietly. "Or does the creative effort really take the place of food?"

"Sometimes it has to," she replied with a smile she didn't
feel. She dragged her eyes away from him, hating the sudden quick beating of her heart as it reacted to the sight and
sound of him. She was just now realizing how lonely she'd
been these past few days, and how much she'd missed him.
She felt a glow inside, as if a rainbow of warmth had suddenly raced through her.

"That doesn't answer my question," he reminded her.

"Oh, sorry," she apologized, "my mind was still on the
Devolg story. No, I haven't eaten."

"Throw on a sweater and we'll walk down the road to the
seafood place," he told her. "It's a little chilly for summer."

"All right."

As excited as a teenager on her first date, she darted into
her bedroom to change. She threw on a beige wraparound
skirt and a green blouse. She ran a comb through her un-
ruly hair. She left off makeup, except for a light touch of
lipstick, and grabbed for her sweater as she went out the
door into the living room.

Hawke was waiting for her at the main door. He was
wearing a pale blue shirt that was open at the neck. Matched
with his darker sports jacket, the outfit gave him a sophis-

ticated look that went well with his masculine attractiveness. Her eyes absorbed the sight, dwelling on the broad, muscular sweep of his shoulders. Why did he have to be so good to look at, she wondered miserably, following him out into the hall. Why couldn't he have been fat and squatty with a face like a toad?

He caught the back of her neck, giving it an affectionate squeeze as they walked outside the hotel behind a group of tourists into the chill night air.

"What are you brooding about, honey?" he asked gently.

She almost told him. It very nearly slipped out, but she caught herself just in time.

"I'm just tired," she said quickly. "Kitty and I hit every tourist shop within walking distance this afternoon."

"You like her, don't you?" he asked.

She nodded and smiled. "I never had a sister, but if I could pick my own, I'd choose Kitty."

He was extremely quiet as the crowd of tourists moved a little ahead of them going down the side of the road while cars jammed together in a steady stream on the highway.

"How much did she tell you?" he asked suddenly, his eyes narrow and glittering as he glanced down at her.

"About what?" she asked uneasily.

"You damned well know about what," he growled.

She jerked her eyes away from his to the colorful neon lights ahead. He hadn't been back a half hour, and already he was trying to pick a fight.

She stopped and turned toward him. "Why don't I go back to the hotel and order my supper from room service?" she asked quietly. "At least that way we'll both be able to enjoy what we're eating."

He stared down at her long and hard. Finally, his hand came up and touched her cheek gently. "I'm being unreasonable, is that what you're trying to tell me?"

"Yes," she admitted.

"Oh, Siri," he said gently, "don't you know why? Aren't you even that sophisticated?"

She looked up at him, puzzled. "Trying to understand you is like trying to read Sanskrit," she observed. "Hawke, what do you want?"

"You, damn it!" he said curtly.

She flushed and turned away.

"Let's eat something," he said tightly, catching her by the arm as he began to walk again. "Maybe it'll improve my temper."

She felt shaken, uneasy. Was that why he'd begun to cut at her so much since they came on this trip—because of a purely physical attraction he couldn't help or do anything about? It made sense, it really did. But what a blow it was to her pride, to be desired only for the arrangement of physical features. It was as if he couldn't see her as a person at all. And didn't care to.

He led her into the seafood restaurant and seated her in one of the colorful red booths beside him. It created an intimacy that she could have done without. She couldn't move without touching him.

The waitress brought ice water and menus, and they studied them silently.

"I'd like the scallops," she said finally, handing him the menu as the waitress came back, "and coffee."

He ordered for both of them, automatically reaching for a cigarette when the waitress went away.

"Will the smoke bother you?" he asked, glancing down at her.

She shook her head. Her hands were wrapped around her water glass as if it were a life jacket, keeping her head above water.

He caught a strand of her hair and tugged it gently, forcing her frightened eyes up to his. He read them, and smiled.

"I'm not going to do anything about it," he said softly, reading the thought in her mind. "You're perfectly safe, little bird."

She looked into his eyes. "I'm sorry for what I did at the beach house," she said in a subdued tone. "It really was the rum. I'd never have done anything like that if I'd been myself.''

His dark brows came together. "You've never tried to interest a man like that before?" he asked.

"I haven't and I wouldn't," she replied. "It's cheap and cruel."

"It depends on who's doing it, and for what reason," he said softly. "I said things to you that I shouldn't have, and I regret them. But I've never lost my head with a woman before. It shook me."

The admission startled her. "But you didn't ...!"

He tugged the strand of hair again, more firmly. "I very nearly didn't let you go," he said solemnly. "It was good, Siri. It was so damned good, I didn't want to stop. I was rougher with you than I ever meant to be, and more intimate. It must be my age," he laughed mirthlessly. "I've never stooped to the attempted seduction of innocents before. And I'm going to take you home tomorrow before I try it again. You're very...vulnerable where I'm concerned, Siri," he remarked with a scowl. "It's damned flattering, but extremely dangerous. One thing I told you I meant—you need to learn about adult relationships with a boy your own age. I'm too old and jaded to teach you in any respectable way. In short, little one," he added with a mocking smile, "I want it all. Not just nibbles."

She blushed, dropping her eyes to the shiny table where her reflection looked back at her. "I shouldn't have come."

"It's my own fault, baby. I talked you into it." He leaned back to light his cigarette, only to have to put it out again as the waitress reappeared with two full plates of scallops, tossed salads, rolls, and baked potatoes.

"Don't dwell on it, sparrow," Hawke told her with a quiet smile. "Tomorrow we'll be home. You'll be back on the job, and swinging at Holland, and all this will seem like a dream."

"Or a nightmare?" she teased with a little of her old impudence as she glanced at him.

"I wouldn't go that far," he said with a considering look. "You left some pretty deep marks on my shoulders."

She blushed to the roots of her hair and gasped unconsciously at the reference. She attacked her scallops with a vengeance, ignoring the soft, amused laughter at her ear.

It was all a game to him, she thought as she ate. Just a game to play with her, and he was a master at it. She wasn't experienced enough to laugh it off, or throw the taunting remarks back at him. Oh, I wish I was five years older, Hawke Grayson, she thought angrily. I'd pay you back with interest, if I had just a little more experience under my belt!

They walked back to the hotel in companionable silence. Siri didn't dare break it, for fear that he'd start teasing her again, and she didn't think she could bear it.

In one way, it would be good to go back home and leave the danger of being with him like this behind. In another sense, it was going to be horribly painful. Now that she finally knew how she felt about the broad-shouldered, husky man at her side, it was going to be all that much harder to go back to the old routine. Having had a taste of heaven, life was going to be very boring for a long time, maybe forever. She glanced up at him, her eyes resting briefly, involuntarily, on the chiseled curve of his mouth. Why couldn't he have been ten years younger? Why couldn't she have been ten years older?

They were alone in the elevator going up to their suite, and she felt his eyes on her every foot of the short climb. He got to the door first and opened it for her, standing aside to let her enter. She started for her bedroom, as she usually did when they came home late. The last time, she thought, this was the last time....

"Siri..." he called gently.

She turned slowly, her sad amber eyes meeting his across the short distance that separated them. His were dark and strange, smoldering.

"Infatuation dies a natural death when it doesn't have anything to feed on," he said. "And that's all it is, sparrow.

You're growing up fast. I've taught you things you should have learned in easy stages, and it's gone to your head, that's all. Don't mistake it for something more permanent.''

She felt absolutely whipped. Was that what it seemed like to him, a teenage infatuation? Did he think her such a child?

"I . . . I didn't say . . ." she faltered, embarrassed.

He jammed his hands into his pockets, his eyes narrowing. "You didn't have to say it. It's written all over you, every time you look at me."

7

S he bit her lip, staring down at her toes peeking out of the sandals, feeling the lump come into her throat.

"As you say," she managed unsteadily, "it's just a... phase I'm going through. It doesn't mean...anything."

There was a muffled curse. "If you keep looking like that, I'm going to carry you over to the sofa and make love to you, Siri! I want you so much, it's like a fire burning inside me, and damn it, you're not helping!"

Her eyes jerked up incredulously to his dark, heavily lined face. The sight of him made her knees go weak. Would it be so very wrong to give in? To feel that hard, hungry mouth on hers just once more, to yield to arms so much stronger than her own...

"You'd let me love you, wouldn't you, little girl?" he asked in a deep, low whisper.

Her lips trembled as they formed the words. "Hawke, I..." she began huskily.

But before she could get them out, the insistent jangle of the phone broke into the silence like an air raid siren. She flinched at the sound.

Hawke turned on his heel and went to answer it. Siri moved out onto the balcony, letting the sea breeze cool her burning skin, settle the throbbing nerves that screamed from disappointment. Through the clearing fog of her emotions, she heard Hawke's deep, curt voice in the distance as he spoke into the receiver.

Minutes passed before he joined her on the balcony. He didn't speak at first, not until he'd halfway smoked a cigarette.

"That was my housekeeper in Charleston," he said. "The overseer had a heart attack this afternoon. I'll have to fly up there and make arrangements for someone to take over the farm until he's back on his feet."

"Oh, I'm sorry," she murmured.

"You've never been to Charleston, have you?" he asked suddenly.

Her heart jumped. "No, I haven't."

"Come with me, Siri."

She hesitated, remembering what had almost happened once before. What if...?

"We'll take the Hallers with us," he said quietly. "I think...we could use a chaperone, don't you?"

"Yes," she managed in a whisper.

He drew a deep breath. "I ought to send you home," he said. "You know that, don't you?"

"I know," she replied.

"But you don't really want to go any more than I want to let you," he added roughly. "I missed you like hell, Siri!"

She turned, her eyes seeking his in the soft light from the living room. It was magic! Sheer magic! Did he care, could he?

He moved away from her, back into the living room. "I think you'd better go to bed," he said.

She followed him into the living room. One look at the set of his jaw was enough to tell her not to argue with him. For all the emotion there'd been in his voice in the darkness, there wasn't a trace of it on his face.

She wanted to ask him...but she didn't dare. She nodded quietly and turned toward her bedroom. Just before she fell asleep, she realized he'd told her nothing about his trip.

The next morning, with Randy and Kitty in the back seat of the big Cessna, they were on the way to Charleston. Hawke's handyman, Charles Simms, met them at the airport outside Charleston in a spacious Lincoln town car and drove them to the farm, which was only minutes away.

Siri watched her surroundings change minute by minute with a bubbling fascination. Charleston was a city of many different faces; it ranged from gorgeous white beaches to cobblestoned streets, where flower vendors and basket-weavers plied their trade; from two-hundred year old homes to modern skyscrapers. Palm trees and crepe myrtle mingled naturally in this city once called Charles Town.

"Looking for the cannons?" Hawke teased as he saw Siri glancing out toward the ocean. "I'll make time to carry you out to Fort Sumter and Fort Moultrie while we're here."

"I'd like that," she said enthusiastically. "Can I fire off a cannon?"

"I don't think the city fathers would like that," he replied.

She sighed. "I never get to have any fun."

The family estate was called Graystone, and once they followed the winding, flower-laced driveway up to the main house, she understood why. The house was built from pale gray stone in a Gothic design, with a soaring portico and columns placed in pairs on either side. A balcony curved over the portico, with black wrought iron railings, and fourth floor over-portico windows completing the Gothic styling. It was a large house, but not massive like some of the residences they'd passed going through the city. It was impressive without being gaudy.

For Siri, as she stepped out of the car and looked around at the neatly kept grounds, at the massive oaks with their beards of Spanish moss, at the river beyond the garden, there was a sense of belonging. It was strangely like coming home after a long absence. And when she turned and met Hawke's intent gaze, the feeling was complete.

The three of them were introduced to Mr. Simms' wife, Mary, who'd kept house at Graystone ever since Mr. Hawke was a lad. She was a buxom woman with gray hair neatly coiled at the back of her head, and Siri had a feeling that she could set a table like no one else.

As they climbed the steps to the wide, immaculately scrubbed portico, Siri noted the big rocking chairs and settees that lined the walls. In the distance, the soft watery sound of the river could be heard along with the swish of the tree limbs touching and the mingled birdsongs. It was like something out of another world; a bower of peace in the world full of turmoil.

"Oh, Hawke, it's heaven," she murmured as they went into the house behind the Hallers.

"It can be lonely," he remarked quietly.

She met his dark eyes. "Any place can be."

Hawke gave them a grand tour, and Siri was flooded with impressions of an elliptical stairway, curved walls, rounded banisters of pure mahogany, and large paintings of previous owners of the house.

"Graysons have lived here for over 200 years," Kitty told Siri, as they followed along behind the men. "In Hawke's den, there's a portrait of the first owner, with a bayonet tear in the center of it. They say a Union soldier used it for target practice when federal troops camped here during the Civil War."

"You and Randy have been here before, haven't you?" Siri asked.

"It was a long time ago," Kitty replied softly, and Siri knew somehow that it had been when Hawke's mother died.

When the luggage was arranged in their rooms, and they'd had a light lunch, they got the tour of the farm. Hawke walked beside Siri, his arm brushing against hers as they first went to the big barn, where a prize polled Hereford bull pranced proudly in a paddock surrounded by a white fence.

"Gray's Fancy," Hawke mused, gesturing toward the huge animal. "The pride of my stock, and he knows it. He's sired five champions already."

Siri cocked her blond head at him. "He does have a macho look about him," she observed.

"You'd have the same look if you carried the price tag he does." Randy laughed. "That's a very expensive ton of beef."

"Don't say that," Kitty cautioned, "you'll hurt his feelings!"

The next stop was the spacious stretch of green pasture where the polled Hereford main herd dotted the countryside with their red and white coats. Siri leaned against the white rail fence and watched them moving lazily back and forth against a horizon of trees.

"The farm covered two counties over a century and a half ago," Hawke told her, while he smoked a cigarette. "Now there are barely a thousand acres left. We raise a few crops, but cattle are our main interest."

Siri gazed up at him. "You haven't been here in a long time, have you?" she asked, so softly that the Hallers, who were several yards away, wouldn't hear.

He studied the glowing tip of his cigarette. "No," he said finally, "I haven't wanted to come near the place until now."

"Could we see the gardens? I got a glimpse of them . . ."

"Come on." He caught her elbow and turned her with him, calling to the Hallers to join them.

The gardens were on the banks of the Ashley River, amid towering magnolia and expansive oak trees with curling lavender-gray strands of Spanish moss trailing down from their lofty branches. The mixing of colors was perfect; the white and pink of the hydrangeas, the violet crepe myrtle, the white snowball bushes, and the pale purple wisteria hanging like grape flowers. It was enough to take an artist's breath away.

"You should see it in the spring," Kitty sighed, "when the magnolias are blooming along with the dogwoods and rose bushes. It's a symphony of color."

"It must be lovely," Siri murmured, her eyes on the lazy current of the river as it wound through the cypress trees at its banks. "What a lovely place to have a picnic."

Hawke turned on his heel, his face taut. "We'd better be getting back. I've got some calls to make about a temporary overseer."

Siri hung behind with Kitty. She knew that Hawke was remembering happier times by the river—maybe picnics he'd shared with Nita in his younger days. She felt a twinge of envy at the thought of how much he must have loved Nita.

Hawke found two possible replacements for his ailing manager before sundown, leaving the interviews to do the next day.

The four of them sat down to a seafood supper that Hawke swore was Mary's crowning accomplishment— stuffed crab and lobster tails. It was the best Siri could remember ever having, but she'd never eaten in surroundings this elegant. Crystal chandeliers hung overhead and old silver utensils and serving dishes adorned the table. It brought the distance between Hawke and her into vivid focus. Looking down the table at him, sitting so majestically at the end of the table in a dark suit, she understood him just a little better. The rugged aristocrat. The plantation master. He'd have been right at home in the nineteenth century.

After the last of the crab was gone, they went into the parlor for after dinner drinks. Siri accepted a small glass of delicately aged French brandy, and sneaked away at the first opportunity to sit in one of the big rocking chairs on the porch outside.

The atmosphere of night in this secluded green paradise was delicious. They were far removed from traffic and the smell of car exhaust. Siri sipped her brandy quietly, drinking in the serenity around her; the low murmur of the river, and the soft chirp of crickets in the thick woods around the house.

"You've got the makings of a country girl," Hawke said at her shoulder.

"Would you rent me about six cubic inches of this and have it mailed to my house?" she asked with a smile.

"You'd miss the sirens after the second week," he replied, taking the chair next to hers.

"Where are Randy and Kitty?" she asked.

"On the phone. Kitty wanted to call her mother while she was in town."

"Don't she and Randy still live in Charleston?" she asked.

"No. They have a home in Savannah now." He sipped his whiskey and leaned back in his rocking chair with a heavy sigh. "Mary has a way with crab," he murmured.

"Mary has gifted hands," she agreed. "Hawke, I never did get to ask you what you discovered about that witness."

"I found him," he replied.

She sat straight up in her chair. "Where? Who is he? Will he testify? Did he . . . ?"

He chuckled heartily. "For God's sake, one question at a time!"

"All right," she agreed breathlessly. "Will he testify?"

"He'll testify."

"Do you know who killed Devolg?" she persisted, leaning across the arm of her rocking chair to intently study his impassive face.

"I think so."

"Are you going to tell me?" she burst out while he emptied his glass in one swallow. He set the glass down on the floor and leisurely lit a cigarette.

He glanced at her with one eyebrow raised. "And make you an accessory?" he asked with mock incredulity.

"Hawke!" she groaned. "You know I can keep a confidence, and you know I wouldn't write anything until you tell me to!"

He smiled at her eagerness. "Remember I told you that Davy Megars had an older sister?"

"Your client Davy?"

"The same. Well, she had a boyfriend, a very jealous boyfriend who knew she was making time with Devolg." He leaned back in his chair and watched the path of a cricket as it crawled jerkily off the porch. "I had a feeling Davy was protecting someone. Youngsters don't generally go around killing other men without a motive. And the fact that his fingerprints were found in Devolg's room only placed him at the scene, they didn't prove he was the murderer."

ˋ "What would he have been doing there?" she asked, her mind nowhere near as sharp as Hawke's.

"Getting his sister out," he replied.

She blinked at him. "You think Davy's sister did it?"

"She had the best motive, from the information I've gathered. Devolg was a known womanizer, and he liked variety. Davy's sister has a nasty, jealous temper. All I need is to get her on the stand for five minutes. I can break her."

It was the way he said it, the confidence in his deep, slow voice, the hardness of his face, that made her certain he could do exactly that. She studied him in the muted light of the porch, her eyes tracing his profile lovingly as he suddenly turned and caught the look in her eyes.

"What are you thinking, Siri?" he asked quietly.

"That I hope you never get me on the stand," she said with a nervous laugh. She finished the brandy and set her own glass down beside the rocking chair.

He turned in his chair to face her, catching the side of her neck with his big, warm hand to hold her eyes level with his, as she raised back up. "I'd never hurt you," he told her. "Not on the witness stand, or in any place on earth."

Her pulse ran wild at the slow, caressing touch of his fingers. She looked into his eyes, and everything she'd ever wanted was within the reach of her arms.

"Woman," he whispered huskily, "I didn't mean for this to happen. But, I need you . . ."

He gently tilted her face and reached across the scant inches that separated them to touch his mouth lightly to hers. She caught her breath as he increased the pressure, shifting his hand to the nape of her neck to force her closer.

"God, it's not enough!" he said in a rough whisper. He moved suddenly, rising to lift her out of the rocking chair, his mouth claiming hers again as he crushed her body against his, burning all thought of protest out of her whirling mind. She locked her arms around his neck, straining closer, returning the fervor of his kisses without reserve.

She felt him drop back down into his own chair, carrying her with him. He draped her over his knees, allowing her head to fall weakly back into the crook of his arm, as he looked down at her with eyes laden with passion.

His chest rose and fell unsteadily against her soft, yielding body, but for all the passion in his eyes, his face was like chiseled rock. Her own breath came quickly, unsteadily, and her lips trembled as she stared back at him.

Sanity returned all in a rush. She vividly remembered the last time he'd kissed her, and what he'd said to her. She had made up her mind that he wasn't going to hurt her again like that.

"May I get up now?" she asked in a rusty whisper. "You...you said last time that you were through giving me lessons."

Something came and went in his eyes, but he erased the hardness from his expression with a slow, lazy smile. "I don't think you need many more, do you?" he countered.

She lowered her eyes to his massive chest in the pure white shirt. "Why?" she asked gently, and he knew she wasn't talking about 'lessons.'

"If you need a reason," he said quietly, "because of this." He caught one of her slender hands and pressed it palm down to his chest just above his heart. The beat was heavy and erratic. "Do you feel it, Siri?" he asked deeply.

She drew a shaky breath. "I...a lot of women must have affected you that way."

"A few." His own hand slid up from her waist to rest not quite intimately at the curve where her own heart was running wild. "I seem to have the same effect on you, sparrow."

"Don't make fun of me," she pleaded in a ghostly voice.

"I don't want to make fun of you. I want to make love to you," he said in a low, quiet voice that made shivers race down her spine.

"You know I've never..."

He laughed softly. "Maybe I'd better clarify that, little innocent. I want to hold you, and kiss you, and touch you. I can do that without taking you into my bed," he whispered at her ear.

"Hawke Grayson, you are the most..."

His mouth brushed against hers slowly, tasting hers in a tender, leisurely encounter that instantly quieted her. Meanwhile, his thumb was tracing delicious patterns on the bodice of her dress, touching and lifting with a strange rhythm that made her tense with unknown sensations.

"You're tense," he murmured. "Are you afraid of me, or is it that good?"

"Hawke..." she protested weakly.

"Tell me, honey."

She twisted, trying to escape the maddening caress of his fingers, but the arm behind her gripped like steel and held her captive, and she moaned sharply, her nails digging involuntarily into his hard chest through the soft fabric.

His cheek slid against hers caressingly. "Your nails are sharp, little cat," he murmured, a smile in his voice.

"I'm...sorry," she managed unsteadily, her eyes closing as she yielded, trusting him even against her will, drugged with pleasure.

"I'm not. Here." He unbuttoned the top three buttons of the silky shirt and slid her cool hand inside it. "Anything goes, Siri," he said quietly. "Anything."

"But...you said..." she faltered.

"To hell with what I said," he growled as his mouth opened on hers. "I want you."

Before she could react to the words, he was teaching her how agonizingly sweet a kiss could be, and she gave up trying to think.

The sound of voices made him raise his head. He looked searchingly down into her misty, amber eyes.

Her fingertips traced a tiny pattern on the warm, bronzed flesh of his chest through the mat of dark hair. "Are you trying to seduce me?" she whispered lazily.

"Not yet," he murmured, "but if you keep that up, I may damned well try."

"Oh!" she breathed. She withdrew her hand with a shaky sigh. "Sorry."

"You still don't know what you can do to me, do you?" he asked quietly. "You sweet, little witch, I step into an inferno every time you touch me."

She searched his face quietly as the voices inside the house drew nearer. "If it's any consolation, you do the same thing to me," she admitted.

"Any experienced man could, Siri," he told her. "Don't let it go to your head."

She dropped her eyes to his chest. "I won't."

"I like the taste of you," he said, holding her close for a moment, "and the way you feel in my arms. But when we get back to Atlanta, nothing will have changed. Nothing, Siri, do you understand?"

She looked up and met his eyes solemnly. "Dad always used to tell me to live one day at a time."

There were shadows of some deep, private sadness in his eyes for just an instant. "That's what I mean, sparrow. For the next two or three days, we'll forget the rest of the world and enjoy being with each other. But the minute I land that plane in Atlanta, I'm going to walk away from you. And I won't look back."

She bit her lower lip. "I…I won't have an affair with you, Hawke," she said self-consciously.

"You're damned right you won't," he said roughly. "I told you before I wasn't going to play fast and loose with you, and I meant it. I won't promise not to kiss you, you impudent little minx, but it isn't going any further than that. I don't want your innocence on my conscience. I've got enough to haunt me without that."

She shifted in his arms, feeling the tension drain out of her to be replaced with a strange, easy comradeship. "Does that mean," she asked, "that I have to promise not to seduce you, either?"

He grinned down at her. "It's only fair. But would you know how?"

"I'm learning. In a few years, look out."

"My God, you'll be devastating," he agreed. He leaned back in the chair and pulled a cigarette out of his pocket, holding it lightly in his fingers. "Will the smoke bother you? If you're going to mind it, you'll have to get up, because it's either this or a shot of whiskey."

She linked her hands behind his head. "Do I unnerve you, Mr. Grayson?" she asked with a smile.

"Yes, Madam," he replied, "you do."

She nuzzled her cheek against his jacket, loving the solidness, the warmth of his body, the deep sound of his voice in the darkness. He was, she thought drowsily, so easy to love.

To love. Her eyes flew open. She gazed across the breadth of his chest to the long porch with darkness at its end. She loved him. For the first time, she let herself admit it, feel it, drown in it. She loved Hawke. And what good was it going to do when he'd already told her how it was going to end? He wasn't a loving man. He could want a woman, true, but Siri wanted more than desire from him. She wanted a thousand nights like this one to lie in his arms listening to the night, and feel a security that had never been hers to enjoy until now, with this man. She wanted children with thick black hair and dark eyes. Her eyes closed. Behind her eyelids, she could feel the warmth of tears brewing.

The Hallers came out onto the porch unexpectedly, and Siri started and sat up. Hawke pulled her down again and held her with one big arm.

"Be still," he murmured over her head, "they're family."

"But you said..."

"Damn it, will you be quiet?" he growled. "Are you ashamed to be seen like this with me?"

"Oh, no!" she said involuntarily.

He smiled gently down at her, and the look in his dark eyes made her want to cry. "Then stop trying to escape. Just act naturally."

"How can I, when I've never been in a man's lap before?" she asked.

The smile broadened. "You felt right at home a few minutes ago," he reminded her.

She blushed. "Beast!"

"That isn't what you were whispering under your breath, either," he whispered as the Hallers came into view. "Come on out," he called to them before Siri could think of a reply. "I'm rocking my *'niece.'*"

"Is that true, Siri?" Kitty teased, a knowing smile on her face.

"No, it isn't," she replied. "He's trying to lead me into a life of sin."

"Don't look at me," Hawke protested nonchalantly. "You're the one holding me down," he added. "A man can't be left alone in safety these days. Brazen young women leaping onto his lap, attacking him..."

"And who attacked who?" Siri demanded.

"Whom," Hawke corrected. "I thought you were an accomplished journalist."

"Of all the..." she began.

"Where are we going tomorrow?" Randy broke in with a grin.

"That," Kitty interpreted, "is called a 'red herring,' in case you didn't know. In other words, time out!"

Siri laughed, relaxing in Hawke's loose grip. "Fair enough. Where are we going tomorrow?" she asked him.

"To Fort Sumter. I'll let you play with the cannons," he added.

"Will you stand in front of one while I play with it?" she asked coaxingly.

Randy and Kitty burst out laughing, as Hawke tried unsuccessfully to turn her over his knee.

It was a lovely, sunny day, and driving down the Battery on the way to Fort Sumter, the Atlantic had never looked bluer. Siri glanced at Hawke across the front seat, her eyes caressing the dark face and hair. He was wearing a red knit shirt with jeans, and she'd never seen him look more handsome. Her own white sundress emphasized her slenderness and her fairness. The contrast between them was striking. She paid so much attention to it that she missed most of the scenery between Graystone and the fort, and wasn't at all sorry.

Fort Sumter faced the ocean, a pale aging relic of an all but forgotten war. The big black cannons still stood guard over the harbor, but the fort's walls were little more than crumbling brick over which an American flag, not a Confederate one, flew proudly. She looked out to sea, feeling the wind in her face, absorbing the faint sea smell as she watched the seagulls in the distance. It was awesome to stand here where so much history had been made. It was impossible to be unaware of those who came before.

Fort Sumter was only one of many tourist attractions they made time to see. Siri's favorite by far was Magnolia Gardens, with its unbelievable number of flowering trees and shrubs, its links with the Civil War and England, and its legacy of almost unworldly beauty.

"It reminds me a little of Graystone," Siri remarked to Hawke, as they strolled over the famous little bridge.

"It should. My great-grandmother fell so much in love with it that her husband created a miniature garden in its image just to shut her up," he laughed.

8

*

The story made her curious, and when they got back to Graystone, she had to go back and stroll through the garden again.

Randy and Kitty borrowed the car to visit their relatives, leaving Hawke and Siri alone. He spent an hour or so with his new overseer before he joined her in the quiet garden, where she stood under one of the monstrous oaks that stood like sentinels beside the river.

He came up behind her, pulling her back against him with his arms locked securely around her small waist.

"What do you think of Graystone?" he asked.

Her fingers curled over his forearms, tangling in the dark, wiry hair. She sighed, letting her body go limp against his. "It's beautiful, Hawke," she said wistfully. "Like something out of a postcard book—colorful and peaceful."

"And lonely," he added quietly.

"Is that why you stayed away so long?" she asked.

His arms tightened, and she felt his warm, hard chest expand at her back. "The world was pretty black for me when I left here the last time. I'd just lost my fiancée—as Kitty told you, I'm sure. And my mother had just been buried. I could hardly bear the sight of this garden. She loved it so." He drew a deep breath. "I had to get away. Somehow it was easier to let Jackson run the farm for me. Even when my father died, I only came home long enough for the funeral. This is the longest I've stayed since. It's also the first time I've been able to enjoy being here." His cheek nuzzled against hers. "You bring the color back into it for me, Siri."

"I'm glad," she murmured, smiling. "Do you think you'll ever come back here to live?"

His body went taut. "Why should I? The house is too big for one man, even with the staff."

"You could get married, raise a family," she said gently.

"In a little over a month, I'll be thirty-nine years old, little girl," he said quietly.

"Does that mean," she asked with mock denseness, "that your advanced age won't allow you to father children?"

"You damned little irritant," he chuckled. "What I mean is that, at my age, it's hard to tell if a woman wants me or access to my wallet."

"Wear old gunny sacks and carry a dented cup around with you for a few weeks," she suggested, "and you'll be able to weed out the ones that want you for yourself."

"I thought Jared said he educated you. Where? At the funny farm?" he asked.

She laughed softly. "Do you really wonder about women?"

"Most men do."

"I mean, about if they're after you because of what you can give them? You're...not an unattractive man," she said, faltering on the words.

"You've already shown me that," he said at her ear.

She flushed hotly, and drew in a quick, shaky breath. "It's...it's very peaceful here. I like the sound of the river," she said enthusiastically.

"You're hedging," he said, and she felt rather than saw the smile on his dark face. His arms tightened.

"Sometimes I think you enjoy embarrassing me more than winning cases," she accused.

"Yes, I do. You adorable brat, you wouldn't give a damn if I didn't have a dime, and I know it." He let her go. "But the timing is all wrong, Siri. We'd better get back. Mrs. Simms will have supper waiting."

"All right." She walked along beside him, enjoying the slow pace he set, enjoying the surroundings of the farm as dusk approached.

"Thank you for letting me come home with you," she said softly. "Everyone needs a green memory to take out and water when snow lies on the ground."

He bent his head to light a cigarette. "From now on, every time I come here, I'll see you," he said.

"Is that good or bad?"

"A touch of both," he admitted with a lazy smile that didn't quite reach his eyes.

"Oh."

He caught her slender hand in his and pressed it gently. "Just enjoy today, Siri. Don't try to live your whole life in a day."

She locked her slender fingers with his broad, warm ones. "Do I do that?"

He smiled. "Constantly."

"I never pretended to be a patient person," she reminded him.

"It comes with age."

"Does it, Methuselah?" she asked with mock solemnity.

His eyes narrowed, his lips compressed. "Methuselah, did you say?" He jerked her body against his, wrestling with her in the shade of a gigantic oak, while she laughed and struggled with him playfully.

He caught the back of her head, holding it steady while he looked down at her. "Let me show you how old I am…" he threatened, crushing his warm mouth down on hers unexpectedly.

With a whisper of a sigh, she yielded to him, her lips involuntarily parting to invite a deeper caress.

He drew back instantly. "Not like that," he whispered roughly. "It's like striking a match to dry kindling."

She leaned back against his hard arms. "I'm sorry," she said softly. "I . . . I'm not very good at this."

"You're too good at it, honey," he said, deadly serious. "Let's go."

She walked quietly beside him, disappointed and a little shaken by his sudden withdrawal, and the hardness that returned to his dark face. He seemed to resent even the small effect her nearness had on him, as if he hated anything that touched or threatened his near-perfect self control. She sighed wistfully. Any day now, it would be all over. They'd be back in Atlanta, and things would be the way they were before the trip began. She studied the ethereal beauty of the estate with eyes that longed for more than just a passing acquaintance with it. How lovely it would be to grow old here, with Hawke. . . .

Just as they reached the house, a silver Mercedes pulled up in the driveway and stopped. Hawke froze beside Siri as the door opened and a tall, slender, strikingly beautiful brunette stepped out of it with a practiced grace. In her clinging white dress and matching sandals, she was elegance personified.

"Hawke, how nice to see you again," the woman said softly, and Siri knew in a blinding flash who she was.

"Hello, Nita," he replied with a pleasant smile. "It's been a long time."

"Too long," she said, batting her long lashes up at him as she moved closer. "Kitty's mother told me you were here. I just had to see you."

"How's your husband?" he asked.

"I divorced him three months ago," she replied sweetly. "I've been so lonely. . ."

"Have you moved back to Charleston?" he asked.

"I'm thinking about it," she cooed. Her eyes darted to Siri, as if she'd just realized she was there. "Who's this?" she asked with a poisonous smile.

"My partner's daughter. Siri Jamesson, Nita Davis," he introduced them. "Kitty and Randy are with us on this trip."

"You'll be in town for a while, won't you?" the brunette asked hopefully.

"Until tomorrow," Hawke said, and Siri felt herself doing a double take. He hadn't mentioned that before.

"Please have dinner with me, Hawke," Nita pleaded with one silky hand caressing his arm. Her eyes were bright blue and extremely seductive. "For old time's sake?"

Siri imagined that he hesitated for just a second before he answered her. "All right." He turned toward Siri, his face impassive, his dark eyes telling her nothing. "Don't wait supper. I'll be late."

"Oh, darling, it's been so long," Nita breathed as she led him back to the Mercedes.

He put her in on the passenger side and slid in under the wheel. Siri didn't wait to watch them drive off. She turned and went quickly into the house. If he'd needed to emphasize how little she meant to him, that was enough. She got the message.

Supper was quiet. The Hallers still hadn't come home, when Siri finished eating and went into the kitchen with Mrs. Simms to help the elderly woman with the dishes.

"Lass, I don't need help, you know," Mrs. Simms told her with a smile.

"I helped mess them up," Siri pointed out reasonably, "and it's only fair that I help clean up. Besides," she added with a grin, "I like the feel of warm soapy water. I never let Dad buy me an automatic dishwasher for that reason."

"A homebody, are you?" Mrs. Simms deftly washed plates and passed them across to be rinsed and dried. "No young man?"

Siri paused. "A friend," she corrected. "No one I want to marry."

"No one except that blind man who comes to visit me every year or so, is that it?" the older woman probed.

"Blind man . . . ?"

"Mr. Hawke," came the bland reply. "Because if he can't see what's written all over you when he walks into a room, he has to be blind."

"He . . . he doesn't know," Siri said quickly. "He can't, not ever. He's already made it very clear that he doesn't have any interest in marriage or a family, and I've made it clear that I can't settle for anything less."

"Ah, a standoff." Mrs. Simms laughed. "Not for long, though," she added with a sly, teasing glance. "I've seen the way he looks at you when you don't notice. It's as if his eyes touch you, lass. I've seen that look in a man's eyes too often to mistake it, but not since that baggage broke their engagement have I seen it in Mr. Hawke's eyes."

"Nita, you mean?" she asked, wiping the last of the plates dry.

"That baggage," Mrs. Simms repeated, "never cared for him, she never did. And now here she comes back like it's been days instead of years and carries him off again. Nothing stupider than a man. I thought he'd had better sense," she added vehemently. "She'll have him trapped again before he knows it, poor thing. You mark my words, men are too susceptible to a woman like that. She gets him so hungered that his mind breaks down. Aye, you can laugh, but it's what happens."

Siri drew a deep, sobering breath. "Maybe that's what I should have done," she said with a wry grin, "but I don't know how."

"You look like you'd be a fast learner," Mrs. Simms teased. "And if you love the man, lass, it comes natural."

But what if the man doesn't love you? She thought it, but she didn't say it. Instead, she sang the praises of the Scotswoman's pudding, and went away with the secret recipe for it.

It was late evening when the Hallers came back, and Hawke still hadn't put in an appearance. Siri knew without being told that he and Nita weren't just talking all this time, and the pain caused tears to form in her eyes as she sat quietly on the porch listening to the night sounds. Had it only been last night that she'd been sitting here when Hawke reached for her and kissed her so passionately that the breath left her body? She drew a shaky sigh. What a bittersweet memory that was going to be.

Randy and Kitty came up the stairs running, laughing, and she envied them their lightheartedness.

"We've been nightclubbing," Kitty laughed. "There's this great little dinner theater downtown, and I don't think I've ever laughed so much in my life. The players were just fantastic!"

"Hawke not home?" Randy asked.

Siri shook her head. "He went off somewhere with Nita."

Kitty stopped in her tracks and the smile left her face. "Nita came here?" she asked.

"This afternoon. Hawke said not to expect him until late," Siri told her with a forced smile. "Don't worry, he's a grown man, he can look after himself."

"How about a drink?" Randy asked.

Siri got up out of the rocking chair and followed them inside for a nightcap. It was after midnight when they stopped talking and went to bed. But Siri lay awake involuntarily until she heard the sound of a car coming up the driveway. When she glanced at the clock, it was three in the morning. And in spite of all her efforts, she listened intently for Hawke's footsteps coming up the stairs, slowly passing her room, before she could let herself go to sleep.

The Hallers decided to spend a few more days in Charleston with Kitty's people, so Siri and Hawke flew back to Atlanta alone. She'd barely spoken to him since their late breakfast at Graystone, instead sharing her bits of conversation with the Hallers and Mrs. Simms, while Hawke sat brooding in his chair.

He unloaded their luggage from the plane and led the way quietly to the parking lot where he'd left the black Mercedes parked when they departed for Panama City. He put the suitcases in the trunk before he unlocked the car doors and turned to Siri. He looked unusually tired, and his eyes were bloodshot, as if he hadn't had any sleep at all—which, Siri thought angrily, had probably been the case.

"Would you like to have a cup of coffee before we leave?" he asked with a stranger's cool politeness.

The temptation was terrible, to spend just a few more minutes alone with him, talking to him, looking at him. It would never again be as intimate between them as it had been during those days on the beach and in Charleston. But she believed in quick, clean breaks, not painful little cuts, so she shook her head.

"Thanks, anyway," she replied with equal politeness and a strained smile, "but I'd better get home and call Bill. What can I tell him about a release date for the information you've given me on the Devolg murder?"

"Give me a day or two," he replied. "I'll send word to you by Jared."

"All right," she agreed.

As she slid into the passenger seat, she realized what he was telling her. *When we get to Atlanta, I'm going to walk away from you and never look back.* Figuratively speaking, he'd just done that.

"Well, when then?" Bill Daeton was growling at her in his office. "My God, Siri, it's been days. I can't wait forever! Do you realize how much it cost us in expenses and your salary to send you on that trip?"

"By the time you deduct it off the paper's taxes," she replied calmly, "probably about thirty-two cents."

"Oh, hell," he grumbled, turning toward the window with his hands jammed in his pockets. "Have you heard from Hawke at all?"

"Not yet," she replied, feeling the pain of having to admit it. "He said he'd let me know, and he doesn't go back on his promises. If you'll remember," she added, "I didn't want to go on the trip in the first place."

"Don't remind me." He turned back. "I'll give you until tomorrow to convince him to let you release that information. If he puts us off any longer, we'll run it anyway."

"Oh, no, we won't," she replied curtly. "I gave word, and I'm not going back on it for you, this paper, or anything else!"

"It's your word, or the flower show circuit," he said firmly.

"I told you before, I like flowers." She stood up. "I'll see what I can do. But no promises."

"You haven't been the same since you got back from the trip," he said quietly. "Want a day off?"

She gaped at him. "I haven't changed," she protested.

"You did that opinion poll for me yesterday without an argument," he replied with a kindly smile. "That's when I knew something was wrong."

She shrugged with a smile. "I just got my feet wet, that's all."

"Keep your shoes on next time."

"You can bet on it."

9
*

Jared wasn't looking well. She watched him at the supper table, really seeing him for the first time since she'd been home. He was pale and quiet, and it wasn't like him not to make conversation.

"Don't you feel well, Dad?" she asked with more than a trace of concern on her face.

"Not very," he admitted with a wan smile. "I don't know what's wrong with me. A little stomach upset, I suppose. Too much restaurant fare while you were gone." His amber eyes held hers. "Siri, what happened on that trip?"

She shrugged, hoping the turmoil inside her didn't show. "Nothing noteworthy. We had a very good time."

"No, you didn't. You look like death standing up, and Hawke's in a shell dynamite couldn't blow him out of." He studied her thin face. "You found out how you felt, didn't you?"

She nodded weakly.

"Did Hawke?"

"Your esteemed colleague revived an old flame," she murmured. "A girl he was engaged to years ago. They were out until three in the morning."

"That's very interesting," Jared said. "Because when I asked him why he looked so haggard the afternoon you two came home, he said he'd been in a bar half the night getting plastered."

She blinked hard at him. "Hawke? Drunk? I can't picture him that way."

"He was the portrait of a man after the night before." Jared smiled.

Siri picked up her cup and sipped the hot, black coffee. "Nita must have really gotten to him."

"Something sure did. But Hawke doesn't seem the kind of man to hold a torch for a woman who stabbed him in the back now, does he?" he asked.

She sighed, putting her cup down and sliding her chair out from under the table. "I'm going to have a glass of sherry. How about you?" she asked with a smile, ignoring the question.

He sighed. "I give up. You can ruin your own life without any help from me, I guess," he grinned. "All right, I'd love a . . . oh, my God!" he groaned.

He grabbed his chest and, white as a sheet, keeled over onto the soft carpet. Siri ran to him, dropping down beside him with a terrible apprehension, as she saw his labored breathing and the pain in his face. Without a word, she made a dash for the phone and called an ambulance.

The waiting was the worst part. Emergency rooms were always crowded, and full of doctors, nurses and aides who never seemed to know anything about any particular patient. Especially when it came to answering questions about a family member.

Siri sat huddled between a nervous expectant father and an old woman waiting for news of her son who'd been involved in a motorcycle accident. It seemed like hours before Dr. Swandon finally came out long enough to tell her that Jared was going to live. "It was luckily just a light heart attack," he told her. "He'll be all right. Go on home, Siri, you can see him in the morning. He isn't going anywhere."

He patted her on the head as if she were still the child he'd delivered so many years ago, and sent her home with a couple of tranquilizers that he made her promise to take at bedtime.

The house was so quiet. So quiet, without Jared in it. She tried to watch television, but it didn't take her mind off what had happened. Oh, God, if she just had someone to talk to, a shoulder to cry on.

The sudden jangle of the telephone interrupted her, as if in answer to a prayer. Maybe it would be Marty, or even Mark, whom she hadn't heard from since she'd been home. Right now, she'd have welcomed a phone call from the devil.

She lifted the receiver. "Hello?"

"Siri?" It was Hawke's deep, slow voice. "I need to speak to Jared."

Hawke! She fought back a surge of tears. If only he were here, and he cared, and he'd hold her while she cried....

"He's not here, Hawke," she managed in a husky whisper.

"All right, I don't have time to track him down. Tell him the Maloxx family decided to settle out of court," he told her curtly, as if he couldn't wait to get off the phone. "And if you want to start getting your story written, I'll probably be able to let you release it by tomorrow afternoon. Davy's sister goes on the stand in the morning. Have your court reporter check with me when court recesses. Goodnight."

The dial tone replaced his voice abruptly. She stood there blankly holding the receiver. Now, it seemed, he couldn't even bear the sound of her voice over the telephone, much less the sight of her.

She put the receiver back down. "Goodnight," she whispered, and burst into tears.

She got up after a sleepless night, feeling somehow more secure in the morning, with daylight outside instead of darkness. She wrapped a thick terry cloth robe around her gown and made herself a cup of coffee in the kitchen. The phone rang as she passed it, and she lifted the receiver automatically. It was Nadine, telling her to remind Jared about his court case that morning out of county. Siri told her as gently as she could about the heart attack, and asked her to contact the judge and let him know, too. Nadine promised to do that, and to go and see him as soon as she could. If Siri had ever wondered how deep the woman's emotions were involved with her father, the tremor in Nadine's normally calm voice told her. She went into the kitchen and made a pot of strong coffee.

Numbly, she sat drinking it, half-heartedly munching on a piece of toast as she tried to organize the day in her mind. The first order of business was to get to the hospital during visiting hours.

The sound of the doorbell disturbed her. She put down the cup of coffee and went to answer it, puzzling at who could be calling at that unholy hour of the morning.

She opened the door and felt her heart skip a beat as she saw Hawke standing there, grim and noticeably disturbed. His eyes swept over her drawn appearance; her tousled blond hair, the flushed freshness of her complexion without makeup, the wide amber eyes that were slightly bloodshot.

"Why the hell didn't you tell me Jared was in the hospital?" he asked tautly. "My God, I'd have been over here like a shot!"

Tears welled in her eyes. "I'm all right," she whispered.

"I can see that." He came in, shutting the door firmly behind him, and pulled her roughly into his arms, cradling her, crushing her against his big body, rocking her slowly from side to side as the tears rushed hot and wet down her cheeks.

"Hawke," she whispered against his chest, nestled like a frightened child in his big, comforting arms. "Oh, Hawke, I needed you," she murmured weakly.

His arms tightened painfully. "You might have told me that last night when I called."

"I didn't think you wanted to be bothered with me," she said miserably. "In Charleston, you said . . . you said you wouldn't look back. . . ."

"Oh, God, don't," he whispered into her soft hair. "I didn't mean for you to try and close every damned door between us."

"It sounded like it."

His arms shifted protectively. "I'll always come if you need me, Siri. At least let me take care of you when I can." She felt his lips brushing her hair. "How bad is Jared?"

"The doctor said it was a light heart attack. He'll be all right, but he's going to have to take it easy for a while," she murmured.

"In other words," Hawke said, "we'll have to tie him to a bedpost for the next few weeks."

"That's exactly right." She pulled away, wiping at her eyes with the lapel of her cream-colored robe. "Would you like some coffee and half a piece of toast?"

His eyes caressed her softly flushed face, the slightly tremulous curve of her pink mouth. "Why only half a piece?"

She smiled with a little of her old sauciness. "Because all I had in the house was one piece of bread, and I've eaten half of it."

"I think I'll pass on the toast," he chuckled softly.

"Afraid of germs?" she teased, turning to start back into the kitchen.

"As many times **as** I've kissed you, little girl, I think it's damned late to worry about it. Don't you?" he asked.

She was glad he couldn't see her face. She let him into the kitchen and poured him a cup of coffee.

"I could scramble you an egg, or fix you some cereal," she offered, setting the hot coffee in front of him at the table. "Have you had any breakfast at all?"

He sat down, his eyes intent and quiet as she sank down in a chair across from him. "I rarely eat breakfast, honey," he said quietly. "Most mornings, I make do with coffee. Finish your toast."

She picked up the cold, stiff bread and studied it distastefully. "I'm really not very hungry."

He eyed the toast with a raised eyebrow. "I don't blame you."

"What time do you have to be in court?" she asked.

"In," he studied his watch, "forty-five minutes. I can drop you off at the hospital if you don't need your own car."

She smiled wanly. "I have to have it. I've got an interview with a senatorial candidate downtown at ten."

"That won't give you any time at all to spend with Jared," he remarked as he sipped the coffee.

"I know." She studied him, noting how handsome he looked in the dark gray suit and elegant, sky-blue silk tie. The silver at his temples only emphasized an attractiveness and masculinity that made music in her mind.

"You're staring again," he said softly.

"I can't help it," she murmured, dropping her eyes to her cup. "You're good to look at," she said in a bare whisper, admitting it at last.

"So are you, little one," he replied, his eyes sweeping over her. "I've never seen a woman who looked so pretty first thing in the morning."

"I'll bet you've seen plenty," she remarked.

"Siri."

She looked up involuntarily to meet his dark, level gaze.

"I didn't take Nita to bed," he told her bluntly.

She blushed like a nervous teenager. "I didn't ask you."

"I know. But it was in your eyes the next morning." His eyes brushed her mouth. "Maybe someday I'll be able to explain to you why I went with her. Right now, I don't even want to try."

"You don't owe me any explanations," she said coolly.

"Don't sit there with that damned cold look on your face and spout pride at me," he growled harshly. "I haven't forgotten how you were with me that night on the porch, and I damned well know jealousy when I see it!"

She closed her eyes on the embarrassment. She couldn't deny it, but she hated having it thrown at her like that.

"Oh, hell," he sighed heavily, "you make me feel like a damned adolescent. I can't even talk to you." He finished his coffee and stood up. "I've got to get downtown to court. Are you going to be home tonight, or has Holland come crawling back?"

She looked up at him with a frozen expression. "I...I haven't seen him lately."

His stormy eyes calmed a little. "We've got to talk. I've spent one of the most miserable weeks of my life looking backwards. We've got to settle this thing between us, Siri."

Her jaw clenched. "I won't sleep with you," she said tightly.

He gave her a slow, calculating look and smiled lazily down at her. "We'll talk about it tonight," he said gently.

"I...I may not be home...." she whispered.

He moved closer, leaning down to put his mouth against hers in a kiss so slow, so tenderly thorough, that tears formed in her eyes at the beauty of it.

He raised his head, his eyes looking straight into hers, reading the turmoil in them. "You belong to me," he said quietly. "We'll talk about that, too."

He started toward the door.

"What about those seventeen years you were so worried about?" she asked in a dazed, choked whisper.

He leaned against the door facing, and his eyes held hers, dark and glowing. "Do you remember what I told you that day in Kebo's, Siri?" he asked. "That if I wanted you, the age difference wouldn't make a damned bit of difference to either one of us?"

She nodded, feeling a surge of light that burst with warm colors all through her body, as she returned that intent look.

"I want you, baby," he said softly.

Her lips parted under the force of her breath, the pounding of her heart, and she wanted to ask him if it was only a physical desire, if he cared... But before she could sort out her whirling mind, he turned and went out the door.

* * *

Jared was pale, and a little drowsy from medication, but he smiled when she came and sat by his bed. He held her hand with a firm, warm grip.

"I'm still alive, in case you wondered," he teased weakly.

"I did, actually," she returned. "I wish you'd told me you weren't well. I'd have made you see a doctor."

"That," he replied smugly, "is exactly why I wouldn't tell you."

"Incorrigible man," she grumbled.

"I'll mend, Siri," he promised. "Nadine came to see me a few minutes before you got here," he added with a grin. "Hysterical. Absolutely hysterical."

"You heartless thing, how can you smile about it like that?" she asked incredulously.

"A woman doesn't get hysterical over a man unless she cares about him," he replied. He crossed his arms behind his head with a lazy smile. "You know, I just may marry that woman."

"Finally, you've come to your senses!" Siri laughed. "I wondered if you'd ever wake up and realize what a jewel she was."

His eyebrows went up. "You approve?"

"I couldn't approve more. You know I love Nadine."

"I've been lonely since your mother died," he added softly. "Nadine's been a shot in the arm. She's attractive, and good company. . . ."

"And she loves you to distraction," Siri finished, with a quiet smile.

He eyed her closely. "The way you love Hawke?" he asked.

She dropped her eyes to her folded hands. "I must be awfully transparent," she murmured.

"So is he," he said enigmatically. "Or don't you know yet how he feels?"

"He wants me," she said quietly.

"You really are blind if that's all you think it is," Jared told her flatly. "My gosh, he's so jealous of you he can't see straight! He has been for years, and you've never even noticed it."

"Jealous...of me?" she asked, staggered by this new insight.

"Murderously. Siri, hadn't you ever wondered why he lost his temper every time you mentioned Holland's name?"

That hadn't occurred to her before, but a lot of things were just beginning to make sense. And for the first time, she felt a sense of hope.

She finished her political interview and broke for lunch, then she went back to the office and wrote it amid a hundred interruptions. She turned it in, started on the Devolg story, working from memory and notes, and finally tracked down the court reporter to ask what information he'd gotten from Hawke.

"Two words," he told her with a grin. "'Go ahead.' He cut the Megars girl into fish bait on the stand. She confessed to the murder five minutes after he started on her. Whew," he exclaimed, "I hope I never have to face that man in a courtroom. My God, I've never watched anyone that coldly efficient with words!"

Or that ruthless. He didn't say it, but she read it in his face. She knew better than most people just how ruthless her father's partner could be, how single minded. What Hawke wanted, he got. And now, he wanted Siri... The thought made her shudder. How was she going to go about resisting him when he was suddenly her whole world? Loving him as she did would make denying that love next to impossible.

She'd just walked into Bill's office to hand him her copy. It was late afternoon, darkness lowering on the city and she'd taken her sweet time with the story because of interruptions, like returning phone calls or chasing down tacky little facts for verification. Nearly dark, nearly quitting time, and she was afraid to go home. It was almost funny.

Bill was on the phone, motioning to her to wait as he wound up the conversation. He put down the receiver roughly.

"Is anyone out there with a camera?" he asked her, gesturing toward the newsroom.

"No," she replied, "most of the day people have gone home. Why?"

"Grab your equipment and get out to Browmner Apartments," he said, "and hurry. The whole place is going up in smoke. I've got Sandy on the scene to get the story. I just need some shots. How about it?"

"I'm on my way," she agreed quickly.

She grabbed her camera and accessories and ran out to her car. She'd be late getting home for sure now. Maybe Hawke would get discouraged and she could put off the showdown until a safer time.

The two-story apartment building was totally immersed in flames by the time she got there. The county fire department had two engines on the scene, and another pulled up about the same time Siri did. Hoses and firemen in turnout gear were everywhere, and the smell of smoke was thick, pungent, and vaguely nauseating.

Residents of the complex were outside in various states of dress, watching the orange flames shooting up into the darkening sky, watching the firemen hold the pressure hoses as they shot water into the building.

Unconsciously, Siri looked for the assistant fire chief. He was new on the job, and she'd known him for several years, ever since he'd started out with the local civil defense unit as a volunteer rescue worker. Herman Jolley was a dedicated fireman, and he'd had to earn the respect of the other men on the detail. He'd done that quite successfully in only six months.

Her sharp eyes focused on his tall, thin body in the metallic turnout gear that protected the firemen from the unbearable temperatures they encountered. He was right at the

ront entrance, just emerging from the blazing complex with
small child held tightly in his arms. It was a perfect shot,
nd Siri moved quickly toward him with the camera raised,
ushing her trailing scarf out of the way as she concen-
rated on the shot. She was clicking away when a voice
houted her name, and the thick smoke suddenly surged into
er nostrils as if she were standing in the flames. A rough
and caught her, ripping the scarf from her neck, beating at
er back.

She whirled in time to see the scarf dissolve in flames on
ts way to the ground, and blinked confusedly at one of the
iremen she knew who was glowering at her.

"You crazy woman," he grumbled, "don't you know
etter than to ease too close to a burning building in a chif-
on scarf?"

"You tell her, Smitty," Jolley seconded, moving in with
a blackened face. "Siri, we've told you about that before.
The picture isn't worth your life, is it?"

"I'll be damned if I know how her mind works," came a
leep, husky, very angry voice over her shoulder.

She turned and found Hawke standing there with Sandy
Cudor at his side. He reached out and snatched the camera
rom her hands, giving it to Sandy.

"Take that to Bill Daeton," he told the young man. "And
ell him not to expect Siri in the morning," he added with
lazing, dangerous eyes. "What the hell was she doing,
Herman?" he asked Jolley.

"Trying for a prize winning shot," Jolley told him with a
grin. "Hit her once for me, will you? I don't like most reporters, but I'd like to see this one live a bit longer. Excuse
ne, folks, I think the fire's waiting for me to come put it
out. These fatheads aren't making much headway."

Jolley sauntered back off with his men, and Hawke glared
lown at Siri with compressed lips.

"If you knew what I felt when I got here and saw that
scarf burning..." He caught her wrist with a hurtful, steely
grip. "You damned little fool, this is the last time. The last

time, Siri! From now on, Daeton's going to put you on the
meeting circuit, or something safe!"

The anger was laced with caring, and she heard that note
in his dark voice. "But, it's my job..."

"Not anymore," he said flatly. "I'm not risking you
again."

"You don't own me, Hawke!" she protested.

"The hell I don't," he replied, jerking her face up to his.

She looked into those glittering, dark eyes and couldn't
look away. It wasn't anger that made them glow like that,
but, what was it? Her fingers lifted to his hard, set face,
lightly touching his profile and the chiseled line of his
mouth, while around them there were the sounds and smells
of the burning building, the angry voices, and the whirr of
machinery.

"If you go on touching me like that," he said gently, "I'm
going to have to do something about it."

"Oh..." She dropped her fingers to his jacket, and her
eyes along with them. "I'm sorry."

"I'm not, Siri," he said quietly. "Let's get out of here."

She followed him meekly to his Mercedes. "What about
my car?" she asked, as he put her in on the passenger side.

"I'll have it delivered back to your house," he said tightly.
"Right now, I've got bigger things on my mind than cars."

They rode in silence back to Siri's house. He pulled up at
the steps and escorted her inside. She took off her sweater
and went to the bar in the living room, still a little shaken by
her experience with the fire.

"Would you like a drink?" she asked quietly.

He took off his jacket and tie wearily, and loosened the
top buttons of his shirt. He sat down heavily on the sofa and
studied her in a blazing silence.

"You could have refused that assignment," he said, ignoring her question. "Were you afraid of coming home,
Siri?"

She poured herself a small glass of sherry and sipped it nervously. "Of course not!" she said quickly.

"You're too pale by far, little girl," he remarked, "and thinner. Haven't you been sleeping?"

"I . . . I sleep fine."

"Well, I sure as hell don't," he said flatly, his eyes narrowing to glittering slits as they swept over her. "I've forgotten what it was like to sleep. Or enjoy a meal. Or watch television. Or any of the other mundane things I used to indulge in before you turned my life upside down."

She stared at him uncomprehendingly.

"Do you want to know why I got into that car with Nita?" he demanded angrily, "when I could barely stand the sight of the two-timing little backstabber? I wanted to show you that those few kisses I'd given you didn't mean anything. That I could walk away from you any damned time I pleased. And I proved it." He sighed wearily. "I sat in a bar until two-thirty in the morning and had to hire a cab to drive me home. I barely made it to my bed before I passed out."

"I've never known you to drink like that," she said quietly.

He looked up and met her searching gaze squarely.

"You've never known me at all, Siri," he told her in a deep, hushed tone, "because you've been afraid to get that close. And I've wanted you so much, for so long, that I feel as if I've had an arm ripped off."

She finished her sherry and set the glass down on the slick finish of the padded bar. "Wanting doesn't last, Hawke," she said shakily.

"Come here and prove that to me," he said roughly.

"What would it prove?" she asked.

"That when I touch you, we make the sweetest fire this side of heaven together," he replied gently. "That you want me every bit as much as I want you. That we're in love, Siri."

Her eyes widened, her lips parted with a note of shock. Had she heard him right? He got up leisurely and reached her in two long strides to pull her body against the length of his, holding her close with two big arms.

"You heard me," he said as he bent his head. "Oh, God, I do love you so...!"

He kissed her with an aching tenderness, a fierce soft tasting that brought a muted whisper from her soft mouth. She reached up to hold him, believing it at last, drowning in the magic of loving and being loved. Tears welled in her eyes, and even as she wept, she wanted to laugh, and cry, and shout her happiness to the world.

He drew back a breath to look at her, and everything he felt was there in his face, in his eyes. The days of pretending were finished.

"I love you," she whispered, testing the words, weighing them, making her own golden chains of them.

"I know." He brushed a stray lock of blond hair away from her flushed cheek. "I knew that day on the beach in Panama City when I held you pinned to the sand and felt your heart bursting under me while I kissed you. You may not remember exactly how you kissed me back, but I went around in a haze for the next week remembering it. You little witch, you left marks on my shoulders that haunted me every time I saw them in the mirror. That was when I had to admit to myself all you mean to me." He smiled down at her. "From that small step down, it was a quick, hard fall to the bottom. I took the Hallers to Charleston in self-defense. I had to have a buffer between us or there wouldn't have been any stopping me. It took every ounce of willpower I had to keep my hands off you."

"I thought you were still carrying a torch for Nita," she admitted, "and I was afraid to let myself feel anything deeper than affection. I wanted to run."

"So did I," he mused. "And I tried. I thought I could walk away from you and live." He sighed heavily, wrapping her closer to press a hard, rough kiss on her mouth. "I hope you like children," he murmured. "I want a son."

She smiled up at him. "Then you'll have to marry me."

"Blackmail?" he whispered huskily, brushing his hard, warm mouth tantalizingly against hers.

"Uh huh," she agreed softly. "So sue me."

"I've got something better in mind...." And he bent his head, passionately kissing her in a loving embrace that meant forever.

* * * * *

AVAILABLE NOW—

the books you've been waiting for by one of America's top romance authors!

DIANA PALMER
DUETS

Ten years ago Diana Palmer published her very first romances. Powerful and dramatic, these gripping tales of love are everything you have come to expect from Diana Palmer.

This month some of these titles are available again in **DIANA PALMER DUETS**—a special three-book collection. Each book has two wonderful stories plus an introduction by the author. You won't want to miss them!

Book 1
SWEET ENEMY
LOVE ON TRIAL

Book 2
STORM OVER THE LAKE
TO LOVE AND CHERISH

Book 3
IF WINTER COMES
NOW AND FOREVER

Available now at your favorite retail outlet.

 *Silhouette Books*®

DP-1A

Silhouette Romances℠

DIAMOND JUBILEE CELEBRATION!

It's Silhouette Books' tenth anniversary, and what better way to celebrate than to toast *you*, our readers, for making it all possible. Each month in 1990, we'll present you with a DIAMOND JUBILEE Silhouette Romance written by an all-time favorite author!

Welcome the new year with *Ethan*—a LONG, TALL TEXANS book by Diana Palmer. February brings Brittany Young's *The Ambassador's Daughter*. Look for *Never on Sundae* by Rita Rainville in March, and in April you'll find *Harvey's Missing* by Peggy Webb. Victoria Glenn, Lucy Gordon, Annette Broadrick, Dixie Browning and many more have special gifts of love waiting for you with their DIAMOND JUBILEE Romances.

Be sure to look for the distinctive DIAMOND JUBILEE emblem, and share in Silhouette's celebration. Saying thanks has never been so romantic....

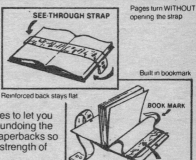

Silhouette Special Edition

proudly presents

Taming Natasha
by
NORA ROBERTS

Once again, award-winning author Nora Roberts weaves her special brand of magic this month in TAMING NATASHA (SSE #583). Toy shop owner Natasha Stanislaski is a pussycat with Spence Kimball's little girl, but to Spence himself she's as ornery as a caged tiger. Will some cautious loving sheath her claws and free her heart from captivity?

TAMING NATASHA, by Nora Roberts, has been selected to receive a special laurel—the Award of Excellence. This month look for the distinctive emblem on the cover. It lets you know there's something truly special inside.

Available now